BEFORE
MY EYES

Also by Caroline Bock

LIE

BEFORE MY EYES

Caroline Bock

St. Martin's Griffin ❧ New York

BEFORE MY EYES. Copyright © 2014 by Caroline Bock. All rights reserved. Printed in the United States of America. For information, address St. Martin's Press, 175 Fifth Avenue, New York, N.Y. 10010.

www.stmartins.com

The Library of Congress has cataloged the hardcover edition as follows:

Bock, Caroline.
   Before my eyes / Caroline Bock. — First edition.
        p. cm.
    ISBN 978-1-250-04558-4 (hardcover)
    ISBN 978-1-250-03567-7 (e-book)
  1. Family problems—Fiction.   2. Schizophrenia—Fiction.
3. Mental illness—Fiction.   4. Politics, Practical—Fiction.
5. Long Island (N.Y.)—Fiction.   I. Title.
    PZ7.B63352Bef 2014
    [Fic]—dc23

                                                    2013032019

ISBN 978-1-250-03566-0 (trade paperback)

St. Martin's Griffin books may be purchased for educational, business, or promotional use. For information on bulk purchases, please contact the Macmillan Corporate and Premium Sales Department at 1-800-221-7945, extension 5442, or write to specialmarkets@macmillan.com.

First St. Martin's Griffin Trade Paperback Edition: February 2015

10 9 8 7 6 5 4 3 2 1

To Mark, Susan, and David

BEFORE
MY EYES

Mark the date. Labor Day. Monday. Nine fifty-eight in the morning. Today I am a lens, a pen, a gun.

Less than a half hour ago, my mother attempted to block my exit. Said I couldn't have the car keys. She had made a doctor's appointment for tomorrow for me and used that as an excuse for why I must stay in my bedroom. I am twenty-one years old and will not listen to her any longer.

I cannot get many places without a car on Long Island, but I could get here.

At the Lakeshore Community Park, one mile from my house, my fingers are slick inside my sweatshirt. Flowers crumple along the sidewalk leading into the park. The grass runs brown and rough under my sneakers. Water restriction signs are posted on trees.

No lake exists in Lakeshore. It never did.

A crowd forms outside a white tent. The flaps of the tent are secured, the space enclosed. Beyond the tent are playgrounds in bright, primary colors: Red. Yellow. Blue. Bleary in the heat are empty tennis and basketball courts. At the far end are baseball and soccer fields, equipped with sprinklers, lights, and electronic scoreboards. It has been a hot, dry, long summer. I am sure I am not the only one pleased this season is coming to an end.

Yet I move up to the tent with a light step. I slept last night for the first time since April—from midnight on, a dead, dreamless sleep.

My eyes dart left and right. I must focus. Straight ahead. Concentrate—and act. I must wait no longer for an answer from the state senator to my letter, my e-mails, and my texts.

Tilting my head, I listen and am met with a ferocious silence. The smell of ozone burns in the air. Rain must be on the way.

I cannot do this alone. I listen, harder. Hear: the whir of insects. My fingers twitch. My skin crawls. I need a cigarette. A cigarette. Coffee. Claire.

I inch behind an old couple, short, withered, gnome-like. They each hold the hand of a girl, five or six years old, with shimmering blond hair, dressed in pink, a tank top with beads and sparkles. This pink is a sign. She is more than a girl. She is a living warning that I am being watched.

Nevertheless, without the voice, I am lost.

In front of me, the old man trips over a tree root. Before he stumbles headlong into the tent, my left hand flies out and catches him. I help him upright. I am nodding at him, the grandma, and the girl. I must breathe. Fix my sunglasses. Push up the sleeves of my sweatshirt. Jam both hands back into the pockets.

Careful.

I latch onto the voice. The voice is with me, faint but nevertheless here. My heart races.

Your deeds will be blameless and wise.

I grin until the edges of my face hurt. The taste of metal singes the back of my throat. I strain to hear. Dig my nails into my palms, cut through the skin, lock the grin in place. I am here to act. To make State Senator Glenn Cooper understand the crucial need for immediate action.

Only you can do this. Be neither of proud heart nor shameful lies.

Out of the corner of my eye: Long legs edge the parking lot. Waist-long brown hair is in focus. She is more woman than girl. She looks lovely. I spin that word around in my head: lovely. But she is not Claire.

Sweat beads along the back of my head, down my neck.

"You must be baking in that sweatshirt," says the grand-mother. "Going to be hot, hot, hot again today."

I shudder.

"I'm going to the beach after this," says the girl. She tugs up her shirt, revealing a bathing suit, pink with sparkles as well. "I'm going to the beach. To the beach." A singsong voice. "I can see myself in your sunglasses." The grandparents beam, nudge her forward.

I know it is a sign. I must be here. The future is here. Violence is both a noun and a philosophical construct. I embody the noun—and the construct—and if I am violence, and I am good (which I must be), then violence must be good or in the purpose of the greater good since my only purpose is to do good. I am wrapped in goodness, an invincible light. My cape. My shield. No one can hurt me. This is my day.

ESTABLISHING SHOT: Lakeshore Community Park. Present day. Morning.

The voice sifts through the white noise and directs my vision. I am the lens. The pen.

MEDIUM SHOT: A flyer taped to the front of a white tent reads "Annual Labor Day Community Fair, ten to two o'clock. Meet State Senator Glenn Cooper."

PAN: Across the parking lot, the volunteer fire department arrives with a display of lights and horns. Minivans and SUVs filter in through the haze and circle like fish in a pond. On the grass, next to the tent, energetic elderly ladies scoot around tables for the League of Women Voters and for the Lakeshore Public Library. The Boy Scouts of North Lakeshore and South Lakeshore roughhouse behind opposing tables. A police car rumbles in and stops alongside the boys. The police officer, freckle-faced, slumping sleepy-eyed at the wheel, finishes his coffee and salutes the scouts.

CLOSE-UP: On the seat next to the officer a gift with a big bow around it. Pink.

LONG SHOT: Survey the crowd like a kingpin, like the top dog. Beam with confidence in the lazy morning light. Own the present and the future—and *CUT.*

CUT.

I blink and squint. Before me, a neon-pink suit strides out of the white tent unexpectedly. "Hi, I'm Debbi Cooper. Hi! I'm Debbi Cooper. Hi! I'm Debbi." She charges at the crowd, shaking hands, saying that her husband, the state senator, and her son are making a few last-minute preparations. "It only should be a minute or so until we are all inside." She is so glad that we have all come out on this Labor Day. She calls a few people by name, says her own again. Offers hugs. Mentions the weather. The lack of rain. The wish for rain. "But aren't we all so, so glad that it isn't raining right now?"

I thrust my hands even deeper into my pockets. I can smell my odor, life-affirming. No water has touched me in weeks, since I was suspended from school in April. Water burns.

Debbi Cooper rushes on to the old couple and the girl, embracing all three. Pink flashes. After a few seconds or more—time has slowed, the sun is beating down on my shaved head—she is asking us all to stand on a special line, if we would like a photograph with the state senator. Only in New York do you stand "on line." I do not approve. Quick enough, she click-clacks back into the white of the tent.

The top of the tent drifts with a vagrant wind. Next to me, a plastic bottle of water is raised to eager lips. I am thirsty, too. Nevertheless, I will not violate myself with plastic.

Bodies shuffle forward. These people do not understand the need for order. The smell of ozone intensifies. I itch. I need a cigarette. A cigarette. Coffee. Claire. I am lost. I want to go back to my bedroom.

Careful. Walk in a perfect way. Smile. Good. All is good.

Finally, the voice is clear and bright and willful. My right hand circles the Glock in my pocket. I stand straighter. Grin harder.

Max
Monday, Labor Day, 9:59 A.M.

The tent in the community park grabs the scent of summer, overripe, wilting, a waiting-for-the-end smell, and I've been waiting all summer for summer to end.

Not that I want school to start. I want senior year to be over, too. I want it all to be over, and something else, something new, to start. I feel like I'm walking through a dream, a muggy, muddied one that will never end. But it has to end. School starts in two days, senior year, soccer season.

My mother strides back into the tent, closing the flap behind her. "Tuck your shirt in, Max. Focus. We have a big morning. You look so handsome in that shirt." I hate the shirt I'm wearing, a polo that she bought for me, a pink polo, boy-pink, she argued. I don't tuck it in.

I kneel down and pet King. He's jittery. He sniffs my hand, licks my fingers. I bury my face in his dog smell.

"Hey, how's it going, Max?" My dad struts through the tent opening like he owns the place, and he does. He owns it. He paid for the tent; the red, white, and blue balloons with his name inked on their sides; and the number-two pencils with his slogan slashed across them: *Glenn Cooper. Vote for your neighbor.*

Send the regular guy back to the state senate. The decent

father and husband. The neighbor who sends his kid off to a summer job, washes his own car (or makes his son, me, do it).

"Can I have your help here, Max," he says. It isn't a question. He expects my help. I'm the permanent, live-in volunteer for Glenn Cooper. He waves pencils at me.

"Max, I need your help," says my mother.

I stand between them, even make a funny movement like I'm being pulled in opposite directions. Neither of them laughs. They train their "disappointed" looks on me. To be quickly followed with their "when is he going to grow up" shaking of the heads at me.

"We have a crowd outside," my mother says instead. "A hot, thirsty one. I hope those bottles of water are staying cold."

She's spent the entire summer working on my father's campaign, speaking at one event after another in her candy-colored suits and high heels. I spent the entire summer being asked, "Is that bottled water cold?" and dragging myself back to an empty house.

"Deb, please," says my father. "What are you worried about? Let's look like we're enjoying ourselves, okay?" My father is a tall, trim man, over six feet, and he's wearing dark blue khakis and a light blue shirt with rolled-up, I'm-getting-to-work sleeves. He swings his arm around her, jostling her, teasing her. "If you can't make it, fake it, isn't that what you always say?"

"You don't take anything seriously, Glenn."

Now he's laying out the pencils with his name in view in

row after row. My mind chatters over this name—*Glenn Cooper, Glenn Cooper, Glenn Cooper,* like it belongs to a carnival barker—until my mother turns to me and asks, "What do you think, Max?"

"What? Water's cold enough."

"This is not about the bottled waters," she says.

I shrug. I try not to think too much these days about anything.

"See, your son's not worried, either," says my father. "You're the only one worried about those crazy e-mails."

"What e-mails?" I ask.

"Don't worry. It's nothing," he says to me. "Anyway, we should have a cop here."

"Where is he?" she asks. "Or she?" Because my mother never misses a chance to pound home that a woman can do anything a man can, as if I didn't learn that from her.

At the back of the tent, two oversized fans throb waves of hot air. We should roll the flaps up, but my father doesn't want to do that until ten o'clock, the official start time.

King whines and flops out on the floor in front of a bowl of lukewarm water. When my parents aren't looking, I'll refill it with cold bottled water. King cocks his head toward me, and even though he can't see me—his blind eyes are watery, weary—I know he knows I'm here. I won't go far. But maybe my mother was right. I should have left him home. I slide my hand down his back one more time, whispering to him, "This will be over before you know it, and then we'll go for a run. I promise." He sinks. My father wanted to put placards on him, reelection signs on his sides. I said no, it was too pathetic, a blind dog begging for votes.

I give King a hug, let him smell me and know that I'm near. He has a bright red bandana around his neck. His leash is tied to the largest table. Little kids love to pet him, and he is gentle with them. Maybe my father will even capture a few "aw, you own a blind dog" votes.

"He's good," I say.

"Better be," says my mother. "Your father is going to pull this election out. Something is in the air. I can feel it."

"Ozone," I say to my father. He fakes a laugh.

"Don't even think that it's going to rain this morning," says my mother, her eyes on the tent flap, her smile fixed. Nothing is wrong. Not in Debbi Cooper's world.

"It's not going to rain, nothing is going to happen from those e-mails or texts, the police will be here, we'll have a great event, and I'll get reelected, how does that all sound?"

"I'm still worried."

"Don't be."

"So what are you doing down there with that dog?" says my mother, turning her attention to me. "Let's get going."

I double-check that King has some leeway on his leash. He is a good dog. He hunches down in his designated space. He sniffs my hand, licks it. I rub his silky ears. He knows how to behave around a crowd.

"I just sometimes think you like the dog better than me or your father," says my mother.

I do.

"Are we going to get to work or what?" says my father to me. "Every other state senator in New York is almost guaranteed reelection. Why not me for a second term? Maybe that should be my campaign slogan, why not me?" He studies the campaign poster. The headshot is a few years old. He looks like an old actor, envious of his younger self. He always said he got into politics because he thought he could make a difference. Even when he ran for the local town board, he said he wanted to take government back from the control of big business and return it to the people. When I asked, what people—the American Indians?—he said I should save it for school, where I was, of course, barely passing American history.

"Look at her. Your mother is one determined woman." He says this to me in a conspiratorial voice as she passes us, concentrating straight ahead, on the tent flap, the exit, the murmuring, curious voices beyond. She hurries outside again, leaving my father and me to finish setting up the tent. We have other volunteers, making sure last-minute signs are in place, handing out leaflets at the local diners. He bends his head, almost knocking into mine, surprised as I am at my summer growth spurt. I pick up more posters to hang somewhere. I could even disappear and say I'm putting up posters, miss this all entirely.

"Most people are probably trying to squeeze one more beach day in even though it looks like it's finally going to rain.

We should all be hoping for rain. But don't say that to your mother."

He snaps his face and name out of my hands. "Don't worry about more posters. We have enough of me in this tent."

I agree. I'm hoping he doesn't want me to help my mother. I don't want to shake anybody's hand. I don't want to smile. I don't want to do anything but maybe take King for a walk. Maybe find my way to Claire's end of town. She liked King a lot. I could tell her—what? That I'm sorry. That she owes me nothing. That I'm an idiot. That I didn't mean what I said, or didn't say, or what I wanted to say didn't come out right. But then, maybe she will show up here, and I should stay.

"What did you do all summer, Max?" my father asks, a short-fused, rhetorical question. He knows what I did.

"I learned how to make an ice cream cone." I flatten my voice into its robot-like frequency. "Vanilla, chocolate, or swirl?"

Glenn Cooper made a point of telling everyone he could: his son was working a "regular" summer job. "Max isn't an intern. He's not a volunteer for my campaign, though I love my volunteers. Max is working regular hours at a regular summer job." Glenn Cooper was going to get New York back to work, and it would start with me, at the Snack Shack on the town beach.

I pick up the pencils, neat in their box, and spread them out on a table like an offering to the summer's end, hundreds of pencils, sharpened to tight points, all with my father's name on them, yellow trees in a great, wild forest.

"What are you doing? Are you even thinking? Do you ever

think, Max?" my father says as I daydream. "Help me out here, Max. Pay attention to what you are doing. And smile. People like to vote for politicians who smile."

"I'm not running for office."

"We're all running."

He straightens the pencils, destroys the forest. My father is especially proud of the pencil idea—not any pencil, as he pointed out, but the test pencil. The number two. In fact, for the last week he's been obsessed with these stupid pencils, ordering more, insisting that they be sharpened. I don't know what he stands for except for sharpened pencils. "Do you think you can handle that job, organizing pencils in neat rows?"

Reelect Glenn Cooper! Meet him here today! Free number-two pencils for school! My father's face and name surround me. I think I'm going a little insane in this tent. Can you go a little insane? Is that even possible? Can I be sane outside this tent? I wonder if she is going to be here today—could I be sane with someone like Claire? Does it matter? Two days, and I'm back in school, back to my old life, except for Claire. Good thing she's at Lakeshore South, and not with me, not at Lakeshore North. I have to think of what I'm going to do. Of course, I could do nothing. She's not my type. Not at all. I hold up a pencil between my thumb and forefinger as if studying it: the tool of my academic failures.

"You going to be okay today, Max?"

I squint at him. I don't know him anymore, this politician father, and he doesn't know me. But I've got to admit—though

I don't, not to him—that isn't about him: I didn't take a pill today. I vowed to myself I wouldn't. Not that I have to keep my promise to myself, but somehow it matters that I do. A lot has changed these past few days, and I need to sort it all out.

"We have a deal," says my dad, breaking into my thoughts. "We are all going to look like a happy family. No worries?"

I force on a smile. "Good?"

"Good." He matches the tops and ends of the pencils into a neat line. "You know something? I want you to just focus on having a great senior year. Getting into a decent college. Being happy."

"Happy?"

"We are a happy family," he says with a hopefulness that stings me. He pats my back. It stiffens.

"I love you, Max, you know that?" He grabs the top of my head and kisses it as if he's bestowing something more on me. He likes to kiss babies, too.

I shrug him off. He chuckles at me. He's often embarrassed at his actions. Maybe that's his saving grace—he knows that we are all acting here, that none of this is exactly what it seems, that we all make promises we don't think we'll keep. I just hope he doesn't make me take the extras to school. I'll definitely fail a test if I have my father's name in view.

"I want today to be a good day. No worries." He distractedly kisses me on the head again. Then, he jogs to the front of the tent, ten or twelve feet, folds open the flap, and acts surprised that there is a crowd of people waiting for him.

One of the people waiting is Jackson's dad. He looks like an older version of Jackson—muscles gone soft, pale hair swept back to cover his bald spot, glancing around like he should be the one who's the center of attention. He's dressed to play tennis. He hugs my mother too tight. Jackson's father knows my parents from soccer and the PTA and from the way everyone around here casually knows everyone else, but doesn't really know them at all. He was the coach of my fourth- and fifth-grade soccer travel team. My father always wanted me to play football—not soccer—like him.

He waves to my father and shouts, "How's my star player?" Every kid was his "star" player.

"Good. Real good," my father rings back for me.

"Way to go," says Jackson's dad to nobody in particular. He spots me in the back near the coolers, and calls out, "Been practicing those penalty kicks, Max?"

I study the pencils like I'm figuring out a puzzle. So I missed the penalty kick. I lost our soccer team—the varsity team—the game. I lost us a perfect season. I don't look up. I hand some little girl in a sparkling pink top a pencil when she asks for one, and then another when she asks for one for her grandmother, and a third one when she asks for one for her grandfather. She clutches them like a bouquet. I have to smile at her when she thanks me as if I saved her from a life devoid of number-two pencils.

My father reaches over to Jackson's dad. The two men lock hands. I hope Jackson won't show up, even though he's always the friendly team captain when his dad's around. Jackson is probably at the beach with Samantha. I can't help myself. I wonder what color bikini she'll be wearing today. I catch a few more phrases from the two of them about "senior year," "the team," and "college." The crowd surges forward. Jackson's father says something about planning to play some tennis before it gets too hot. He steps to the side, sipping his iced coffee, as if the coach once more, following the action from the sidelines.

My mother claims my father and draws him into the crowd. She greets what seems like every single person with a hug. My father prefers the double handshake, one hand over another, which says, "You're important," without him having to say it.

In the back of the crowd are Trish and Peter. Both of them look confused that they are in a tent and not at the Snack Shack, where we spent all summer together—the fat girl, the sped, and me. But I don't want to think of them like that anymore, even if Trish is over three hundred pounds and Peter is in special ed classes. Claire didn't think of them that way, at least last night she didn't. I wave them over. Trish must have made sure that the shoelaces on Peter's work boots were tied. In fact, both of them look like they could be going to church—Trish in a long, flowing sundress and Peter in a short-sleeved, button-down white shirt and pressed black pants. She's holding his hand, leading him toward me.

I swipe the sweat off my upper lip. I should have shaved this morning. But I wanted to save my weekly shave for Wednesday, the first day of school. I feel rough and grungy in this pink polo. Feel like this is a mistake, me coming here at all. I tell King,

"Sit." Yet as I rise, he does, too, dragging the folding table with him one or two feet, screeching it along the floor, throwing off pencils and balloons and pamphlets with my father's face on them, a mini-disaster. King stops, knowing he's made a mistake. He flattens into the dried-up grass.

I scramble to reorganize. My father breaks away from my mother and hurries over. Instead of berating King, or me, he helps me fix the table. You see, my father is just an ordinary guy—I'm sure that's what everyone is thinking—a working guy, with a kid in high school and a blind dog. He even taps King on the top of his head. A breeze eases through the humidity. My father whispers to me, "Don't worry about this. It's showtime. Smile."

I don't smile, not yet. I know I have to get myself into the "game" today: smile, shake hands, be the good son. I rub my back almost as a habit. No matter what, I am playing on the varsity soccer team this fall. Nothing is keeping me off the team.

I scan the crowd, thinking of Claire again, thinking of last night. She could kick the ball. In the moonlight, in my backyard, her running reminded me of her swimming, strong and swift, those long, long legs—and what am I thinking? What would the guys—what would Jackson say if I start bringing someone like Claire to the parties? I mean, she's pretty enough in her own way. Old-fashioned. Too tall. Probably reads a lot and likes school and doesn't have a lot of fun, in the way the guys on the team define fun, though right now the word sounds like it's full of lead and sour milk. Better not to get involved with Claire. She wouldn't fit in. There will be plenty of girls in my own school to hang out with senior year. Better to make this decision now. I look around the tent for something else to organize. I now want everything in straight, even lines.

The last person I expected to be here is here: Barkley. His shaved head is slick with sweat. Why didn't he show up last night, especially after he made such a big deal about being invited? And why is he here now? All summer at the Snack Shack, Barkley called teachers and politicians like my dad "con artists." I busy myself with the pencils. I don't want him to talk to me and say something stupid about the pills I bought from him.

I make like I'm busy. Even with the flaps now open, and the fans whirring, I feel like I'm running uphill or swimming against another riptide. I'd actually like to go for a swim, one last swim in the sea before school starts. I want to see how far out I can go—past the breakers, off the continental shelf, out to where the ocean is wide and clear. Glancing up, no sign of Claire. Better if she doesn't come. I don't want her to think that Barkley and I are friends.

He's in the gray sweatpants that he has worn almost every day to the Snack Shack: stained, stiff, stinking. If he pulled his hands out of that sweatshirt for all to see, I'm sure they'd be rough, his fingernails thick with dirt, as if we spent the summer working fields and not serving up ice cream, hot dogs, and bottled water. He's not moving from the center of the tent. Usually, he doesn't smile much. But this morning, his grin is wide enough to make me think that something is wrong. He removes his sunglasses, wipes the sweat off the reflective glass with the sleeve of his sweatshirt, and his gaze deadens on me.

People move in slow motion.

"Does anyone need a cold water?" Debbi Cooper asks the crowd in the tent. "My son has bottled waters in the back, if you'd like one. Like a cold bottle of water?"

My fists clench. The smile stays fixed. My mouth is dry. My tongue, heavy. I am ignored. Jackson's father, the soccer coach who left me on the bench in fourth and fifth grades, ignores me now. He weaves over to greet Debbi Cooper with a kiss—big, fake. In his possession is an extra-large iced coffee in a clear, plastic container.

I wade through.

ZOOM IN: Max, a lanky, athletic, seventeen-year-old boy with shocks of dark hair and blue eyes. He waves from the far reaches of the tent. I make sure he is not signaling her—Claire. But she has not arrived. I must tell her about today if she does not witness it for herself. She must not hear from Max. Nevertheless, I hope he is feeling good. Even weak men should not feel pain. I hope he popped one of those pills that I sold him the other day. I hope that I helped him.

CLOSE-UP: Two women speak without listening to each other. They are talking about the state senator. How they never vote but are voting for him again. How they never "do" these things, but he's Glenn Cooper. Our neighbor. And isn't he good-looking? And such a nice family. They rub their spindly fingers down their tanned arms as if for some reason these thoughts chill them. *CUT.*

When I do today what I must, forces greater than State Senator Glenn Cooper will recognize me. Crowds on red carpets will greet me. Claire on my arm. I understand that the personal is political. Yet I am more than personal. I am more than political. I believe in the end of plastic water bottles to save our seas, in grammar as the basis for a well-ordered society, and in speaking truth to power. I am more.

Inside the sweatshirt pocket, fingers curl tight around the metal.

Walk perfectly, the voice reassures.

CLOSE-UP: Max raises his chin—a dare, no, a beckoning.

Search for what he sees through the crowd. At the raised tent flap entrance, a flash of strong bare legs. She is dressed in a white T-shirt, tight cutoff jeans, and flip-flops. No makeup. Clean skin. A question in her eyes.

You must be heard. You will be seen. Action, the voice incites. The heart is on fire.

State Senator Glenn Cooper is having his picture taken with neighbors. "Smile for the camera," he says.

I smile hard. The Glock is out. A scream arcs. "A gun," someone shouts.

My throat is raw. A plastic water bottle spins toward me. The world falls away.

I am the lens, the pen, the gun. The voice directs.

BEFORE

Claire

Water, bluish-gray, splattered with sun, and me, swimming with long, strong strokes, the only one out here. I duck my head into the water and swim harder. The tides are pulling me out, away from the beach, which is scattered with families on blankets and under striped blue-and-orange umbrellas, rented for the day. I swim on, imagining I'll soon be at the other shore, the one I can't see but I know is just ahead, across the Atlantic Ocean. Greater forces—the tug of gravity, the moon in its orbit—guide the tide. I steer through the sea, but the unseen controls the tide. Water buoys me. I float. I dive through the waves, hold my breath, and shoot up for air, but the break between sea and air shifts, and there is more water. My lungs tighten. I swim toward the light. Breathless. Airless. The light shifts on the surface. My eyes blur. I swim harder and, finally, break through the sea and gasp for air. I know I should turn around, go back to the familiar shore, find my little sister, Izzy. The waves pitch higher, the tide more insistent, and the light dips from clear blue to purple-black. Lightning cracks overhead. I swim faster. My arms and legs fail. I'm weak. I don't know how I found myself so far out to sea. I don't know how I got here. I don't know why I thought this was a good idea. Wasn't I supposed to be the responsible one? Wasn't I supposed to be the one taking care of Izzy? I scream. She signals me back as if this is a game. She runs off. *Help!* But no one is there. The blankets and umbrellas have been packed up, and everyone on the town beach has fled for safety. A wave smacks me, knocks me underwater. I can't see or breathe. *Help*—the sea sears my skin, my eyes. My mouth tastes seawater, broken shells, silver fish. I can't scream. I gasp for air. *Help.* Waves pound over my head. I am as alone as I have ever been. I don't deserve to have my summer end like this. I did nothing to deserve this. I should have done something wild, something unexpected, something that made somebody notice me. A wave, as broad as a football field, smacks me down. I'm grasping for light. My arms are ripping from their sockets. The waters churn black and dark and cold.

I feel an urgency to save that girl, and perhaps even a greater desire to let her drown.

It's a dream. And I know I'm dreaming.

I'm in the Atlantic Ocean, and somewhere else in my mind, I'm in my bed. I can see myself as if through a lens, and I am letting myself drown. I am there and not there. I am in the sea. At the same time, I'm in my bed, under the woolly muck of my inky purple blanket, crocheted by my mother for my sixteenth birthday. I feel someone pulling me up and out, and in fact, I hear my name—Claire Wallace—from afar and then near.

I swim out of the dream.

I jolt up ramrod straight. My room, its disorder of dirty clothes and lilac walls and writing notebooks, surrounds me. It's morning. I'm drenched in sweat and tears. In a daze, I wipe my hand across my cheeks, across my dry lips. I'm tangled in the wool, breathing in short, hard intakes as if I'm in water, as if I'm still drowning.

I shake the dream from me, literally, flapping my T-shirt from my body, wanting to change into something clean and fresh, but no one, meaning me, has done the laundry yet this week. My hair is frizzy and heavy around my waist. The birds are going wild, tripping through the trees. If I opened the window any wider they'd fly in, or I could fly out. I am not dreaming. Lying in bed, with my eyes open, I can't be dreaming. Yet a woman's voice rings in my head. Or rather, it's the memory of her voice. My mother was always impatient, always saying: *Let's go, let's move it, no daw-dling, when I say it's time to go, angel, it's time to go.* Not angry. Just hurried. Just wanting to get on to the next thing. There was always somewhere to go. I can remember the voice—never soft, never quiet, oversized like her. She was, or is, tall like I am, had chestnut brown hair like I have. She never did any more with her hair than run a brush through it. Twenty-five hard strokes with her walnut-handled brush, a square, sturdy brush, and she was done, and it was like a mane—thick, loose, wondrous.

I wrap my blanket around me. I imagine lavender, but the scent is faint.

I can do this. I can get out of bed—in control, in charge.

A voice calls to me. This one I know for sure isn't part of the dream. "Come on, Claire, what do I have to do? It's time to get up. It's time to go."

Please. One day. All I want is one full day at the beach, one day without wheelchairs, without the reek of bleach and urine and boiled vegetables and bodies struggling to walk a few painful steps, to raise a hand, to smile.

"Your mother counts the hours until she sees us."

Three months ago, the beginning of the summer, my beautiful mother had a stroke, an aneurysm, a brain vessel burst. I turn that word over in my head all the time, "vessel," an old word for a container, but this vessel carried blood, and it broke apart as if in a storm, causing damage—brain trauma and paralysis of her left leg and arm.

I'm not opening my bedroom door for my father. I'm not going out and visiting my mother at that rehabilitation center today. I want her home, back to normal.

My father, once a strong man, gives the door a weak push. The locked door, hollow, cracked, streaked with fingerprints on the inside and the outside, holds.

In the mornings, my father goes to work as an accountant. In the afternoons, he visits my mother. This has been the routine all summer. After three hours at the rehab center yesterday afternoon, I couldn't stay there any longer. I couldn't bear to kiss my mother good-bye on that parchment-white skin. I said we had to go—I lied and said I had to meet friends. My father wanted to stay. I demanded that he drive Izzy and me home. He did, then returned to her.

"Claire?"

I don't know when he came home and went to bed, or if he did. I'm pushing him too far. I know it.

"The insurance has run out," he says on the other side of door, heaving one last time against it.

Why should a sentence so bland sound bad, or scary? *The insurance has run out.* What does that even mean?

My father is not someone given to long explanations or speeches. He likes numbers and columns. He likes things to add up. "I'm scrambling to see if we can borrow more, borrow more against the house. I'm trying to make the numbers work. But nothing's working—"

"Borrow?"

"The insurance has run out," he repeats, louder, through the door, as if this should make sense to me. He never asked me to do anything around the house, but I've tried to keep up with it all, even though sometimes it feels like a race I can't win: grocery shopping; making sure we have breakfast, Izzy and I, and dinner; and vacuuming and dusting. "The insurance has run out and I can't make the numbers work, not now, not this week. It's the end of the month and next month's payment is due. But you don't need to worry about this. You have enough to worry about, but the insurance has run out and I don't know what to do." Something hits the door—his fist? His head? He's pounding his head against my bedroom door.

"Take Izzy," I say, softly. "Can't you take just her today?"

"I don't want to take Izzy without you. She's too young for all this."

"She's six," I say, knowing that sounds dumb from a seventeen-year-old.

I wish I were "too young." I know I'm being horrible. But I hate the rehabilitation center. I hate going there. I hate having to smile at her and pretend everything is going fine, that I'm happy to be there, that it's a happy day to visit my mother at the rehabilitation center. I'm holding it all together, but I can't smile.

"Come on, Claire, for me."

I do everything for him. Cook. Clean. Take care of Izzy. I wrap myself into my blanket.

He sucks in more breath.

"It's going to be over ninety-five degrees again," I say, going to my door but not opening it. We couldn't take my mother outside yesterday, it was sweltering. Yet the inside of that rehab center was airless. A thrum of machines and moans swept down those long corridors—and I could barely breathe. Izzy sang "It's a Small World" with my mother, struggling out the words. They must have sung that song ten times. Yesterday, I was there forever, stuck to a plastic chair, pleasing no one, watching dust swirl in the heat, and mouthing without sound, "It's a small world after all."

I can't go there today. I won't. I deserve a day off.

And I can't open my bedroom door now. I don't want to see my father. If I see him, if I look him in the eyes, I'll cave. I'll go to the rehab center. Maybe I will insist that we bring her outside to the courtyard, no matter the heat. I'll work with her on standing. I can support her. Upright, with a cane in her good hand, Izzy always cheering us on.

However, if she stands, I will see how much thinner she is, thinner than she has been since Izzy was born, even thinner than she was before Izzy. I'll see that she's all loose skin, as if vital organs have been sucked out of her. She will not have the strength to walk and talk. It will take all her concentration to struggle, left foot, right foot. After a few steps, my father will want her to sit. They may even argue. She is determined to walk. Soon enough, we will have to ease her back into her wheelchair. I will have to sing with Izzy "It's a Small World," until all other songs—all other *sounds*—are banished and I'm without images or words.

"Why don't you take a day off from visiting, too?" I say to my father in a whisper, as if not going to visit my mother can be a secret between us. "And a day off from work, too?"

"I can't," he says. "I haven't worked a full day at the office since this happened to your mother."

He hasn't taken a day off all summer. He's pasty-pale and exhausted. "All you do is work," I say, without adding—and visit her.

"All I do is work, Claire? I don't know if I can afford the rent on my office space anymore. Or the mortgage here." Right before my mother's stroke, he was forced out of his corporate job. He set up his own income tax preparation business, but I know it's been hard, even though he was always saying at first that it was the best time to go into business for himself.

"I don't know if I can do this much more, Claire. I just don't know. I know I should go to the beach with you and Izzy. I know I should do more for you two girls—" His voice breaks. "But the insurance."

I can't bear his tears, again.

I drop the blanket away from me, feel like I'm molting. But I'm not becoming anything else. I'm not a caterpillar turning into the butterfly. I fling open the door. "I'll go with you."

He is disheveled, even more than I am. He's in khakis and a wrinkled polo shirt with a stain above the pocket. I almost want to say that he should take off his shirt and I'll wash it, but he may not have a clean one. Our laundry is like a spore, one attracts another, one towel, another. Who knew three people could produce so much laundry?

Yet I have everything else under control. I wake up, make breakfast, vacuum and dust. I vacuum and dust every day. I am good at that. The entire house. Every day. But the laundry piles grow. Dishes, too. But laundry more. My father turns to leave me.

"I'll go," I say again, louder, as if he can't hear me. His eyes wander over my head, as if someone else, anyone, is going to exit my bedroom. He never looks at me anymore. I'm not sure what he doesn't want to see. Unfortunately, I'm hard to miss. I'm five-foot-nine, broad-shouldered, wide-hipped, long-legged, over-sized, not fat, just everything else. My mother used to say that someday, I'd find a boy who would appreciate me. Not here. Not in South Lakeshore, or across town, in North Lakeshore. Not here, where size zero is a goal as specific as a top-tier college. "You're athletic," my mother always said. I am not athletic. I'm too big on top, too bouncy, though when no one is looking I like to run. I like to swim. I need to do it more. My mother always said that she should exercise more, but she never did, and look what happened to her. She was overweight; she had high blood pressure; she was prediabetic, or so I learned afterward. She was forty-three years old when she gave birth to Izzy and gained fifty pounds from her pregnancy. She was always asking me to go for walks after dinner, and I was always refusing. In some way, this is all my fault.

My father gazes down the short hallway as if he expects my mother, or anybody else, to come save him from talking to me. "You're right, Claire," he finally says. "You don't have to go. You shouldn't go. Your mother and I have to figure out what to do next."

"Please, let me go?"

"Don't go for me."

"I know how hard it is on you, isn't it?"

"On all of us."

I think he's going to hug me, or I think I should hug him. If we were another family, we would. Instead, he inspects his shoes. They are scuffed. My mother would tell him that they needed to be shined. She'd even polish them for him because, she'd say, your father isn't good at remembering to do things like that.

"I don't want you to go. None of this adds up. None of it makes sense. I can't make sense of the numbers."

"What's going to happen next?"

"Too many questions. It's better that you don't go today. I need to do this alone—or just with your mother. Just her and me need to figure this out."

He blames me, too. I don't do the laundry, don't remind him to shine his shoes, and I didn't call 911 fast enough for my mother.

He sighs. "Why don't you go to the library with Izzy today? It will be nice and cool at the library. Just be careful, that's all. Watch your sister." His face is big and jowly and loose. His dark curly hair is grayer at the temples than I remember it, from yesterday or the day before. He needs a haircut, too; my mother would make him go to the barber. He comes home later and later each night and eats alone—cold fast food from paper bags. My mother would yell at him about that. Before, we'd always have dinner together—almost every night—my mother was big on sitting down to dinner, no television, no telephone, no anything, just the four us. I realize now that it was the best part of the day, the four of us around the kitchen table. I was always wanting to hurry and she'd always tell me to slow down. It was the only time of day she seemed to sit. I'd always want to get to my friends. Now, I haven't seen any of my friends over the summer, and of course, my best friend, Sara, moved to Washington, D.C. She was the only one who understood how important my poetry is to me, how serious I am about it. So I don't even really have any true friends. Except for Izzy, I've spent the entire summer alone.

"Just promise me you won't go to the beach. Go to the movies. And even there, make sure you keep an eye on your sister."

"Don't I always watch Izzy? Haven't I spent the whole summer watching Izzy? What else do I do except watch Izzy?"

"Just be careful, that's all I'm saying. I don't want you at the beach. I heard that the undercurrent is particularly bad right now. Your mother would never forgive me if something happened to Izzy," and he adds, "or you."

"If we go to the movies, I'll need at least twenty bucks."

He drops his shoulders, sinking into himself, a big man made small. He reaches into his back pocket and yanks out a worn-thin wallet. Inside there is one bill. He hands it to me. I don't even want it. I should have gotten a job this summer like everybody else. But I take it. "You're sure?"

"Take it."

"I'm going to do all the laundry today."

"Go have fun. You're right. Go to the movies. It's the last weekend of the summer. Your mother would want you to have fun. Life is too short. Didn't your mother always say that?"

His voice catches.

My mother never said that. She said smarter things, and not just because she was a psychologist. I correct myself: She is a psychologist still, isn't she? Does a stroke take away that, too?

I curl the twenty-dollar bill into my hand, wanting to be that fun-loving, easygoing girl who hangs out, has a good time, is game for anything and everything. I want to be somebody else.

Max

Spend your summer having to work at the Snack Shack at the town beach. Work with freaks: Trish, Peter, and worst, Barkley, who smells like rotten eggs mixed with seawater.

Study, when forced, to take the SATs for the third time, even though you're going to screw up again anyway. Write at least fifty versions of the introduction paragraph of your college essay.

Keep your dog locked up in your bedroom. Your mother doesn't want the dog running through the house all day while they are focusing on your father's reelection. You agreed to this. But you didn't think King would be locked in your room for months.

Imagine you are on the field again. It all started with the last soccer game of the season. You were playing mid-field, and you went flying on the grass, landing flat on your back. It was the first game your parents watched from beginning to end that entire spring. They hadn't seen you hit hard before—you had been caught in more than one slide, elbowed more than one time—but this time when you went down, you blacked out, only for a few seconds. When you stood up, everybody cheered, your mom the loudest, breaking your name into two syllables: Maa-ax. And you didn't want to show weakness or pain. Coach never wanted to hear complaining, even though you'd been hit harder than you'd ever been in your life.

You were given a penalty kick. Walking to the line you felt like a steel rod had been rammed into your back. The kick spun high, toward the corner, the left corner, just as the coach had you practice a hundred times. It flew—a white-and-black bird—too wide, shot off the goalpost, and missed the net. You would have had a perfect season without that loss.

Afterward, you were on your knees. Your mother and father were leaping out of their chairs, emblazoned with *Reelect Glenn Cooper, your neighbor.* At home, they wanted you to go to the doctor, and you went. The doctor checked you over for five or ten minutes tops, and said that you should take it easy, take over-the-counter meds, and return in a week or two. Your father had to be back in Albany and your mother had to be at a fund-raiser, and you nodded and agreed. Later that night, you borrowed one of your father's prescription pain pills for his back. That's when you started taking a pill, now and then.

Even now, eight weeks later, it sometimes hurts as much to lie down as it does to stand. Now you need something, again, to stop the pain. You need to wake up. You need to walk. You need to stand all day at work. You need a pill, now and then, even when the pain isn't there, just to keep the memory of pain away, to dull your senses, to float instead of walk or stand.

Singing. Chirping. Not mermaids. I don't know why I wake up thinking of mermaids: too many days at the Snack Shack. Sand in my brain just like it's embedded in my skin. No, not mermaids. Frantic birds sensing rain, I hope. Not mermaids at all, I say aloud to myself as if I have been submerged. I surface slowly from sleep enhanced with over-the-counter pain and sleep aids. Lie in a pool of sweat on top of my plaid bedcovers. Lie still. One last weekend to go at the Snack Shack on the beach, and I am done.

King, loyal black Labrador retriever, stretches out beside me. He should be sleeping in his crate in the corner, according to my father. But I rarely make him go in the crate. King is the first and the last dog I will ever have. I couldn't bear to have a King II. My mother once told me about a hotel in New York that has always had a pet cat. If the cat's male, it's named Hamlet; if it's female, it's named Matilda. If I were to die, would my parents just come up with a Max II?

Yup, maybe they would: Max II. But I couldn't have a King II. No dog could replace King. I wipe my slick hands down his black coat from head to tail; being rubbed by me is one of his favorite things, but these long strokes are as much an attempt to dry my palms, pull myself out, save myself from mermaids.

King shifts his snout from the pillow we are sharing and sniffs my hand. He would know me in the blackness of a cave or mine, or grave. He licks me. Now I'm wet from him, too. I think of kisses, of a girl kissing my face, finding my mouth, and drawing my lips to hers. Of course, I know it's my dog. I try to push him off my bed. He digs in. Instead, I stretch. Feels strange to stretch. I'm two and three-quarter inches taller than I was in that doctor's office. I could say three inches. I'm three inches taller.

I close my eyes and think about the girl I've been thinking about all summer: short, real short, only about five feet tall. I should call her petite. She's blond, swinging blond hair, and in a different string bikini at the Snack Shack at least three times a week, each time the bikini somehow magically growing smaller over glossy skin, until one day, perhaps today, she'll just show up naked. Her name: Samantha, never Sam or Sammie, only Samantha to her friends. I'm not one of her friends.

King groans, or I groan first. But he's just hungry, castrated and hungry, and I'm—what am I? I heave upright. His ears, alert, hear my movement, and he anchors himself onto four legs.

My mother is always saying I'm the most handsome guy she's ever met, but she's my mother. I have dimples, you can only see them when I smile, and blue eyes with 20/20 vision, and splotches of acne made worse from a summer eating hot dogs and soft swirl and sweating from every pore. I play soccer, varsity. Other than that, I'm ordinary, very ordinary, contrary to what my parents, the extraordinary state senator and his wife, want to believe.

I rub my lower back. One pill would do it. But I can't risk taking another pill from Dad's supply. Nothing over-the-counter is strong enough. Every day at work, I spend the whole day, or at least my eight-hour shift, standing, serving so-called customers, pathetic, moronic, sorry job that it is. I need one pill.

King shifts, raises his head, barks at the rustle of trees against the windows. I wish I could open them wide, and let some fresh air in for him. The central air is blasting a cold breeze, and my parents would kill me if I opened a window. But then, I never knew how hot summer could get until working behind a grill.

Two more days of work, and then Sunday—and Sunday night, the party. I groan. This is the last weekend before my last year of high school. I wish I could take a pill and have the whole year be over. My back tightens. Sunday night is my mother's annual birthday party for me. Will it be the last? I shouldn't even be having a party this year. She always gets me a huge cake and I don't want a cake this year. I don't even like cake. And I don't want to see any more of my so-called friends. But maybe Samantha will come, if I ask her. Maybe she'll show up in her bikini, one of the pink ones, I muse, easing onto my back, feeling sore and bruised, smelling the sea off my skin, even though I showered as soon as I got home last night. I can almost feel the pounding of the waves, hear voices calling out to me, not mermaids, I don't even know why I think of mermaids, it's the echoing of kids wanting ice cream swirls, demanding cold bottles of water, shoving sandy dollar bills at me. Ice cream. Vanilla? Chocolate? Or swirl? Two bucks. Water? Two bucks. Yes, it's cold. It's always cold. Vanilla? Chocolate? Or swirl? Two bucks.

Water? Two bucks. Yes, it's cold. It's always cold. Will I die say-ing those words? Will they be my last? Yup, they will be.

One more weekend. One last weekend.

I'm going to talk to Samantha today. I'm going to ask her to my party.

I've got to admit it, my head is clearing all too fast. I want to wake from sleep slowly. I want to keep focused on Samantha in her bikini or, better yet, another image: Samantha at the Snack Shack without a bikini, with nothing at all. Right now I want to be alone, not with her, but with the image of her strolling up to the Snack Shack all blond and tanned. I once overheard her tell her friends that she was a size zero. Can you be less than zero?

A rap at my bedroom door wipes out Samantha. "Time to get up, Max." My mother. I am never alone. Next to me, King scrambles. Barks at the closed door.

Now she lowers her voice. "What did I say about that dog, Max? Please quiet him down in there."

"Deb, he's a dog," says my father from somewhere behind my mother. "Maybe he should be let out of this room?"

"As long as we are in campaign mode, I can't have that dog all over the house. The way we are going to win this election is to be focused and organized. Isn't that what we agreed to, Glenn?"

All my life, she's been the PTA mom—president of my ele-mentary school PTA at one point, even the president of the Board of Education. My mother encouraged my father to run for office. Two years ago, people were eager to vote for change, anybody but the incumbent, and my father, to my surprise, and even to my mother's, I think, won. He won by a 1 percent margin, by fewer than two hundred votes. Winning is winning, he always said to me, my father, the former high school quarterback. There are no losers in this family, he said to me on election night.

King growls. Something instinctual in him says to protect and defend. I wish I had his instincts. I sense what he senses: my father is on the other side of the door. I can hear him breathing and hesitating. I pet King down with, "Good boy. Good dog. I'm going to get up and feed you in a minute." He turns to my voice as if challenging me to do it now. I'm not up to any challenge. I can feel the crack of every vertebra. A vise clamps down the center of my back.

When King leaps off the bed, I gasp for breath. If I lie still, the pain will subside. If I had a pill—I'll take something over-the-counter as soon as I get up, and not just two, I'll take three, three is a lucky number. But if I had one of my father's pills, I wouldn't be feeling any pain. I wouldn't feel anything. Maybe I could take one more without him noticing.

I hold my head up, dig my elbows into the bed, and steady myself. *Steady. I can do this. One last weekend.*

King is on alert. A fly lurches by his head. With a bolt, he snatches it between his jaws. Good boy. I tell him to stay, that I'll be right back, that I'll walk him in five minutes, as if he understands all this. He seems to understand. He swallows the fly and raises his blind eyes toward me. "Good boy." I open my bedroom door, and in the hall, my father is twitching his thumbs. He's sending a message off, probably the first of many to his staff. He has two identical devices, he says, so he can keep his personal life and business separate, and he doesn't know how to work either one smoothly. His thumbs jab at the screen.

"What are you trying to do?" I ask.

"Forward texts."

"I didn't know you even knew how to text."

"I don't."

"Let me."

He hesitates. He's clueless about this stuff. I know it, and he knows it. "I got it, Max. Don't worry."

I shrug. I have no interest in politics. None at all.

"I'm having my staff draft a reply to these, but they need my input. Damn it, I don't think what I sent made sense . . ."

I slouch against the wall.

"You okay, Max?"

"Just need this summer to be over."

"Me too," he says, distracted by the device in hand, flickering and buzzing, the fly you can't kill in the room.

Barkley

I do not sleep.

No need. I check again. The Glock model 19 is in the bottom of my desk drawer, under the stack of schoolwork, specifically under my fifth-grade book report, "Soccer in Many Countries," on which Mrs. Larkin noted, "A plus. Perfect grammar."

I stare at my keyboard. Letters invert. Lose their proper location on the screen. Better to compose with a pen. The computer is for games. The pen understands that there are rules. The pen fits into my hand as well as the semiautomatic pistol.

I double-check the bolted security locks on the inside of my bedroom door. All is well. I turn up the music: metal, guitar, drums pounding. Reverberations. I do not even need the actual sound. I can listen to what is in my head and be fine. Absolutely fine.

My parents, of course, worry about school, but I will go back. I will return to a university, not that community college, that false city upon a hill. Not those teachers, those con artists of grades and procedures and rules. I am the future that they have been waiting for. I will teach them.

It was remarkably easy to buy the Glock. I drove out of state to a gun show. I listened to the voice. *Careful. Smile. Walk perfectly. Purchase the Glock 19.*

I shared my official New York State driver's license with them, offered the funds earned from all my summer work at the Snack Shack as well as assisting Jared, and purchased the gun, legal and unremarkable. Once you turn twenty-one, the world opens up to you.

On the other side of my locked bedroom door, my mother and father hush each other, believing that I am in bed, asleep. I have spent the last ten hours and fifteen minutes at my desk, in the game zone. The world is at war, enemies at every turn. Yet I can split myself. See myself from the outside, at the computer, and hear my parents, now tap-tapping on the locked door, urging me to wake up.

My mother is sure to be impeccable. She is a gym fiend, petite and naturally athletic. She is a perfectionist about her looks, her work, her home. Her goals in life are: a size zero, another promotion, and me. I am her project.

"He hasn't showered in I don't know how long. I'm telling you, something is wrong, Dan."

"Nothing. He's working hard. He's an unbelievable kid."

"Exactly, but he's got to take a shower. How long has it been? Two or even three months since he's showered?"

"Can't be."

"Dan."

"You're not with him every minute of the day, Kate."

"He is breaking my heart."

A perfect heart. Perfect blood pressure, cholesterol, body mass index, she will tell anyone that admires her, and she is often admired.

"Nothing is wrong, Kate. Stop being overdramatic. This is all part of growing up. He's an awesome kid."

My father likes to unfurl words: Awesome. Unbelievable. Phenomenal. I am often described this way, and it has become meaningless. He speaks, but is no longer heard. He is indiscriminate with language, throwing around adjectives like confetti.

He, like my mother, is in advertising sales at a cable television network, different networks, neither of which I will watch. In fact, they only watch the commercials, not the shows. For these cable networks, they sell sixties, thirties, and fifteens. This is the breakdown of commercial airtime. Their lives are measured out in units of seconds. Air is not what they breathe but what they sell. We create new meanings when we must, but how can I listen to these people who sell air and time?

"Not showering all summer, Dan? Shaving his head? Asking us about guns? Something's got to give. You know what's going to give? Exactly. Me. I'm going to give."

I shoot one last enemy alien on the screen in a blaze of light, and turn away. Life is about the odds of survival, about the seconds in the minute in which to make a decision.

"Believe me, he's a good kid. An amazing kid. He's just a little caught up in those video games."

"We should threaten to take them away, shouldn't we?"

"He downloads them from the Internet."

"He's online for hours. I'm talking seven, eight, nine hours at a time. That can't be normal. Is that normal?" She does not wait for an answer; she has it. "Exactly, it's not normal."

"Okay, maybe it's the games. Or it's the Internet. Every other parent blames that, why shouldn't we? He likes these games, I don't know why. Don't all the kids? It's not like he's going to go out and buy a gun. Believe me, he's not." My father sighs. He is careful to retreat from her perfect wrath.

"Will you talk to him, Dan?"

"I'll talk to him, but I think you're overreacting."

"Exactly, I'm overreacting. Your answer to everything." She bangs on the door. "Barkley, honey, time to get up. You okay in there? Mommy and Daddy have to get to work, but we want to make sure you're going to be home tonight so we can talk."

Where else would I be?

My father pops open his first diet soda of the day. He drinks diet soda all day. We all have our addictions. His addictions are diet soda and outsized adjectives.

"I'm up. Getting ready for work," I finally call out as I relock my desk drawer.

"Is anything wrong, Barkley? Answer Mommy."

"Nothing is wrong."

"See, Kate, he's up. He's getting ready for work. And why are you talking to him like he's a kid? I got to tell you," and here he raises his voice so I know that he is really talking to me, "that's an awesome young man in there. He spent his whole summer working. You think jobs like his, at the beach all summer, are easy jobs?"

"Now you're blaming me for making him work?"

My mother pushed me to take this job after I was expelled from the community college. I wanted to join the army or navy. I found a recruitment center. They gave me a slew of tests. But they know nothing, the army. The navy. The Defense Department. The government of the United States. They told me I was unfit for service. I didn't want to hear it—not from someone behind a desk—not from someone who never shot a gun.

I plan to be a filmmaker now—to control the images and the sounds. I should dream big. Small men dream small. Be a famous director of superheroes, the next generation of a Batman or Superman or Ironman, and in my spare time advocate for the environment. In interviews, I will say that the reason I create is to save the world by any means possible. At that community college there was an intro to cinema studies class—and a waiting list for the class. I will not be wait-listed again.

"I just think he's plain old terrific," says my father in too loud a voice. "And we should be telling him that. You hear me, Barkley?"

More bangs on the bedroom door from my mother, wanting me to come out, to inspect me. I growl under my breath. The dank smell of sweat, skin cells, dying off, and saltwater comfort me.

Her rapping stops as abruptly as it started.

"I'm telling you, something's wrong with our son, Dan.

Why, all of a sudden, is he hanging out with that nephew of yours?"

"What do you mean?"

"You know what I mean. And your father."

"You worry too much, Kate."

"And what about your father?" I can detect everything: her shallow breaths, his thrumming reluctance against a can of soda, the whoosh of central air chemically scented with roses, and the sense that we may lose it all in a blink of an eye. "Have you done some more thinking about him?"

"No, he's dead. And I have a lot more to worry about right now. I have that trip coming up to L.A., and I feel my whole job is riding on it. Can we look into this after Labor Day? Come up with a strategy?"

"Exactly, he's dead," she says. "Didn't he kill himself with his hunting rifle?"

"I don't know, Kate. Nobody ever said. My mother wanted him buried in a church cemetery, and that couldn't happen if it was a suicide."

"Nobody ever said what it was. Dan, open your eyes, there's history here. Your family's. We need to look into this."

"I was never very good at history," says my father, a lame joke.

"And that nephew of yours. Jared. A pothead. I've smelled it on Jared, and so have you. So, what exactly am I missing? We have to face facts, maybe our son is into drugs. Maybe we have to consider that. What do you think of that? He's very close to that nephew of yours."

Tell them that you abhor drugs. You do not pollute your body. You will not be found floating in the oceans of the world like an empty plastic bottle. You will walk perfectly. You will show others the way. This is the voice of rationality in my head.

I hunch over the screen. My father never hunches. He is a trim man with a swagger. He wears crisp, monogrammed shirts; expensive ties; and even more expensive designer suits. He wears it all like they're brand-new or borrowed, his shoulders stiff as if to say, "No one is taking this suit from me."

"Let me tell you, I know young guys like Barkley and like Jared. Barkley is not Jared. He's not into anything like that. We're living the dream here—great neighborhood, fabulous house, good jobs, and I plan on doing everything I can to make sure I stay in this dream. Jared's had a hard road with my sister's divorce. Maybe it's time we trust Barkley?"

"Exactly. I don't trust anybody, is that the issue?"

"We are going to miss the seven thirty-six train," my father says with finality. The soda can crunches and crashes into the far-off kitchen garbage. "Let's continue this later? Timing is everything in life."

I have to hand it to my parents—time is both precious and a commodity.

They never miss that train. The world ends if they miss that train into Manhattan. Ninety-eight percent of success is showing up, or so says my father.

Even more so, their morning routines—the workouts on the elliptical machines, the cans of diet soda, their Long Island Rail

Road—define them. I even respect them for their adherence, no matter what, to their schedules. "We love you, Barkley," says my mother. "You hear us? Answer."

Neither of them waits for a reply. The front door slams shut. And the interior assault, the surge, the rush, begins. I rub my hands over my head. The precision of skin instead of hair sends chills. No need to shower. No need to change my clothes. I find my sunglasses and take a few moments to align them evenly across my face. I even practice smiling with them on. Film directors wear glasses like this. All the world is reflected off these glasses. I am safe behind them, readied and armored for my own ascent into the outer world.

Everything about the beach is anticipation.

Izzy can't decide what she should wear: The pink bathing suit? The pink-and-white? The pink one with stars? I've made her swear to tell our father that we went to the movies.

"Wear your favorite," I call out from my bedroom to hers next door.

"They are all my favorites," she says, laying out each one on her floor, studying them. "Which one did I wear last time?"

"Green with frogs. That's my favorite."

"That's my favorite, too!"

Sometimes I wish my life were like Izzy's again. That the biggest choice I had to make was like hers, over a bathing suit: pink with stars or green with frogs? I have to help her into the bathing suit, which is perfect on her. Her build is the exact opposite of mine and my mother's. She's wispy, delicate, and fair. I brush her hair into a ponytail, and she insists on a pink rubber band—as she reminds me, her absolutely favorite color.

But I'm fine. I can handle all this. It's a mantra I've repeated to myself the past three months.

I yank on my dark blue Speedo. Unlike Izzy, I have three bathing suits: light blue, dark blue, and orange. I have no favorite color. I hate to shop for myself. Nothing ever fits right. Even at six years old, Izzy is a better shopper than I am.

I hurry into the kitchen. No one has done the dishes in a week. My mother would make us French toast or scrambled eggs with bits of green pepper and tomato for breakfast. She would know how to get the laundry washed before it piled up in baskets like used-clothing donations nobody wants. She would be able to get Izzy into her bathing suit, brush her hair, spray her with sunscreen—and get the dishes done—before noon. Before we go, I'll push the vacuum through the house and make sure all the windows are open wide. I'll dust her tables crowded with knickknacks on lace doilies, and at least the house will smell like my mother's house, of summer breezes and lemon oil.

"Izzy? If you don't come now, I'm leaving you." I shake some stale cereal into the last clean bowl. Before my mother had her stroke, I never had to think of dishes, or laundry, or the sun burning Izzy, or me.

There is the "before" for everything. Before the stroke, my mother worked as an adolescent psychologist, part-time. My father always kidded her that part-time meant full-time to her. She loved her job, though. She'd run through the day. She did everything fast—her job, her cooking, her talking. I don't ever remember her still, or sitting, until I saw her lying on the bathroom floor, by the toilet, that morning.

One minute *before* she was fine.

Izzy was in her bed. My mother had woken up with another headache. But she hadn't even drunk her morning coffee. The kitchen was full of the scent of fresh coffee.

"I'm taking a cup of coffee," I said from the kitchen. I had just started drinking coffee in April, on my seventeenth birthday. I liked it fresh-roasted with cream and two sugars, the same as my mother. I had convinced her to spend a little more and buy "organic fair trade" beans.

"I want to blow-dry my hair, so I'm unplugging the coffee pot," I called out to her. I didn't want a fuse to blow again. This house is old and the rooms boxy and tight, even the electricity seems to be set up for a time and place when everything moved slower. My mother never complained, even though, if anyone asked where we lived, she often conveniently dropped the "South" part from "Lakeshore."

That late May morning, I hung in the kitchen for a moment or two longer, daydreaming, breathing in the coffee as much as drinking it, running my hands through my tangled hair, thinking about nothing, and everything, a moment when my mind filled up with the enormity of myself. I heard a crash but I thought it was something else—the garbage being collected— roofers on top of someone else's house—I wasn't paying enough attention, not to my mother, not to someone who was always there. She always had everything under control. That morning, I had one of my writer's notebooks out, a black-and-white composition notebook, nothing fancy, and was thinking about a poem, or a string of words, or I don't know what.

"Before" is a strange, curious word—both prior and next—both what preceded and what is about to happen—both memory and what will be. "Before" is the kind of word my English teacher would spend lots of time on as if there were time in the world anymore for one word, any time for anything but what has to be learned now. And the *now* is over and gone in a blink, without a moment to reflect, or to foresee what's coming at you—because there's always something else.

Now, I can't stand the smell of coffee. I can't drink coffee. I can't eat coffee ice cream or fancy desserts like tiramisu. I can't hang out with everybody else in the local coffee shop. One minute, she was fine. I didn't hear her fall. I didn't hear her body hit the floor. The world was all there, too much with me, and I wasn't paying attention at all.

And when I found her, when I finally finished that cup of fair-trade organic fresh-roasted coffee and wanted to blow-dry my hair, I don't even know how many minutes had passed (the ambulance guys asked, and I could only guess: Five? Twenty?). I didn't even know what I was seeing.

My mother was on the floor. Her body was sprawled on the tiles. Her body had hit the floor.

My father would later point out that I had Red Cross first aid training, as if bandages and antiseptic could have fixed her. My mother had made me take those classes so I would be prepared to babysit. I didn't want to babysit; I never babysat for other families. Didn't I have enough of little kids with my own sister? However, to make my mother happy, I took the course.

Yet that morning, I only stared at her. She wasn't supposed to be on the floor. She was supposed to be getting dressed. I had to blow-dry my hair. She was unconscious on the sea green tiles. Her purple toothbrush was next to the sink, and I thought: I have to brush my teeth. My mouth tasted of night, pasty and leaden. I almost reached for the toothpaste first. Instead, I bent down, I'm sure of it, and touched her hand. Her fingers were already stiff. I said, once, softly, "Mom." She didn't move, and I put my face next to hers as if the problem were that she couldn't see me.

Why didn't I run when I heard her fall? Why did I waste time? Why did I hesitate? If I had helped her sooner, would she be like this?

Later her doctor said to me that she might have had a series of small strokes before the bigger one. He couldn't be sure. He did say that she was at the hospital in plenty of time for new, life-saving medicines, which she received. Her life was saved.

But maybe I could have done more.

I pick up the hairbrush, her hairbrush, and sweep it down through my hair, once, twice, at least twenty-five strokes. I'm facing the mirror, but I don't truly see myself because if I look I'll see her. I hear her deep, smooth voice say my name. *Claire.* She named me Claire, telling me my name meant "clear and bright" in Latin. She's saying my name to me as if I'm her lifeboat in the wide empty sea. I close my eyes and hear my mother telling me to brush the back of my hair: *Make sure you get out all those knots, Claire. Make sure you brush at least twenty-five strokes, angel.* I want to see her. And I do. I see this: Her hair is chopped off at her neck. Her eyes are red-rimmed, naked without makeup, unfocused. She wears glasses instead of contacts. She used to hate wearing glasses, even the violet ones, which she once thought of as "funky" and now just look weird and oversized on her. Her good arm, the one that can still rise and fall, is scabbed, scaly, bruised black and sickly yellow from the intravenous needles, and it reaches for me—

Stop it! She will get better. She will come home—restored, that's the word she used, like an old piece of furniture. But that doesn't sound right. She'll be home and everything will be back to normal. She promised. That's enough.

I open my eyes and brush, hard.

Max

"Vanilla? Chocolate? Or swirl?" I ask the kid, even though it's way too early for ice cream.

"Chocolate?"

I wait him out.

"Vanilla?" He's nine or ten. His swim trunks hang on bony hips. His hair sticks up from sand and sea. In his fist is a crumpled up, sweaty ten-dollar bill, clutched in a way that says: I don't have to care about money. He's North Lakeshore all the way.

"Swirl. How about swirl?" I offer. I remember being his age, being given money, trusted for the first time to return with change, and I remember the lecture afterward about being careless with money. I may be North Lakeshore, too, but my parents, especially my dad, care about the so-called "value of a dollar."

"I hate swirl," he shouts at me.

"Vanilla, then?"

"I hate vanilla. Got any other flavors?"

I stare him down. "Vanilla or chocolate or swirl."

The beach is quickly filling up with more kids like this one, kids who will all run over throwing dollar bills at me like I'm in a cage. My mother used to bring me to this same beach, and it hasn't changed much since then. Every winter, there are warnings about sand erosion, about the ocean reclaiming the shore, about the barrier of land between the rest of the land and the Atlantic sea washing away, and one recent October there was even a major hurricane. Ninety percent of Long Island lost electrical power. The tide rose across Ocean Parkway and upended it. Water surged into houses. Even those that had always been far enough from the ocean or bay were flooded. And yet every summer, we are back.

Of course, the larger state park has more shoreline, more room for everyone to spread out, and it's only a mile or so west of here, past the dunes. Anybody can go there. Some even take buses from I don't know where—Queens or Brooklyn or other parts of the city. I never go there. Nobody goes there, it's too crowded, and of course, we have our beach.

You have to live in the town of Lakeshore to go to this section of the Atlantic Ocean. You have to pay an annual fee and show identification to a group of teens, the ones with the easy jobs, sitting in an air-conditioned tollbooth out front, checking town passes. What everyone loves about this setup is that it feels exclusive. It's the same water, the same sand as a mile to the west. I think some people, my parents, even believe the problems are over there, not here. They believe that there is a line you can draw in the sand—on one side you're from Lakeshore and you're safe, even if you're from South Lakeshore.

I've got to admit that within the boundaries of the town beach the North Lakeshore high school kids don't like to be seen with the South Lakeshore high school kids. An outsider wouldn't know who's who to tell the difference, though of course, we all know.

Some days our town beach is twice as packed as the state park, but it is packed only with people like us.

Trish bustles around me. She's in her usual defiantly striped tank top and shorts, as if saying to the world, "Nobody is going to tell Trish Nelson what to wear, even if she's nearly six feet tall and over three hundred pounds."

"Excuse me, sweetie," she says, as if I'm the one in the way.

Trish is the type of girl I'd never talk to in school, would pass in the hall and look through as if someone her size could be invisible, though I don't know if there are any girls in my school who have quite her heft and attitude. She's South Lakeshore all the way. She's not someone who lets you ignore her. But then, I had to spend my entire summer working with her in the twelve-foot-wide Snack Shack at the edge of the town beach.

"I'll get this, sweetie," she says, saving me, again, from a nine- or ten-year-old boy who can't make up his mind. Not much different from sixteen—nearly seventeen—year-old boys. That's why it's better, sometimes, not to think at all.

I want to tell the kid that it doesn't matter whether he chooses vanilla, chocolate, or swirl. His life doesn't hinge on that decision. But I remember when it seemed like it did. Now, nothing I decide matters. I didn't want to work here, but my father had a friend who was connected and I got the job without even an interview. My father made me take this job.

"Your mother knows you're asking for ice cream at ten in

the morning?" asks Trish. "You want to grow up and look like me, sweetie?"

"I won't," he says.

"You won't?"

"I'm a boy."

"Yes, you are," she says, giving him a serious look, making him blush and throw back his thin shoulders. "So what kind of ice cream do you want, big guy? Vanilla or chocolate?"

He is suddenly shy with her size and intensity.

"I like chocolate," she says.

"I like chocolate, too."

"Chocolate." She gives him the biggest chocolate cone the kid's probably had all summer. "Two bucks, sport."

I squint out to the ocean glistening in the sun, and wish I were anywhere else.

The kid hands Trish the ten and almost forgets to wait for change. She's good, though. She calls him back. Sometimes I just put it in my pocket—as a tip, that's how I think of it. If anyone remembers, or if a mother sends a tearful kid back, I always give up the money, making the kid feel guilty, like it was his fault for being careless and stupid and a kid.

Peter is another "coworker." Even in my head, I put the word in quotes because I can't reconcile that he and I are both in the same job, being paid the same wages. Of course, he's happy he has the job. He likes the job. This job is a challenge for him—unpacking water bottles, wedging them down into the tubs of ice, making sure that we have enough ice from the ancient ice machine clunking out cubes in the back. The only strange thing about him at first sight is the work boots. Everyone else wears sneakers to the Snack Shack. One of the rules is no flip-flops. But there's no rule against wearing big yellow work boots on summer days. Peter clomps around the Snack Shack in his size-thirteen work boots, ready and willing to lift, carry, or stack.

Barkley usually shows up at some point. He's twenty-one years old and sees himself as the "assistant" manager. That's a title he gave himself. He's the same as me and Trish and Peter, except that he closes up when Phil, the manager, isn't around, and Phil is never around. In fact, Barkley was the assistant manager of the varsity soccer team when I was a freshman. As far as I could tell, he was in charge of water for the team. So maybe it's something about the title. I didn't know him that well, but all summer he's been acting like we were, and still are, friends, and I'm trapped. I've got to admit, today I wouldn't mind him showing up. Not that I need him for the Snack Shack. Any moron could run the Snack Shack. But I'm thinking of taking him up on something else.

"Peter! Do you need help, sweetie?" shouts Trish. "If you need another hand, you have to ask!"

He's grunting, carrying twice as much as he should be, helping me out, really. Ever since he found out that I hurt my back playing soccer, he's offered to load up the water bottles and ice from the back. I could lift if I had to, but Peter gets me out of the extra work.

"Max, I'll take care of Peter," says Trish. I guess today she's decided that she's in charge. "You take care of Daisy."

I hate Daisy. That's what we call the soft serve ice cream machine. Trish is much better with it. I'm not mechanical. Her pours are neater. Boxes of a thick, milky substance have to be dumped into the back of Daisy several times a day, and somehow, it comes out as ice cream. But Trish knows the tricks to Daisy—when she's empty, how much to pour in so the ice cream is creamy and smooth and doesn't melt before the kids leave the Shack, which only means that they'll come back crying.

"You guys are my best friends," says Peter to nobody. He tends to talk to the floor, or to the walls. He has issues with eye contact.

"We're not," I say, lifting a stack of water bottles out of his arms instead of dealing with the ice cream machine. I also hate having Trish order me around, even though I've got to admit, she's good at it. "After tomorrow, I'm never going to see you again. And can you deal with Daisy, Trish? She hates me."

"Why am I loved by those who shouldn't love me?" Trish asks in her over-the-top philosophical way. But she goes to the ice cream machine. The insides smell sour.

"Now what's your problem, sweetie?" She's speaking to the machine.

"We're going to see you," Peter says to me. He spins toward Trish for confirmation, knocking over the cartons of swirl mix. They crash to the floor. Lucky they weren't opened yet, or the day would be totally ruined. "Aren't we going to see Max?"

Trish picks up the boxes for Daisy with ease. She could probably bench-press more than I could, too. "He just means that he's going back to school—and so are you."

"But we can be friends even if we are in different schools. Can't we, Max?"

I shift the water bottles down to the ground. There is no answer for this. I don't want to answer. I don't want to be friends with him or Trish. I want to erase this summer.

"Can't we, Max?"

How do you tell someone like Pete that these kinds of friendships don't last, that they weren't made to last more than the summer even in the best of circumstances, and these certainly haven't been the best. That some friends aren't meant to be, except in stories, or books. You miss a penalty shot and no one wants to talk to you, and maybe you don't want to talk to them, either. You want your own oblivion, and they don't understand. You don't answer their texts or even answer the messages of the one or two who venture to call. None of this has much to do with Peter, but you know you won't be friends with him past tomorrow. I close my eyes. I want to be inside my own head, nowhere else.

"Didn't we have a great summer together, Max? We'll still be friends after it's over, won't we?"

You won't answer his messages or take his calls. You will never see him again. But I hear myself saying into the dead space between us, "Yup, Peter. We'll be friends."

Claire
Friday, 11:00 A.M.

"Izzy. Let's go. Now. I'm ready to go. We have to get out of here. Let's move it. Let's go."

Focus on getting out the door. Lock the door. Get in the minivan and drive away as if you're never coming back.

On the ride to the beach, Izzy, in the backseat, asks, "Can I open the window, Claire?"

"No," I say automatically.

"I want to taste the ocean."

"You can't taste the ocean."

"I can. My lips can lick the air."

I know my mother and father hate me to drive Izzy around with the windows open, even if she is mashed into her too-small toddler safety seat with her seat belt across her six-year-old chest. But I love the image of her "licking the air," and so I say, "Yes, go ahead. But stay in your seat."

I unlock the window and she zips it down. She shifts to the edge of the seat. Her hair swoops behind her. She laughs. Her mouth open, she licks the air.

I smell the ocean before I see it—like a hot burst in my mouth. The sky is bluer here. I always think the beach should be farther than it is, that it should be a long trip, because when I was Izzy's age it always felt that way. I forget sometimes that we live on an island and that water, the Long Island Sound to the north and the Atlantic Ocean to the south, surrounds us. Unlucky cars slow down to pay the tolls. Those cars go off to the right, to Jones Beach, the state beach. I head the other way, toward our town beach. The parking lot here is less crowded than the others down Ocean Parkway. I flash our town pass.

"Promise me again, you're not going to tell Daddy that I brought you to the beach?" I nod my head to her, urging her to imitate me, which she readily does.

"I never told the other times. Did I?"

"I don't think you did."

"I am not going to tell anybody, not even me," she repeats.

I park the whale of a minivan. Across the parking lot, we hold hands, race-walk. My beach bag jostles against my shoulder. Cars shoot around us, and soon we are running, our ponytails loosening, the sea salt caught in our hair. Ahead of us is the tunnel that skims under Ocean Parkway from the parking lots to the actual oceanfront. The tunnel, short enough, is dark, damp; it's a passage to another world. On one side is endless heat, on the other the ocean breeze. On one side, pavement, on the other, sand.

When I was Izzy's age, I was scared of the tunnel. Even then, it had no lights and water dripped down the concrete sides, no matter how dry a summer. Bugs drowned in its stagnant pools. My mother would encourage me to run, meet her on the other side. She wanted me to be brave, she said. Screams would echo, my own and of other kids. All of us were sent running through the dark. Now, I plunge in with Izzy in hand. No one permits the little kids to run loose anymore. We all have bags and chairs and children in tow and somehow we hold on to it all. I'm still a little afraid of touching the walls, of the quick darkness, of the stench of urine mixed with sea and coconut sunscreen. I wonder if my mother felt fear and just hid it from me.

Izzy tugs loose, races ahead of me.

Packs of families swarm by me. Mothers pull wagons of gear with them—they are prepared not just for a day at the beach, but for a lifetime, with coolers, blankets, chairs, umbrellas, and sets of underwear and shorts and T-shirts.

I bump my bag against the shoulder of one girl striding in her black bikini and silver flip-flops toward the beach. She gives me a look that says, "How dare you touch me," until even she sees that I'm no one, no one she needs to be worried about, and then makes a face and rolls her eyes and fixes her lipstick as if that's what the real problem is. I never understood lipstick on the beach. Hers is hot pink.

"Izzy," I say, realizing I've lost sight of her.

She'll know to wait on the other side. She's a smart kid, starting first grade next week. Sweat stings my lips, mixes with the sea air, and I can taste salt as if I'm melting. "Izzy! Wait up!" I say as if I can see her. She's disappeared among the bare legs and portable freezers and carts packed high with supplies. I break into the sunlight.

Along the boardwalk and onto the beach, in a trick of light, people meld into other people. Girls in bikinis swim together—not really swim, they don't go in the water; but they walk in schools together, a flutter of legs. The guys in the baggy, long swim trunks crash into the water as one; they plunge into the waves headfirst, and rise, flexing their abs and running their hands over their flat, hard stomachs. I hurry along the boardwalk searching for my sister, for a little girl in pink—no, in green with frogs—and curly blond hair. She is lost. The girl in the bikini with the pink lipstick slithers past with her friends surrounding her, all of them in bikinis and lipstick.

"Izzy!"

Once when I was Izzy's age, my father brought me to the beach alone (I don't know where my mother was, since they rarely split up), but I was with him one moment and then I wasn't. I turned around and he wasn't there. Sea gulls, hundreds of them, had landed near me in too-still lines. Until then, I was going along on the beach, certain I'd find my father. But these birds had black beady eyes that didn't blink. I was sure they would snatch me up and drop me in the middle of the ocean. I would be lost and never found. I screamed, "Daddy." And every father looked like my father: dark curly hair, muscled bodies strong enough to pick me up with one arm, a bathing suit that was blue or green and had a pattern on it like palm trees, a soft belly and a broad chest matted with lots of hair, thick enough to comb. I ran from those sea gulls certain if I ran fast enough I'd find my father. I was lost for what seemed like hours. My father swore to my mother it was only for a half hour, an hour tops that I was missing. But in that time, a half hour, an hour, I knew that the only one who could save me was me.

"Izzy!"

I catch my reflection in a pair of mirrored sunglasses. I look like I'm falling apart, hair out of my ponytail, beach bag overflowing. He tilts his head, seeing me, watching me watch myself. In the reflection of his sunglasses, I'm all wide brown eyes. I'm distorted, elongated; but he doesn't turn his head or take off the glasses, and I wonder if he's looking for someone, too. He has a shaved head and a cold grin.

Then, from behind him, Izzy appears. She races toward me: giggling, dashing to my side, and jabbing her hand back into my own. "Slow poke," she cries out.

"Don't do that again."

"Do what?"

"Run away from me."

"I'm right here," she says. "Anyways, I'm not afraid."

"I'm not afraid, either," I say, though I am angry at the fear welling inside me. I take a deep breath. The heavyset, bald guy trains his mirrored sunglasses on us. I look down toward Izzy. I've seen enough of my distorted image.

"Yes, you are, Claire," says Izzy. "You're always afraid something is going to happen. To me."

I exhale. We're here. It's going to be a blistering day. I am not afraid.

The girl in the black bikini and silver flip-flops slides by with her friends. She winks at Izzy and ignores me. She's barely raising her legs, more gliding along the wood and sand. Strangers are always attracted to Izzy, commenting on her heart-shaped face, her quick smile, her blond curls, how happy and precocious and adorable she is.

"Someday I want a bathing suit like that," says Izzy, pulling toward the other teenagers. "Why don't you ever wear a bathing suit like that, Claire?"

"I like the frogs on your bathing suit more," I say to her, tickling her tummy to make her laugh, which she does.

"Beach," says Izzy.

And I wish I were a kid again. I don't want to be the responsible one anymore.

"Beach," she repeats, as if trying to be reasonable.

I am waiting for the day to end, and the day after that, and for school to start and end, and for the day when I go off to college and leave you, though you will always be my little sister and I will never really leave you. I need to go. I need to know if there will ever be one person, that's all I really need, one guy who will look at me and understand me. And kiss me. I have to add that. I'm probably the only seventeen-year-old in North or South Lakeshore who hasn't been kissed in a way that says you're the only one I'm thinking of, looking at, seeing.

"Come on, Claire. You're just thinking too much. You're going to hurt your brain."

"That's what Mommy always said—or says. She's still going to say that, isn't she. I still think too much."

"If your head wasn't screwed on you'd lose that too, Claire."

My mother used to say that, too. And Izzy is repeating it with the exact exasperated tone as our mother. She's also tugging on my arm. I force myself to focus on her. "Did you ever lose your head, Claire?

"Not yet."

"Why'd she say that?"

"I was a daydreamer."

"Aren't you still?"

I don't have time to dream in the day. I'm shaking my head. I'm not a daydreamer anymore. I'm practical. I get things done.

"Can we hurry up?" she's saying in her grown-up six-year-old voice. She shakes my arm.

Why do I feel like turning around and going home? Going into my room, locking the door? Anything could happen here. We are too exposed. "Stand still," I say to my sister and spray more sunscreen on her from top to bottom, emptying the can.

"If we don't hurry up, we're going to miss the ocean, Claire."

She looks at me, smiling, pleading. There's no other adult to tell her—or me—what to do. I look around as if to double-check that my father—or mother—aren't suddenly appearing. We are alone, and I realize, free, *free:* unfettered, unburdened, unleashed, I think, running through synonyms at top speed, for at least today.

"What are you waiting for, Izzy?" I say, kidding her, dashing along the boardwalk without her, squinting into the sun, resolved to have a last day at the beach that will sustain me through the winter.

I expect her to follow me. But she stands there, alone, looking panicked into the blinding sun, as if I am going to leave her. "Izzy, come on. Let's go," I say, and her thin legs scamper to me. She entwines her fingers through mine. She swings our arms together. I am never going to have a moment alone again, am I? We walk, our hands locked, toward the far end of the boardwalk.

The Atlantic Ocean stretches before us, miles to the east and miles to the west. At the far end to the east is beach, ocean, and more ocean, and at the far end of the western horizon is New York City with its skyscrapers and bridges in miniature, like a model, against the blue-blue skies. Before us is the chance to be lost in ourselves.

"Look," Izzy says, pointing back toward the restrooms. I hope Izzy doesn't have to go to the bathroom already. It will take us a half hour just to get her bathing suit pulled down and back up.

"He talked to me." She points to the bulky guy with the shaved head and mirrored glasses, now pacing near the men's room.

"What did he say?" I ask, focusing instead on the beach. I like to lie near the edge of the crowds, near the dunes and sea grass.

"He liked my bathing suit. And he wanted to know your name, Claire."

"I hope you didn't tell him."

"I told him: Claire Wallace."

"So you didn't give him my middle name, too?"

"I'm sorry, Claire."

"Did he want to know your name, Izzy?"

"No."

"Good. Don't tell strangers your name."

"I didn't! I said I told him yours."

"I got that." I glance back toward him again, but now he's gone into the bathroom or the crowds, become a shadow in the light. "I'm sure he's harmless, just another guy who likes to hang out here."

"Claire, when are we going into the water? Can we dive in? Can we dive right into the biggest wave? Can we? Can we, Claire?"

I should warn her against the dangers of the sea. I should tell her to be cautious. I need to let her know that I am in charge, that she can't be running off. I'm the grown-up here. Instead, I whisk her onto the blistering sand, each of us doing a little dance. I shoot to the left and dash between blankets, jumping over other people's shoes and sandy towels and bare legs. I shouldn't be running, but I am, and she's following right behind me, screeching and laughing. I lick the air. Taste the sea in my mouth.

Max

"You load the ice in, Pete." I snag a cold bottle of water out of the freezer and roll it along my face. The sun beats down. This day is never going to end.

"Okay, Maxie," says Peter with a loopy smile, as if he's been thinking of this retort all summer. He hates being called anything but "Peter," except by me.

"Maxie?" I say back to him as if I'm angry. "Who you calling Maxie?"

"You," he says, staring at the floor, as if I'm mad at him.

"I like 'Maxie,'" says Trish. "How'd you think of that, Peter?"

Peter shrugs, proud of himself. "He called me 'Pete.'"

"Hey," I say as if I'm angry. In fact, nobody has ever called me "Maxie." Most kids, guys on the team, call me "Cooper." If you didn't know me, you'd think that was my name. "You can call me 'Maxie,' Petey. Yup, only you."

Trish snorts. "If I need you, I know how to call you. I'll whistle, sweetie." She whistles off.

I slump against the back wall and slug down the water. They've been okay to work with all summer, Trish and Peter, not that I want to admit it to them. Peter loads more ice in with a crash and a wreckage of cubes bouncing off the never-washed wood floors. He's smiling, kneeling down, cleaning up his mess.

He's done more than his share of work. I look out to the beach, to the ocean, gulping the water down. To the side, Trish snaps the ice cream machine back in place and, calling out that we need more cones, leaves Peter and me for the supply closet in the back. We also need hot dogs for the grill. But the grill is Barkley's job and there's no sign of him.

A line suddenly forms in front of the Snack Shack, and at the front of it is Jackson.

"Hey! Hey! Petey. Petey? You hear me? You see me? Over here. I'm right here. Come here. Your job is to wait on me. You know that's your job, isn't it?"

I can't deal with him today. Jackson. He was always one of the tallest kids in our grade, and he must have passed six feet this summer. The captain of the varsity soccer team, his hair is styled after European soccer players, shaggy-long, and streaked blonder from the sun. I run my fingers through my hair. I don't think I even combed my hair today. Last time Jackson was here I took off into the men's room, pleaded a break. He looks like he has spent his summer sleeping with every girl who will sleep with him, which is most, judging from the rumors at school. He gets to drive a BMW to the beach, unlike me with an old Jeep. My father says that he can't have his son driving a nicer car than most of his constituents. I turn half away, fiddling with the ice cream machine as if something is wrong with it again.

"Where's Cooper? Or the Bark? They didn't leave you in charge, did they?" He says it again when Peter doesn't answer. "They didn't leave you in charge? Are you in charge, Petey?" On the surface, he sounds like a reasonable customer. However, I've noticed for the first time that he likes to repeat himself, as if, having said something once, it makes it more clever to say it again.

Peter crashes the rest of the ice into the box. Overflowing, most of the ice scatters around my feet and into the corner, milky white, like field mice.

"How about it, Pete?" he asks. "How about it?"

She laughs next to Jackson. Not Trish. Trish is nowhere to be seen. Anyway, Trish's laugh, also off-key, is arguably nicer, at least until you see that it's coming out of the three hundred pounds of her. This laugh is streaming out of Samantha, in her shiny black bikini today. This is the same bikini she wore last Friday. I wonder if she has racks of bikinis with the names of the days pinned onto them.

"Can I help you?" says Peter, gripping the empty bucket of ice.

"Can you help me?" Jackson asks, and then asks again, as if this is a rhetorical question, and not Peter trying his best.

I cringe. If I could make myself smaller, lose the new two and three-quarters, almost three inches, I would.

Peter bites his lip, glances back. He knows I'm there, about ten feet behind him, in the shadows. I don't think I have the free will to go to the front. I don't care what Mr. Morrison, my history teacher from last year, said. I don't believe in free will. I'm staying back here.

"Petey?" says Jackson, whistling at him like he's a dog. "Petey, come here."

Peter steps forward. He's willing to do his job but he's not smiling. He looks back at me, and I shrug. It's his turn at the counter, isn't it? I mean, if we took turns.

If Samantha wasn't there, if it wasn't my last Friday, my second-to-last shift, I'd go to the front counter. I send mental messages for Trish to return. She's probably having a snack. She likes to sneak off and eat. In fact, I've never seen her eat anything in front of me except an occasional ice cream. I just see the telltale signs on her shirt or around her mouth. But when she eats ice cream, she eats fast, faster than I've ever seen anyone eat ice cream, a daze of productivity.

Peter is rocking forward, toward the counter, and then back on the heels of his oversized work boots. He does this when he's nervous. And his shoelaces on his left foot are untied. He could trip. I should tell him to tie his shoelaces.

"Can you help me?" says Jackson. "Do you think anyone here can help me?"

"I don't think he can help you," says Samantha to Jackson. Her hands rest on her bare hips. I cringe, hearing his words echoed in her mouth. I pummel the side of the ice cream machine as if that's what's needed.

"Maybe he can help you, Sammie. Petey, do you want to help Sammie instead of me?"

He's the first person I've heard call her Sammie.

Peter tips back and forward on the thick heels of his work boots. He does this when he's nervous or unsure. He's smiling now; it's a confused, eager, sad smile.

Samantha, a.k.a. Sammie, is laughing.

Peter doesn't know what Samantha's done to make Jackson laugh, but he attempts to laugh, too. Maybe she made a face about Peter helping her. She hasn't made a face at Peter all summer. She just floated down the line in her different color bikinis. But she never came around with Jackson. This is the first time. She's been turning up all summer by herself, and I've been waiting for the right moment to say something more to her. Now she is laughing with Jackson. She is laughing at Peter, or at me. I need to go forward. I don't need to be a hero or anything. But I have to go to the front. Do my job. Help Peter. But I can't. I can't because I can't believe what's happening—Peter is peeing his pants right there in the middle of the Snack Shack. It's only a dribble, but it's seeping through the front of his shorts and down his leg toward the untied work boots for everyone—for Jackson and Samantha and me—to see.

"Oh my god, Jackson! Look at that! I can't look! But look at that!"

"I don't think he can help either of us, Sammie." Jackson laughs hard.

Peter is frozen to his spot, more surprised than anything that he has no control over this situation. He looks from Jackson to Samantha to me, with an expression of shock and embarrassment and pain. But something odd happens; Samantha decides somehow that this is an affront to her, as if Peter is doing this on purpose.

"Make him stop," she says to Jackson.

"Oh man, Petey, come one, this is disgusting. Disgusting.

Totally. Disgusting," says Jackson, changing his stance, coming forward in front of Samantha as if she suddenly needed protection.

"Hey!" I shout out.

"You got to clean that up, Cooper," says Jackson, as if daring me to go on offense.

Samantha smothers her eyes into Jackson's chest. "Get it out of here."

Peter doesn't move, and neither do I.

I don't know if the "it" is Peter or what—that he made a mistake? That he had an accident? I glance at Samantha and wonder if she's playacting or if this is for real, this act with Jackson. I want to be able to picture her in her bikini, or even less, without thinking of this. She looks up at Jackson, almost a foot taller than her. Her eyes flit from him to Peter as if this could be a contest. She giggles. His arm snakes around her shoulder.

"Petey. Petey," says Jackson in response. "Petey, come here. Now, you going to take my order, or what? You going to take my order now? And then you can go like a good boy and clean up."

Peter contemplates his untied work boots, now both of them with the laces limp across the sandy wood floor. He's saying, "Sorry. I didn't mean to. I didn't mean to, really. Max? Sorry. I didn't mean to. But he was calling me 'Petey' and that's your name for me, not his. I'm sorry." Now it's him repeating his sentences, as if everything in this world needs to be said twice to be made real.

"Peter," I say quietly, "go in the back. I'll take care of this."

He stays at my side as if I need help.

"Hey, Cooper, been practicing those penalty kicks?" Jackson throws at me. He doesn't expect an answer. "I think I've convinced Sammie to come to our first game. She'll be new to school this fall—eleventh grade—moving up from Lakeshore South, and she's all worried about making friends. I said she shouldn't worry, we're a very friendly bunch."

I say nothing. Samantha clings to Jackson. The two of them go off, into the hot sun, toward the back of the Snack Shack. And while Peter is saying: Maxie, Maxie, Maxie, over and over until I can scream, I'm watching Samantha and her bikini bottom being claimed by Jackson. Everybody else on line is wondering what is going on. Why is Peter standing there like that? Maybe, they're wondering, like I am, why some people are cowards and others are not.

"May I please have two bottles of water?" the next girl on line asks as if I would consider not selling her water. She's the same height as I am and has a striped towel thrown around her neck for cover, even though she's wearing a plain one-piece bathing suit. Not someone from Lakeshore North. Not the kind of girl I like. Not Samantha. Not the kind of girl Jackson would pay any attention to, I'm sure of that. Not the kind of girl guys like me look at much. She clutches a younger girl's hand tight in her own. I'm surprised when she says something else to me. "I think you should help your friend." Her voice is low, husky even. No giggles from this girl.

"Me?" I say as if she's talking to the wrong person. "He isn't my friend." I glance over at Peter. He's shaking and looking like he's going to cry. All Peter can do is stand there. The floor, I realize for the first time, is uneven, on a slant, the planks cracked, with sand spitting through. Ants truck across the wood in a line, more industrious than anyone in this place. Peter rocks back and forth on the heels of his work boots, stinking, going to topple over, with his shoelaces dripping down the sides of his boots.

I pull out two bottled waters for her. They aren't cold. Instead of complaining, she says instead, more urgently, "You should help him."

She has brown hair, a lot of it, and brown eyes, wide and fixed on me. I can't help it. I blush. This look is way too intense for me, and she's too tall, too big a girl, not big like Trish, not fat, but not Samantha, packaged in her bikini.

"Peter, go to the back," I say, looking at her, not him. "I think I have an extra pair of shorts in my gym bag. You can wear those."

But he doesn't move. I have to turn and whisper, "It's okay. Go, Petey."

"Really, Maxie?"

"Yes, go change." He shuffles off, shielding the front of his pants. "And make sure you wash your hands, too."

That broad-shouldered girl with the gold-flecked brown eyes and mane of hair, with her front teeth slightly crooked, is looking optimistically at me. I hate that look. I focus instead on the little sister. "Anything else?"

"Ice cream, Claire?"

So her name is Claire. Not even a cute name like Samantha or Sammie.

"Later," Claire says, stroking her sister's head. "It's too early for ice cream." She flattens a twenty-dollar bill out as if she's reluctant to give it up. "I don't have anything smaller." She abandons the money between us, waits for me to pick it up, which I do, smoothing it out even more, pretending to glance at the bill, as if it is counterfeit, but looking at her look at her sister. She is definitely not my type, not the kind of girl I like.

"Next!" shouts Trish, now barreling up beside me with a towering set of ice cream cones, as if she's the one who has been kept waiting.

"Is there anybody here who can help us? My kid is thirsty. And he wants an ice cream," demands a father stepping forward from behind Claire. I wonder where Barkley is. He has a tendency to disappear when the line gets long. Trish helps the father as I make change for Claire.

"Thank you," she says, as I hand her change back to her. She counts it again before hiding it away in the bottom of her beach bag, a cheap green bag used for recycling.

"Next," I say, but I'm still looking at her, and she's looking at me, until her sister pulls her back toward the sea.

"Vanilla," says the kid at the front of the line with his father. "No, chocolate."

"Make up your mind," growls the father. "I'm not going to stand here sweating all day like a pig. Get my kid a swirl."

"I don't want a swirl," wails the son.

"Chocolate? That's my favorite, sweetie," says Trish.

"Next," I say.

"Bottle of water," says an old guy with a ponytail. "Make it a cold one." He laughs to himself like we haven't heard that line all summer.

After a few minutes, Peter appears back at the counter in my black-and-white athletic shorts and knee-high soccer socks, with his yellow work boots, still untied. It's going to be a long day. I kneel and double-knot Peter's laces.

Barkley

From the back of the Snack Shack, over the shield of the swinging doors, I train my sight on the little girl and her sister.

I have seen them twice. This must mean something. The same little girl. She told me that her name was Elizabeth, that everyone called her Izzy, and that her sister was Claire. Only a pink rubber band marked the little girl, no pink on the sister.

"Barkley, you working the grill or not?" calls Trish. "Can you stop acting strange and grab more hot dog rolls from back there? There's a line out here."

There is always a line in front of the Snack Shack. But I want to help her. Trish is my friend, even if she will attend that community college, and I will not. Everyone here at the Snack Shack is my friend or colleague. Perhaps "colleague" is a better word. We are collegial. It's almost like we are at our own college, Snack Shack U.

"Barkley!" Trish plants her arms on those hips and shouts.

Cases of bottled water surround me, atoms in man-made forms—they should be blown apart, destroyed before they destroy us. Nevertheless, I am forced to sell bottled water. Don't they know all that plastic gets dumped out to sea? That fish get caught in the plastic? That plastic bottles will be submerged in the world's oceans into the next millennium? All they care about is whether the bottle is cold. I must get asked that question a hundred times a day: Is the bottled water cold? Get me a cold one, will ya? Cold, I said, come on? Reach in and get me a real cold one. Is the bottled water really cold? I count the bottles. I do this every day, sometimes twice a day, sometimes every hour. I am efficient. I once told Phil, the manager, who never shows up except on rainy days, about my objections to the bottled water, about my cause.

Makes money, he said. Everybody drinks water, he said. Finally told me to shut up, and I did, for he is a little man of no consequence, no talent, no skill, and there was no use wasting my intelligence on him. He does not know that I have a direct link to the state senator. I e-mailed him. Texted him. It took all my powers of concentration to work the keyboard. A ban would tackle two problems: no plastic in the ocean and no more stupid questions about how cold the bottled water is. I am awaiting a reply to my messages, upon which he will certainly agree and act.

"Barkley! Sweetie, you are driving us crazy," shouts Trish from the front counter. "You are moving in slow motion today. What are you thinking? Please, we need your help."

I want to be a help to her. I grab a tray of hot dog rolls. I have no issues with hot dog rolls. White. Enriched. Only a few days old. I swing back through the doors to the front.

The little sister and Claire are gone from the front counter, lost into the crowd. My heart races. This must not be so. White light bounces off the ocean. I must find her. I wish I could wear my sunglasses at the Snack Shack. Without them my eyes are naked and raw. Light strikes them. I am exposed.

"Hey, Bark, bring those rolls up here," shouts Max Cooper.

"When are you going to hit the showers, sweetie?" asks Trish. She does not require an answer. She has asked me this at least once a day since the thirtieth of June, and I have never answered her. I wish I could help her. Find a magic pill to halve her size. I should ask Jared; he must have something. Nevertheless, I sniff under my arms. Affirm life. I stopped showering after the incident at the community college. Droplets of water felt like spiders running up and down my arms. The shower was somehow making me less clean. I cut back on showers, from once a day to two or three times a week, to a burst of water once a week—I felt like I was being burned—and then only on my hair, and then I shaved my head. I smell alive. I dump the hot dog buns next to her and Max.

"Don't you ever smile, Barkley?" asks Trish. "How about just a little smile, for me?"

"You threw a few dogs on the grill and disappeared again, what's the deal, Bark?" says Cooper. This does not require an answer, either. He is insincere and sarcastic, unable to have an honest conversation. I have tried to help him over and over. "We need more hot dogs now."

I go for the hot dogs and return.

"I peed my pants," says Peter to me as I set up the meat near the grill. "So, I'm wearing Max's shorts." He must be pleased with himself in the soccer shorts, as if just wearing them means he could ever play the game. He could not even be an assistant manager to the team like I was. Not him.

Peter stumbles forward, trips again, the third time this week. His body hits the floor. I would help. First, I must feed dogs to the grill. I feel like I am watching myself working, outside myself, looking in. A body is hitting the floor.

Cooper helps Peter up, braces him. "Hey, Bark, the dogs are burning on the grill. Go, Bark." He howls at me, barking like a dog, teasing me in the way so many others have in my twenty-one years.

Peter must feel compelled to follow—some men are always followers—and howls "Bark," too. He throws back his head, hair unkempt, and shouts out, "Bark! Bark!" like a cheer, egged on by Cooper, in such a way that it must sound funny to them. I am the only one not laughing, not saying anything, everything silenced.

"Hey, Bark—" Cooper touches my shoulder, a violation of my sovereignty. I swivel toward him, focus in, as if from inside a long tunnel. "We're only kidding you," he says. He shrugs. Offers me a smirk, dimpled, the kind the girls must like. He is excusing himself. He is thinking that small men can truly kid bigger ones, as if the weak can truly bully the strong, as if he does not know who supplied him with the magic pill, and who is waiting for him to ask to buy more, because they must always buy more.

"Something wrong with you, Bark? Say something."

The dogs sizzle. The meat pops. Lean forward on the counter.

To the left is a grease-stained sign: *All Employees Must Wash Hands.* Surrounding me is the skirling of sea gulls. They have landed on the roof of the Snack Shack, lurking over our garbage. We live in chaos. We serve up hot dogs.

Max

After all day at the Snack Shack, without turning any lights on, making as little effort as possible, I fall down on my bed and King stretches out beside me. My room is freezing, a shock to my system after the Shack. Every muscle, even behind my eyes, pulses. My skin feels gritty. I stink of burning meat and grease. With one hand, I stroke King. He is grateful. Maybe I should see if anyone else is around? Maybe Samantha? *Yup, like she knows who you are, Cooper.* King pants along the length of me. Maybe it's better to be alone. Maybe this is the way it's always going to be from now on. Maybe I'll die alone. I scratch a bit behind King's ears, I want him to know that I love him, even if I wished he were a girl in a hot-pink bikini—stroking me.

"Don't worry, King." My voice sounds hazy and far away. His ears perk up. It takes a second for me to hear what he hears: my parents, both of them. If he could dig a hole right there, he would. He knows it's better to hide if my parents are heading for me. I lead him off the bed. He shimmies his way under it. I drop the side of my comforter down to conceal him. It's his hiding place that everyone knows about.

Down the hall, my mother strains to lower her voice, which of course only makes it ring more clearly. This afternoon, this pill doesn't seem to be working very well. No gentle fog. No cat's paws on my brain. No float. And worse yet, my parents are talking about me—and pills.

"I thought you were going to throw away those old pills months ago," she says to my father.

"I only need them when my back hurts, that's why I went looking for them."

"Your back hurts again? Should we call the doctor?"

"That's not the point, Deb. The point is—they're missing."

"Are you sure? Maybe you lost count. Your mind is on so many other things."

I reach for King's collar. I should take him for a walk. Get out of this house. Now.

He doesn't move from under the bed. It's time to be fed, not to go for a walk. He's smarter than me.

"I'm going to talk with Max," says my father.

"What has this got to do with my son? Don't bother him now. He just got home from work. He must be exhausted."

"I'm exhausted, too. I should be focusing on the campaign, not on this."

"Yes, you should be focusing on the campaign," she agrees.

"Somebody's been taking these pills, Deb. And if it's not you, and it's not me, who is it? The dog? Get out of my way. I've had enough. He's checked out of this family, and maybe this is the reason for it."

King whimpers. I've got to admit that I don't have the energy to fight my way into the kitchen. Get his food. I really just want to sleep.

"Please, Glenn. This isn't really about Max, is it? This is about you and your fear that you are going to lose this election. Maybe you should go public with those e-mails and texts? Get a few sympathy votes."

"I can't go public with them."

"Why?"

"I want to stay focused on my issues. I want to campaign on my terms. This nut is going on about pollution, water pollution, plastic water bottles, and I don't know what else. Maybe it's a plant—just to distract me? I don't know. But it's not my job to save the world's ocean, too, is it? He's a nut. And I don't want to lose focus, and I don't want to give my opponent an issue that she can jump on. Okay, Deb? Let's worry about our son."

My father swings open my bedroom door. I'm not allowed to have a lock on it, one of his many rules, or it would be locked all the time. "Have you been taking my painkillers?" He acts as if he is a prosecuting attorney on one of those crime shows. "Have you been using them, or what? What the hell's been going on this summer? See, Deb, he comes home and all he wants to do is sleep in here with that dog. We should have known something was up. He even looks guilty. I can't have this. I have to have a son who can stand next to me, not someone who can't even stand up."

"That's a good line, Dad. A son who can stand next to me."

"Stand up."

"Max," says my mother, but I see her smiling a little. She likes when I'm clever like that.

"Stand up," my father repeats as if I didn't hear it the first time.

So, I stand. Fine.

"Look at this, he's exhausted from having to slave at that horrible Snack Shack all summer," says my mother, coming to my defense.

I study the ceiling, at a constellation of spider webs in the corner of my room.

"Stand up straight when I'm talking to you."

"He's worked all day, Glenn."

"Stand up," my father says, right in my face, as if he is still in the army.

I throw my shoulders back.

"Did you or did you not take any of these pills?"

I look straight at him and lie. "No." I may not be able to talk to the girls in bikinis at the beach, or even to that girl Claire, but I can convince my father and mother of anything.

"What do you think we are, idiots, Max? You think I'm a schmuck? Am I a moron, Max?" He breathes down on me. "These are heavy-duty narcotics. Prescription pills. For my back."

"This is our son, Glenn." Her voice rises. "He's an honor student."

One semester I made honors. I'm not an "honor student." I had a mix of Bs and Cs on my final report card for junior year. My guidance counselor said I should consider community college "even though" my father is a state senator, as if that should make a difference in my grades.

"Max, are you okay?"

"Tired, Mom."

"Tired?" my father repeats with a curt laugh. "Hard job? You don't know what hard work is. Being in the army is hard work, going to law school at night is hard work, campaigning is hard work. Trying to change this state, this country for the better is hard work."

I'm waiting for my mother to say, "Save it for the voters," but she doesn't. I've got to admit, he looks true blue saying this. He says it like he believes it, and maybe he does. He grew up with a widowed mother in an apartment in Queens, played football, and joined the army out of high school. I've heard the story a hundred times how he went to college and then law school at night after serving in the first Gulf War back in the 1990s. It was there, in a war no one remembers, that he hurt his back. My mother showers him with an expression of adoration, of zeal. He's charging forward, on the field, going for the goal, going for the win. She wants him to win, for me to win, for us to be the kind of family others want to be. She set our whole life up that way.

My father scans my bedroom. King rustles under the bed. "Your father probably just lost count of the pills. How many pills do you have left, Glenn?"

"Who the hell knows how many? That's not the point, Deb. You think I'm an idiot, don't you? It doesn't matter to you that I'm a state senator, that I don't need a scandal with my son popping pills? I already have enough problems."

"Like what?" I ask.

"Don't worry about my problems. Don't you have enough to think about? How's that college essay going? I want to see that revised opening paragraph."

"I'm working on it."

"I've had enough of this," my mother says, as if this has all been resolved. "I'm going to make dinner now. Is that okay, Max? Okay, Glenn? We have a lot of good things coming up for this family. Max, you have your birthday party coming up."

"I don't want a party."

"What's this? You always have a birthday party over Labor Day weekend."

"Mom—"

She snaps back to my father. "And Glenn, you have your Labor Day rally at the community park. Max, you're going to be there and help your father win reelection?"

This isn't really a question. I have no choice but to be there. Always the negotiator. The family's true politician.

"Good," she says, without waiting for an answer. "Wonderful. Glenn, let's not make this a bigger thing than it is. We have bigger things to worry about, don't we?"

She hurries down the hall with a furious clicking of heels. I pick up my musty, dog-haired comforter from the floor and spread it back on my bed. His eyes bore into me. My back tightens. I want to crawl under the bed with King.

"Why'd you take them, Max?"

"I didn't take them."

He raises his chin. I raise mine.

"You're lying to me. Don't lie."

"I won't." But, of course, I am lying and he knows it, and I know it.

"You know I'm hurting, too, Max. I may not win the election."

"Would it be so bad not to win?"

"I want to win. I have things I want to do, that people sent me to Albany to do."

"Like what?"

"I don't like to lose, Max. I'm someone who's won, who's always won. It's us versus them out there. But for the first time in a long time, the 'us' is hurting."

"Who's the 'them'? Aren't they hurting, too?"

He scrutinizes me as if I've asked the stupidest question in the world. I don't understand why it has to be us versus them, why the world has to be divided into winners and losers.

"The whole world is hurting, *Pop*." I grab King's leash. "Excuse me, I have to walk my dog before dinner," I say. "I don't want him pissing in my room again, right?"

King growls like a wolf in a cage. But he won't come out unless I lead him with my hand. I've got to admit that he's smart, maybe smarter than me.

"Only a kid like you would pick out a blind mutt and then want to keep it."

"Excuse me," I say, standing in front of him.

He shakes the orange pill container in front of me.

I remember when I was small and sick with the flu or something and had to take a pill. He crushed it into a cup of warm milk. He stayed up with me. He fell asleep at the end of this bed—him, not my mother. She always said she needed her sleep or she couldn't function. He was up with me, stroking my legs, making sure that whatever was wrong with me would soon be fixed. I don't know what he wants from me. One minute he wants me to grow up, get a summer job, help with the campaign, and in another, he won't let me have a lock on the door and I'm under interrogation.

"I'm going to flush this down the toilet. You got me? I expect this to be the end of it. We love you, Max, your mother and I love you."

"Flushing prescription drugs down the toilet, that isn't good for the environment. The drugs enter the water system."

"So you do think you're smarter than me?" he says. "Let me be very clear about this. These—and all the others—are going down the toilet. Call the EPA."

I'm not smart at all, I want to say, only his son. He blocks me from leaving.

"Dinner smells good, doesn't it?" he says. "You're going to be at the Labor Day event, Max? We need to show a united front as a family."

I lock eyes with him.

He takes that as a yes and says, "Smart boy," and shifts away as if he hates looking at me. I don't care what he says. I see it in his eyes that he wishes he had another son, one that wins.

In a moment, he is in the main bathroom. The toilet flushes, and a shudder runs through the house as the pills are driven into the ecosystem.

The scent of frying hamburgers wafts down the hall. I used to love my mother's hamburgers, juicy and slick with onions on the side. Tonight the smell makes me angry. During the last two years, she stopped cooking. She was always taking the train up to Albany to meet my father for some event. I was left with money for takeout. I don't need to sit down with them for dinner now. I can't look at them now.

King rubs against my legs. I clutch at his collar. Even blind, he finds my face and licks it.

Claire

We stay as long as we can, after most of the families leave, tugging their wagons off the beach, the wagons now piled with wet, sandy towels and half-asleep children seemingly more of the sea than the land. In their wake, upturned plastic sand buckets remain. Fresh-dug holes spill over with seawater. Sea gulls forage the garbage. And the oceanfront reverts into the empty place it should be.

I hurry a sleepy Izzy toward the minivan. I think that we'll miss getting home before my father. We'll end up getting caught in traffic, our hair knotted with sand and seaweed, our skin scaly with too much sun, our mouths singing: we are mermaids.

Yet in less than a half hour, our minivan slips into the driveway, the lone car. I call my father on his cell phone and leave a message. I thank him for the wonderful day at the movies. I warm up leftover macaroni and cheese, add a few raw carrots to each of our plates. I don't know how my mother grocery shopped. I can't seem to figure out how much to buy, or what to buy, or when to buy. Izzy loves bananas. But somehow the ones I purchase turn instantly brown and soft, and then what do you do with them? We have piles of brown bananas and I don't know what to do with them. We've lived on macaroni and cheese for weeks, but I have it all under control. However, tonight neither of us is very hungry. I make sure Izzy has her bath, using the last of our mother's bubble bath, and change her into one of her princess nightgowns. I don't remember ever having a princess nightgown. I fluff out her blond hair. Next to me she is fair, adorably freckled. She slips her skinny arms around me and kisses me for the tenth time or more today. She's easier with her kisses than I ever was.

Curling up in her bed, she smells like a mix of sea and lavender. All the lights must be on. All the teddy bears must be lined around her. Blond curls and valentine lips, I think again for the tenth or twentieth time, she's going to be gorgeous. I sigh. "Go to sleep."

She pops her head up. "When is Daddy coming home?"

"Soon."

"Can I stay awake for him?"

"Sure," I say, knowing she'll be asleep in ten minutes. "Just close your eyes."

She lays her head back down with her eyes wide open. "Sometimes I can't remember her before, can you?"

"It's time for sleep now."

She studies my face so hard I have to turn away. "I know who she used to look like."

I pick up her soggy bathing suit from the floor.

"You. She looks like you, Claire."

"No. She doesn't look like me." In her bedroom mirror, a glimpse of my face, burned brown from the sun with its chapped lips and peeling nose, almost confirms this for me. I don't easily remember what she looked like before.

"You do. You look exactly like her."

I have to get her to sleep. I don't want to have this conversation. Not now. I don't want to think that to Izzy I look like our mother. I'm not her. I don't want to be her.

Izzy flops back on her bed and slips her hands behind her head. "Where do you go when you die, Claire?"

"I told you."

"I forgot."

"You don't have to worry about dying."

"But I want to know. When I die, will I go to heaven? Will Mommy be there when I get there? Will she be all better?"

I can't do this tonight. I just can't. My father should be home. He should be the one answering these questions, or not answering them, as is usually the case. I'll make us dinner. Do the laundry, even. But not this.

"Mommy isn't dying so soon, and neither am I, and neither are you."

"What's heaven like, Claire?"

"Why are you asking so many questions?"

"I like asking questions. You do, too."

"Let's talk about something else. Did you have fun today?"

"I always have fun at the beach. But I am going to have more fun tomorrow."

"Why?"

"Every day I try to have more fun," she says, as if I'm the six-year-old.

"We're both going to have more fun tomorrow."

"But Claire, I still want to know. What happens when you die? What happens to your skin? Do your bones become like dinosaur bones?"

Everyone says that Izzy is one of the most verbal kids they've ever met. Sometimes, I wish she were a little less verbal. "You don't have to worry about that for a long, long time."

"Sometimes I dream of her, and it's before she had the stroke."

"Izzy, you have to go to sleep," I say with desperation. I want to go into my room and be in the dark on my computer.

"When I die, will she be in heaven?"

"She's not dead. She's in the rehabilitation center." My voice has an edge. I don't want to talk about anyone dying.

"I know that. But when I'm dead," she persists, "will she be there? Will Daddy? Will you?"

"Yes. But no one is dying."

"Everybody will be in heaven with me," she says, happy and matter-of-fact in her logic. "Guess what I'm going to wear in heaven?"

"You're not going to heaven for a long time. You have time to plan your outfit."

"Just guess. What am I going to wear in heaven?"

"Elizabeth." She knows I use her full name when I've had enough.

"I'm going to wear my bathing suit in heaven—not the one with frogs that I wore today, the pink one. Are you allowed to do that? Is there an ocean in heaven?"

"Elizabeth, there's an ocean in heaven, okay? Now, I'm going to my room. Shout if you need anything," I say, and what I think is: Please, please, go to sleep already. Please let me go. Please let me be for the rest of the night by myself, alone, without dreams of my mother, or dying, or even heaven.

Izzy scoots under her blanket, made up of alternating squares, berry purple and yellow, knitted by our mother in the last months of her pregnancy, the needles tapping and clacking every evening for weeks. She didn't have to look at each stitch. She didn't even have to stop and count her lines. She never knitted things with holes in them, never got frustrated, never had to unravel lines and start all over again. I don't know if she'll ever be able to knit like that again. I press my face into Izzy's blanket, baby-soft and lavender-scented, my mother's scent. Her knitting runs across my face in perfect, tight stitches.

Izzy tugs the blanket to her chin. I kiss her tonight on her forehead six times, one for each of her six years.

"I can't wait to be seven," she says, and I almost scream in exasperation. "You know why, Claire?"

"Why?"

"Because then you'll give me seven kisses every night, won't you?"

I want to give her another kiss right now, but I know what it's like to wait and plan for things like that.

"Will Mommy be home for my birthday? Please say yes."

"I can't," I say. "Do you want another kiss?"

"No," she says. "Just leave the light on. One more thing, Claire."

"What?"

"Did you double-check the front door? Daddy is always saying to lock the door, that you never know," she says, sounding like a grown-up. I don't ever want her to turn seven.

"Checked and double-checked."

"What is it that 'you never know'?" she says, drifting off.

"I don't know."

"Maybe I'll dream of Mommy tonight," she says in a sleepy, faraway voice.

I hurry out. Take five, six steps into the darkness of the hallway, before I hear, "Claire? Claire?"

I can't do this. I've been with her all day. I can't be mother and father to her. I don't say anything. I want to go—anywhere, or at least be alone to think and write.

"Claire?"

I suck in my breath. He should be here now. He should be dealing with her. What if he doesn't come home? What if it's only her and me? I push the fear down.

Her voice calls out, louder now. "I love you, Claire."

I breathe. "I love you more, Izzy."

Barkley

In the pitch black in front of the computer screen, the brain filters information at full speed. I must connect with her. She is my vision, my creation. Filmmakers would label her the ingenue. The naive young girl. The one who must be taught. She is mine to teach.

Next to me, the super-sized bag of corn chips and jar of hot salsa are half-emptied. May have to venture out for more. Must feed the body.

I type with one hand and eat with the other. The body and mind are two entities, paralleling each other, an independent and dependent clause. The body needs food to keep it satiated, calm in front of the screen. The mind must roam free.

Words jump on the screen.

I found her in a half dozen places on the Internet, and I am now at her blog, inside of her words. Claire's words. Stare at the particles, verbs, nouns, split infinitives, until they are in straight, even lines. I am reading a poem from Claire. My Claire. I absorb each syllable. I am not alone. I am with her.

The voice intrudes. Correct me: instructs. *I will sing of mercy and judgment. That is a poetic line. That is truth.*

Her poem is not about mercy or judgment. I say this aloud, to the voice in my head. Problems arise with the poem. Not that I am a professional critic, yet even I can see beyond the words: the grammar is arbitrary.

Who makes the rules about where to break the line in a poem? Is there a rule book, like in sports, to consult? I understand from my private studies that there is a format for scripts and one must follow it or be punished by the film industry.

The words waver in and out of focus. I stare harder.

Is there a rule about periods versus commas versus semicolons at the end of the line? Doesn't a semicolon connect two independent clauses? Didn't my English teacher at that community college call semicolons the bastards of grammar and want them banned from papers? If there are no rules of grammar anymore, what does that say about our society? Have we given up even the basics of how to control our poetry?

I eat faster, more chips, more salsa.

Neurons ping my brain like an electrical storm. I shiver. I am in the center of the storm. Charged. I can smell ozone, a rarified acrid smell of fire in open skies. My left hand falls away from the chips. The back of my throat scratches for a cigarette and coffee. Cigarette. Coffee. Claire.

I never used to like coffee. I started drinking it at school, at that community college. One cup in the morning to get me going, and then, by the end of this year, spring semester, I drank ten or twelve oversized cups a day. I had a hot coffee in my hand when the English professor pressed me to sit down, to calm down. I was calm. He asked me to interpret the white spaces on the poem. One cannot read the invisible; one cannot read space.

Skewered beliefs in space and connections and metaphor. And the coffee flew out of my hand, struck the professor in his face and arm, seared him. I apologized. My parents apologized. I am bereft of apologies.

Pound down the last of the chips.

Behave wisely, and so will our friend.

I have no friends, I want to scream: I am alone in my room. I have a gun in my drawer. I have bullets. But it would be insane to scream that out loud.

I fling the plastic bag to the floor. Scatter crumbs like broken shells. Waves crash over me. I am drowning at my desk.

Behave in the perfect way. The path is straight ahead.

I breathe from the gut. My head hurts, but the voice soothes. Before me, the words on the screen are, suddenly, straight and true. Focus, hard. The poem is for me to decode, and only I can do this, only I can understand her. Claire must know this.

Claire

After checking on Izzy, now sleeping, I lift back the plaid curtains and search out from the front window for a sign of my father. If it were up to me, I'd strip all the faux early American—the flowered, the crocheted, and the cross-stitched—from the house. Strip this living room down to its bare essentials. My father won't let me store away even one embroidered pillow.

I try my father's cell phone again. I don't even bother leaving another message. I notice dirty dishes in front of the television in the den. I don't think they were there this morning. I carry the traces of him—my life is filled with dirty dishes—into the kitchen sink. I circle through the house, clean the plates, leave the kitchen spotless, double-check that the back door is locked, hurry around the kitchen to the front door, and double-check that lock, too, not that my house would be the first one on the block that anyone would ever think of breaking into. If someone wanted in, all they had to do was push through a flimsy window screen. One of my father's many cutbacks this summer was air-conditioning. I ram the swollen living room window up even farther as if that will cool down the house.

I press my face against the screen, wish for a breeze. I expect to see my father appear out of the shadows, into my sight, up the pathway of fieldstones. Nothing stirs, except the wings of crickets and the howling of dogs. The night is inside as much as outside.

I cross my arms, squeeze myself into my center. I throw my shoulders back even though they ache. My mother was all legs and curves and bounce, I mean she is, or will be again. I shake my arms loose as if swimming wildly through air. Nothing seems to fit me right anymore; my pants are too short, my shirt too tight. I feel like this is somebody else's body. If it were up to me, I would have a different body, bared to essentials—only necessary nouns and verbs, maybe an occasional adjective, never an adverb—a body, lips that someone would kiss. I feel like some revelation should be at hand. I move across the living room, past the two wing chairs, hers and his, pulled up close to each other, empty these past months. He should be home, but does it really matter? If he were home, he'd be in the alcove off the kitchen, watching some movie, something black-and-white, something with the sound turned up so as to compensate for the grim lack of color. He doesn't watch sports, doesn't care which baseball or football team wins or loses, like other dads. He likes happy endings, and that's why he says he watches old movies. If he doesn't come home until late tonight, we'll do fine without him.

I switch on the outdoor lights. Two dim bulbs flicker on and moths swoop in around them. We haven't been using the outdoor lights, also trying to cut back. But perhaps tonight he'll need them to find his way home. A car slows down before driving off. Something in the shadows, something shifts; hear a cry, another dog, long, lonesome. One outdoor bulb pops and dies out, and then the other—like what I imagine two gunshots would sound like. I flinch. A wave of darkness ripples over the house. I listen for Izzy. Silence. Finally, finally, on the couch, I am alone, unfettered, unburdened, unleashed . . . unconnected, unmasked, untapped, unseen, shifting through the shadows.

I won't be home.
Will be very late. Don't worry.
All is well here.

The message looks like a haiku by someone who can't count syllables.

No xxoo, no love. It is from my father, who hates all electronic communication, rarely e-mails, never texts. I don't know this person anymore. I punch in his cell phone number. I reach a robotic voice informing me that his box is full. I couldn't leave a message if I wanted to leave one. There's no connecting to him even if I could. I'm going to ream him out when he gets home, I think to myself, and realize that I'm suddenly sounding like the adult.

I type: Where is "here"? When will you be home?

His answer doesn't make sense: YMRRIQOW. I bet he's typed on the wrong keys and pressed send anyway. He'll be home when he gets home. Then I'm going to tell him that I've had enough. I don't want this feeling of being grown up and not grown up, ruptured from my old self—into what? Old enough to take care of the house, take care of my sister, to have all these responsibilities and yet not have any of—*of what?* Any fun? Any friends? I want a guy who wants—*what should he want?* What do I want? I just want a guy who isn't my father. A guy who doesn't need me to take care of everything. But who would want someone like me? I run my hands through the length of my hair and then across my lips as if checking that I'm whole. I know that I don't need my father or some guy. I can do this all just fine. Except, isn't there something or someone who will make me forget who I am—let me be someone other than the good daughter and sister—let me imagine that if I stood on the shore, the distance between the sea and the possibility of land was only as far as I could swim.

I get rid of my father's misshapen word. Go to my blog. And I am surprised by a message in my comments. Usually no one comments on my posts.

"Very thought-provoking poetry."

Thought-provoking? I've never had a comment other than from a handful of friends on the school's literary magazine—and my mother—on my blog. The comment is from Brent. I don't know a Brent.

"Thank you!" I write back, thinking that he must have randomly found my blog.

In a minute another comment snaps in. "I like your use of metaphors," he adds.

That will be that; we'll move on. But it's not.

"'She is I; I am her.' Was this poem to anybody special, Claire? I understand if it's hard to talk about your writing. I find it hard, too. I have to tell you, you should use a period instead of a semicolon. They lead to disorder, not order."

He's quoting the first line of a poem that I wrote earlier in the spring, immediately after my mother's stroke. Is he a writer, too? Is that why he's reading my blog? I really need to know who he is. And he has picked my favorite line in the poem.

"There is so much there. Like you are inside of these people, on the outside but looking in."

That's exactly how I feel: I'm observing the world, taking mental notes, on the outside, close enough to see but far enough away. I peer at the screen, waiting.

Nothing. Blank. White.

"Where did he go?" I say aloud. I study his sentences. He likes to write in full sentences like me.

But he's gone as randomly as he found me, he's gone—leaving me hanging, alone, listening to the crickets. The sweat beads at my neck. I throw off my blanket.

Finally, after a long minute or two, he adds another comment. "I want our conversation to be private, is that okay with you? May I call you? I found your phone number online, too."

His voice in my head is clear: gentle, halting, questioning, and shy.

The house phone rings and I race for it in the kitchen.

"Claire?" he says. He sounds just like I thought he would.

"Do I know you?"

"No," he says after a pause, as if he wants to be sure and careful.

"Are you in high school?"

"Not in high school," and then he adds, "not anymore."

I knew it. I just hope he's not an old guy. That would be too weird. That would mean I'd have to hang up.

"If I don't know you, I shouldn't be talking with you. What's your last name?"

He tells me, and I hang up on him. I'll show him. But nothing comes up with that name on any search. This makes him more intriguing, absorbing, captivating—synonyms pile on one another.

Here is someone new.

I see if I can call his number back, and I can. It's local and knowing the phone numbers in North Lakeshore, I can tell it is from that part of town. I hope this isn't a prank. But he urgently asks, "Claire, are you okay?"

The shadows on the kitchen wall dance behind me. I am small against the exaggerated shapes of trees and this makes me feel slightly disoriented. The outlines grow, tremor, monstrous. "I didn't find out much about you," I say, breaking from the shadows. I turn the kitchen lights on.

"Not much to find out. But I am concerned about you. Are you okay?"

My white T-shirt is clinging, damp. My hair is wrapped around the side of my neck. Everything inside me is tight and knotted, but I like hearing his voice. "I'm okay."

"I sometimes feel like I'm standing at a window, looking out at the world. Or, I am a bug. Like Gregor Samsa? Kafka, do you know Kafka? Are you still on your blog? I am going to send you a link to a picture so you'll see that I am not vermin. You won't be able to download it, but it's the best picture that I have. Claire, is that okay?"

"Slow down. I shouldn't be talking with you."

"Claire."

"I don't know you."

I return the phone to the receiver carefully, and trace along the walls to my bedroom, thinking: this is strange. Kafka? Of course I know Kafka. I had to read his novella, *Metamorphosis,* in eleventh grade, about a traveling salesman who wakes up one terrible morning as a bug. Who is this guy kidding? Believe me, if he thinks that I am some naive little girl, he has something else coming. I'm not clicking on any links.

I check in on Izzy, who is curled up in the corner of her bed. Unlike me, she is a light sleeper. Her head is thrown back on her flower pillow. She's tangled in her sheets, one thin leg on top and one lost inside. I straighten up the sheets and say to myself: *I love you more,* knowing I'm saying what my mother always said to me. *I love you more.* Izzy doesn't know that these are our mother's words. My mother always said that, like she always called me angel, even when I wasn't acting like one, like purple was her favorite color and lavender her favorite smell. There are things I remember about her, but other things I don't, like her face before the stroke.

Back in my bedroom, I climb back into bed but ignore the laptop. I scramble for a pen and some lined paper. I can write the old-fashioned way. Wasn't I going to try to write a haiku? Five, seven, five, isn't that the form? Five syllables are all I need for the first line. But I can't think of five. All I can think of is: I'm not going to click on his link.

I turn off the lights. Once again, I am alone in the house with the shadows.

After a half hour or more, in the dark and quiet, hearing his voice in my head say, "Claire," I reach out and click on the link.

He's older than high school, maybe in college, twenty, or twenty-one even. He has dirty-blond hair and sideburns. He's striding across a campus with red stone buildings in the background. He is lanky and lean and muscled. He's not exactly smiling. Maybe he hates having his picture taken, like me. And he's carrying a book at his side. I can't make out the title, even though I zoom into it; the book is turned into his side. It's not a textbook, a slim paperback. His face is upturned toward the camera—forthright and intelligent and sincere. I think my mother would say he was interesting looking, if not a bit rakish. She used to like words like that: rakish. I zoom into his hand, the one curled around the book. It doesn't have the heft of a textbook. Maybe it's a graphic novel, or maybe a classic? Kafka? I inspect the picture closely. He doesn't look dangerous or weird at all. And he is tall.

The phone rings again, and I hurry for it, thinking only:

I don't want it to wake up Izzy. But part of me knows, I want to hear the voice attached to that photo.

"Claire," says Brent. "Where were you? I was worried. Did you get my picture?" He almost sounds as if he's been running, or maybe it's me.

"I did." I'm not about to tell him he's not hideous. I don't want him to think I care that much about how he looks. "How old are you?" I ask instead.

"Twenty-one."

"You know how old I am?" Once he learns how old I am it will probably be the end of this conversation. He won't want to deal with a high school kid, even a senior.

"Old enough, Claire."

"Sorry. Seventeen."

"Sorry? You are very mature."

I don't know how he knows these things about me. I feel like I've gone from a kid to a grown-up in one summer.

"Do you know what it means to take control? To be free, Claire?"

A car rumbles down my street and I rush to the front window, but it's not him. Not my father. "Brent? What time is it? It must be late. I have to go to sleep—don't I? Don't you?"

"I understand. Maybe we can meet someday, Claire?"

"Maybe."

"Maybe?" he repeats.

"It will be up to me if we meet."

"Claire, one must listen to one's inner voice."

What I do is listen to him exhaling sharp, short breaths into the phone for a moment more before I ask, "Should I go? To sleep, I mean?"

"I never sleep," he says.

"I wish I never slept."

Claire
Saturday, 12:15 A.M.

HAIKU
by Claire Wallace

Free, untouched. Freely—
unmasked, understood. Freedom—
undone, unraveled.

Barkley

Saturday, noon

The sun, high in the sky, strikes hard. I sweat. My sunglasses streak. The world is blurred. I retreat to a sliver of shade along the concrete wall of the men's restroom. The damp from the showers or toilets sears my back. I feel different. I'm running on coffee and cigarettes. Coffee, cigarettes, and Claire.

Claire is the only one who knows that my true name is Brent. In all my hopes and dreams and plans, I am Brent. After this summer, I will be known by that name. I will do what so many others in Hollywood have done: change my name, reveal who I am truly meant to be.

I pace along the concrete wall. Max Cooper said noon, right here, before his one o'clock shift. He has the money, he said. I am trying to be helpful, to be here on time. I am never late to a promised engagement. I was never late to class, not to one class at that community college. I would show up early, even, wait in my seat for the professor. Never late for class. Perfect attendance.

Finger inside my pocket. Individual pills nestle in plastic bags. Jared, my cousin, has been supplying me with them all summer. He's pushing me to distribute more. Even give them away—the first time. Samples. "Get them hooked. Like big fat fish, it shouldn't be hard, Barkley?"

Jared has marked the bags with handwritten labels. Dumb

titles. The ones in my pocket are Big X and Gators. Jared drove down to Florida and visited doctor after doctor, hunting for prescriptions, complaining of an aching back. I did not want to participate in this. But he said just once. Then once became twice, and then there was money for things that I needed. And so I bought things that I needed: extra-large coffees, a gun. I have money for my own trip at the end of the summer. I could go anywhere. Los Angeles. It is the only logical choice. Claire must come with me. I nod my head like I'm listening to music, but what I'm hearing is the voice, not Jared's voice of course. His is high-pitched and anxious. The voice is calm, ringing of truth. *O when will you come with me?*

I wipe my head dry with my sleeve. Unlike me, Jared has pockmarked skin and shoulder-length hair. His ice cream truck plays music at decibels prohibited by the city. His policy is: kids first. He sells ice cream out of one window and pills out of the other window to anyone who looks over eighteen, a lot of parents.

Jared has never even received a parking ticket. Always makes his ice cream cones like towers. Always gives out free sample of ice cream to kids. He makes his profit from the pills.

Do I think for a minute that I should not be selling? I plan to use proceeds to leave Long Island and attend film school on my own terms, not my parents' terms. My life will not be wait-listed.

And everybody is selling something. Or at least, this is what the marketing professor taught. Turn on the television or the Internet and all you see are ads. Everybody is selling something.

America is capitalism. America is the free market. The business of America is business. That was his marketing 101 class. Taught by someone who had lost his job in corporate America. What else did the professor with the cheap haircut say? America is about a sucker born every minute, or was that history class? I was never late for class, not once, not even the day it snowed and classes were canceled. I was there.

Jared calls the doctors' offices "pill mills," interesting terminology in our post-industrial age. Mills were once places in America where steel or cloth was produced. We appropriate terms from the past, give them new meanings. This is how our society progresses, or not. We manufacture little steel or cloth, but have "pill mills."

When I first said this about words, about their new definitions, in the English class, the professor called it "provocative." He liked to use words and phrases like this. "Thought-provoking. Provocative. The rules we live by are under fire. Even simple rules. One has to start with definitions, doesn't one?" That's what he said. He never used one word if he could use two.

My field of vision narrows. Sand flies bite at my ankles. "Hey, Bark," comes a voice from behind me.

Cooper is wiry, muscled, and something else. Taller. Now at the end of summer, we stand almost eye to eye. He will be even more competitive on the varsity soccer team this year.

Once I was the assistant manager to the varsity team. But I could never make the team. Nevertheless, my father said I would be an "awesome," "unbelievable," "phenomenal" player. He urged me to work harder. It was a lie. At least I was there at every game, never late, not once. In eleventh grade, I was briefly given the job of keeping track of the team stats. They became jumbled and confused. The coach asked me to be in charge of supplies instead. Now I count water bottles at the Snack Shack every day and I am fine with arithmetic. Nothing is wrong with my counting skills.

"Barkley, what's up?" He shifts his gaze left and right. "Everything good? Can't believe I'm here at the beach early today."

"Sure," I respond with care. "You are one great employee." Nevertheless, I must clarify. "You said you would be here at noon."

"What time is it?"

"Not noon."

"You didn't have anywhere else to be, did you, Bark?"

"You are looking good, Max." He does not look comfortable at the compliment, or maybe it's with me using his first name like we were friends.

"Last day."

"You are working second shift to closing."

"Still thinking you're the manager?"

His voice may be friendly, his eyes are not.

Beware, my friend. He is not listening. But we know better. We know who has the ideas; we know who is the one who holds the future. You are the one. Only you do. You walk perfectly. Smile.

I adjust my sunglasses. But I cannot smile. I can only focus on Cooper. See into him and understand that his motives are less than pure. Blue eyes range under heavy dark brows, a nervous, hungry pose. "I have exactly what you need. I am here to help you."

"Good!"

Cooper speaks in exclamation points—like he is overcompensating, slapping me on the back with every sentence. "I have a back that feels like it's been stretched on a torture rack."

"I want to help."

Cooper leans into me. I back away. He is not allowed to touch me. "Are you sure these are prescription, Bark? I don't do drugs. It's just not my thing. Are these from a doctor?"

"Dr. Jared" is the joke my cousin makes. But I am not good at jokes. "Maybe this is not a good idea," I say, testing the demand.

"For who?"

"Not a good idea."

"Not a good idea?" he repeats, as if this is ironic.

I do not like it when people repeat what I say. Thoughts must be original. The pills go back in my pocket. I do not like or appreciate irony, or repetition.

On the beach, a hundred yards or so from us, people stake out a plot of sand, the essence of capitalism, the illusion of owning the land and sea and air. I scan over the bikinis, tensing. I have learned to beware certain colors, that they represent warnings and signs like weather flags. Red flags indicate a high hazard from surf and current. Yellow or green flags, and you should exercise caution. My warning sign is special to me—pink.

"Barkley, you okay, man?"

A boat bobs at the horizon. I follow it across the beach and spot her at the edge of the crowd, off by the dunes, on a purple-and-white striped towel. A much younger, blond child runs around her. The little sister in a bathing suit with pink stars. And then from the ocean waves: Claire.

I zoom in on her: Claire, dripping wet, rises from the crest of a wave. She is not in pink. Claire is a girl who, I am sure, would never wear pink. Now that I have her, I know I have always wanted Claire, the one who writes poetry, the quiet, lonely one. I know loneliness. I know sadness. Her breasts push against the top of her bathing suit. My father's words echo, "Big tits," and I block them out. I do not want to hear *his* voice in my head. I listen for the other voice, but I am alone. I suck in a breath, smell disinfectant mixed with seawater. Everything reeks of low tide, of downed ships.

Cooper shifts from one foot to another. He may be the state senator's son, but he lacks focus. "Do you ever think of the politics of it all?" I ask him.

"Of what all?"

He is as unhearing as his father. "Of who we are? Of what we want? We all came from the sea, didn't we, Max?"

"What are you talking about?"

"Your father is running for reelection, isn't he?"

"Everybody knows that."

"But does Glenn Cooper know who controls his chances?"

"Who?"

"People like me." I close in. "Maybe even me." Max Cooper

backs up against the wall outside of the men's bathroom as if giving me a clear shot with my mind's camera. He offers me an inconsequential smile. I continue, "He has to listen to me."

"Hey, he has to listen to everybody—except me." He glances side to side as if someone is watching us. No one is. I know he wants his pills, but as the representative of Glenn Cooper, he has to listen to me now. And Max Cooper is full frame: sweat breaks across the bridge of his nose, the dimples disappear, the skin is unevenly scorched by the sun, peeling, blotched with acne. My mind's camera films all imperfections.

"All politicians are con artists. Aren't they?" I ask with rhetorical intent.

"I thought you said last week that all community college professors were con artists?" He offers me a meaningless laugh.

"I am talking about consequences here."

"Hey, no disrespect, Bark, but I really don't want to talk about politics right now. That's all we ever talk about at home—about how to win. And that's not why we're here, is it?"

"What else is there? We all want to win."

"Yup, we all want to win."

"Nevertheless, first you have to listen."

His sight levels with mine. "I'm here. Do you have the pills or not?"

At the water's edge, Claire is being buried. The little sister dumps sand along her arms and legs, rivulets down her skin, golden tanned skin, none burned. Rough grains of sand mesh with the skin, alight, flecks of fire. Claire must be careful of the tide coming in, of the unexpected turns of the sea. Even now, its momentary glassiness is a false calm.

He looks to where I am looking, to my Claire. He is not allowed to look at her. Not allowed. Not. "I have to tell you something," I say deliberately, wringing his focus back to me. "I have a gun."

He does not respond. It is as if he is thinking or hesitating. Max Cooper has faltered before, on that last game penalty kick. I was there in the stands, observing the game, and he thought a second too long, and failed, a wide kick.

"Cool. A gun? Do you go out to the rifle range? I think it's in Relville."

I shake my head. I have no knowledge of a rifle range.

"My dad is a vet. He goes there sometimes. Always says he'll bring me, but hasn't yet."

I wait for more. I want questions or curiosity. I want an eager mind. But he's distracted by Claire, or by the sea, or by the failings of our fathers, or his father, a failure, or worse, a man of false promises. I am walking past him.

"Where are you going, Bark? I thought we were good."

I do not understand. Good? Good requires evil. Good is not an abstract but specific actions. I dig my nails into my palms. The nails are long enough to cut the skin. Max Cooper is spinning a web of words, pale words. Nothing is "good" here.

Max

We aren't good.

From the front of the building drifts the whiff of hot dogs wallowing on the Snack Shack grill, a summer's worth of fat and grease. One more shift, I think to myself. One more, and I am done. I'm never coming back. And this news about a gun. What's with that? If Barkley wasn't so harmless, I guess I'd think it's strange that he's telling me has a gun. But when he bought a new computer, he went on and on about it for two weeks as if no one else had ever bought a fully loaded gamer computer. I don't want to even ask him about what kind. Maybe his family goes hunting. Or maybe his dad has time to bring him to the rifle range. A slight wind off the ocean rises but doesn't break the heat. The waves are especially high and rough today. I should let him go. I should dive in, swim, and then finish the shift—and the summer.

"Come on, Bark," I call out. He's slouching down along the concrete wall to the men's room. He's fish-faced with pinched lips. He bulges out of his sweatshirt. He looks like he's been packing away the doughnuts all summer. His shaved head is waxy-yellow. This morning, his face looks particularly bloated. The rolls on his neck are tattered with day-old beard. I feel like I'm seeing him for the first time close-up, though we've been working at the Snack Shack together all summer. If I didn't know him, I'd be scared. But I kind of feel sorry for him. No one likes him. He doesn't seem to have any real friends. Yet truth be told, all I want is to just buy the pills and get through my last shift. But Barkley is slower than Peter. Barkley is my parents' nightmare, and maybe mine, too. Community college dropout, works part-time for the town, lives at home, spends all night eating junk food, on his new computer, or so he says.

He stops at the end of the wall and turns back to me. I can buy the pills and get out of here. "I'm worried about you," he says.

"It's not like I'm going to make this a regular thing."

Barkley sweats. He looks like he's been swimming. However, I don't think he's been near the ocean all summer. He strides back to me. "You know you grew this summer? How tall are you now, Cooper?"

"As tall as you, Bark."

"That tall." He says this blank and hard. I've had enough of him. "Bark, what do I owe you?"

"Nothing."

"Nothing? Come on, Bark. I don't need another favor."

"Terrific," he says. "Twenty bucks a pill."

"Twenty?"

"Exactly."

"That's a lot of money," I say, stating the obvious.

"Invite me to your party, and I'll throw in two freebies."

"What party?"

Waves crash. Kids squeal. A lifeguard's whistle shrills. This is taking too long with Barkley, though, in a way, time feels like it has stopped. I am never leaving this men's room door. "Give me two pills. That's all I need," I say, jamming all the money I have on me into his sweaty palm. Forty dollars. I just want the pills and want to get away from him. "You sure these are good?"

He glances down at my money, smoothes the bills out in his palms, counting one at a time as if he needs to check for counterfeits. "The party?" he says, with no emotion in his voice.

"I don't think you'll know many people if you come to any party of mine."

Scanning the packed shoreline, I think of an old line, "It's so crowded, no one goes here anymore." However, there, along the edge of the dunes, with her little sister, is that girl from the Snack Shack line again.

Something about her. She has legs. I mean, she had legs yesterday, too. I don't think anyone would ever call her fat, but she's not one of those super-thin anorexic types. Curves, that's it. She has curves and breasts she can't hide even in a boring one-piece bathing suit.

"Is that girl coming?" he asks. He points out toward the girl with the curves and her little sister.

"What girl? There's nothing but girls on the beach today. I don't see which one you mean."

Of all the girls in bikinis, clustered with their girlfriends, why is he picking out her? Strange that he'd pick her out of all the girls, all of them in bikinis, all of them clustered with their girlfriends, lying on their backs, glistening with sunscreen, all of them—except for Claire—in the barest of the bare, I shouldn't even be thinking of this because I'm getting hard, a chronic condition of working at the beach. That's the last thing I want Barkley to see. Yet even that girl is spreading lotion down her arms and across the top of her bathing suit, carefully, methodically. I bet she smells like coconut and the sea—and I just have to get away from Barkley. Go for a swim. Behind us, someone flushes a toilet with a roar. The sidewalk burns through my sneakers. "Just give me two pills, that's all I need."

Barkley's fingering my two twenty-dollar bills, rubbing them against each other. I step toward him, close enough to smell a stomach-churning mix of eggs and sweat and disinfectant on him like he sprayed himself with Lysol instead of showering.

"So what do you plan to do with that gun?" I ask, wanting to avoid talking about the get-together.

"I'm awaiting orders," he jokes.

"Cool," I say because I just want to buy the stuff from him and go. He probably doesn't even have one. I've heard him say he was on the varsity soccer team. No, he was the *assistant manager* to the team. If Barkley wants to say he has a gun to impress people, so be it. It doesn't do anything for me.

"What about the party?" he asks, easing closer. "I heard it was tomorrow night."

I shrug.

"Your annual end-of-summer birthday party?"

His eyes are even more than beady; they are dark-ringed like he hasn't slept, and darting left and right as if he can't focus on any one thing for more than a second or two.

"Everyone's talking about your party, Cooper."

"Everybody?"

"Jackson."

I did invite Jackson and the team.

"I think I'm the only one you're not inviting, Cooper, and I'm helping you out here."

"Just give me the stuff, Bark. Okay? If you want to come to the party, come to the party."

"Stop calling me Bark."

"Stop calling me Cooper."

I don't think I ever said to anyone to stop calling me "Cooper." I say this right to his face. It feels good. "Got it, Barkley?" I pull his whole name out. I guess no more barking at him, either, though he doesn't say that. I'm tired of that, it's old, it feels like something a stupid kid does.

He doesn't respond, but I'm not surprised. He didn't respond to a lot of remarks this summer. He just tunes it all out. Now he won't even look at me in the eye. With his dirty fingernails, he digs out two plastic bags. Inside one bag, two dozen or so pills lie pure white. They look like real pills. An *X* for some reason is handwritten on this plastic bag. He transfers four pills to the empty plastic bag, and I don't say again that I only need two.

As if in response, my back arches and aches more. It takes all I have not to pop them immediately into my mouth, not to slide into nothingness right in front of him. Instead, I stuff the plastic bag into the side pocket of my backpack.

"We're good, Barkley?" I say, stepping away from him. "We're good. No worries." I want to be able to keep buying from him. I just don't want to be friends.

"We are good, Max," he says, blocking my way. "No evil here."

"I got to go, Barkley. Get in some sun and sea before my shifts starts." Maybe take a pill.

"Don't be late for your shift."

"Yup. Don't be late," I repeat. "Who put you in charge?"

He laughs. "You know I could be."

"Hey," I laugh, too, because I want to get out of here. "What stuff are you using?"

"None. Ever." He has this psycho salesman grin on his face. I bought these pills from him and somehow transferred power from myself to him.

"Ever think what a strange word 'good' is, Max?"

I feel caught in an undertow, unable to stand straight. I've got to go. I can't stay here with him.

"Is it only an absence of evil, Max?"

"Haven't thought much about it."

"Do you ever think about grammar?" he asks.

"Am I going to be tested?"

"I'm just trying to be helpful, just trying to be friends."

He lets out a breath that could topple you. Off the horizon clouds gather, maybe the first hint that a storm to break this damn heat is on the way.

"You're going to miss seeing me every day, Max." He slips back on his ridiculous mirrored sunglasses. "You're going to miss Barkley helping you out. But we'll stay friends, right? I have what you need."

I look right into the sun. My irises burn. "Maybe I'll go for a swim. Maybe, today, you should go for a swim, too?"

"I don't swim, Max."

I wish he would stop saying my name—first or last. I sling my backpack over my shoulder, duck past him, and spot her again: the girl with the curves. She's in the ocean. Her back is broad and strong. Her hair cascades down past her hips. The ends of her hair dip into the sea. Her little sister skips out to her. They are hand in hand. Now Barkley slips off his sunglasses and looks to where I am looking. My head pounds. I really need a swim before I start my shift. I want to run along the shoreline toward her. Dive in right there, into the biggest swells. I should warn her about Barkley being trained on her, though I'm staring at her, too, so maybe there's something wrong with me. Maybe I shouldn't be looking at her. I don't know her. I have other places to be, don't I? I have to keep focused on—on what? The future? The day ending, that's all I care about. The weekend ending. Work ending. I care about endings, not beginnings. I don't need to start anything up with any girl on the last days of the summer when the wind will pick up, when the beaches will empty, when all this will be forgotten, or never remembered, not even that last sight of her. I keep on following her as if I need that last sight. But I don't go after her. There's no reason to, is there? So Barkley and I, we just stand outside the men's room, until she disappears, diving headlong into the highest wave.

Claire

I plunge beneath a wave. I can't catch my breath or see anything in the muck. Seaweed, or a jellyfish, slides coldly across my arm. The ocean floor is swept from under me. All I can think of is how my father finally reached me and let me know that there is absolutely no more money for the rehabilitation center, but he was trying to work it out. He spent all night there at some special training. He said he'd explain later. I can handle this wave. I know the sea.

But I don't know what this all means about my mother—and in the waters, I lose Izzy's hand. I reach for it. I'm lost in the spray and the undercurrent pulling me out to sea, gasping for breath, my mouth full of saltwater and sand, and *Izzy!*

The wave rushes out to sea.

Behind me, sprawled in the surf is Izzy. She's tossing her head, digging her hands into the sand, and loving the waves' crest over her legs. She reaches for me, and I lift her up into my arms.

"I'm a mermaid," she says, a strand of seaweed wound about her leg.

"We should get out. Take a break."

"No," she cries. She stays in my arms.

We've been in the water for at least two hours, the wind rising and the waves growing rougher.

I know I shouldn't be here. I didn't tell my father that I was taking Izzy to the beach even when I could have on the phone call. But why ask when I know what the answer will be? A distracted, angry, don't-you-ever-listen-to-me no. And the true answer is: I don't have to listen to him anymore or even lie and feel guilty for the lie. I can do what I want. I don't have to be scared of the beach when the things to fear, to be really scared of, aren't outside, aren't here in the water, or atop a mountain even, but in ourselves: a tremor, a headache, a morning when smells or sounds are unfamiliar in the most ordinary and familiar of places.

I lay Izzy on our blanket. We're isolated, out by the edge of the dunes, which is how I like it. We haven't had two straight days at the beach all summer. And it's one of those days you think will last forever. That you want to last forever. Why can't there be more days like this?

"Let's rest," I say, though I don't sit beside her. I stretch my arms toward the sky, then toward the sea. She jumps up and copies me. I breathe in the sea, deep into my chest. So does she. I dig my toes into the wet sand at the edge of the tide. So does she.

A wave rushes in and out to sea, molding our feet into the sand.

I want to go back into the sea. Alone. I want to swim by myself like I used to when I was on the swim team, butterfly division, fast and sure. I want to swim like a butterfly. Swim and fly. Izzy looks ready to rest for a while. Her eyes droop. I cover her with a towel to shield her from the sun. She'll be fine for a few minutes.

"You sit down and wait for me right there," I say to her. "Don't go anywhere. Wait for me right here. I'll be five minutes, or less." Five minutes without tethers to Izzy.

"Five minutes," she says, holding up her hand.

"That's all."

"Okay, five minutes," she says, seriously.

"First, let me put more sunscreen on you." I spray her down, tickle under her arms, make sure her shoulders and the small of her back are protected, too, place her in the middle of the towel, and make sure she promises to sit right there and wait for me.

Then I run toward the sea, crash through the waves. Most girls I know don't like the ocean. They love the beach, not the water. The ocean whips your hair, leaves sand in the roots, ruins your makeup, and is oblivious to how good-looking you are or are not. Those girls are anchored to their towels. Those girls are moored near the lifeguard, half a beach away. I don't understand those girls and never have. But that's okay. I've always been invisible to them.

The sea is mine.

On shore, Izzy is shouting, or maybe she's singing to herself again. I can't hear her, only the roar of the ocean and the beat of the tide. My ears fill with water. I shake my head left then right, making it worse. She's waving her hands over her head. Her bathing suit drips from her slim shoulders. The pink stars on her flat front bounce. Her curls spring around her face. She's fine. I shout back to her, "I'll be right out," but before I can raise my arms I'm hit by a wave, a big one.

The roar of the ocean, of my heart, drowns out all. Yet I swim to the surface; I'm okay. Izzy's shouting, but I can't hear her. I aim to swim to her. She is my focal point on the shore, a hundred or so yards away, to the left of the rocks. But another wave strikes, hard like a bullet, crashing crest and foam, churning ice cold, flinging me to the ocean floor. This time, I can't find my footing at all. I'm tossed down, scraped along the bottom. I twist. My legs are pulled one way, my arms another. I need air. I need to get back to Izzy. *Izzy!* I try to swim to the surface. I can't push against the current. I have an irrational thought: *My mother is swimming toward me. She will save me.* My eyes burn. Blackness. Another wave strikes. I open my mouth to protest, to scream, and saltwater rushes in. I'm swallowing the sea. I choke, gasp, gag, strain for light, and plead for air.

Barkley finally leaves me, and I am alone down near the dunes and the water, deciding that I will take one perfect pill and swim. I'll float on the pill—and on the sea. I'll swim alone for fifteen minutes or so. The sun blisters the top of my head. All the summer light refracts off the sand in a haze.

All I want is immersion into the dark and cold sea—and a little white pill.

I maneuver the plastic bag out of my backpack, and a little kid, the one who's been with the girl-with-the-curves, careens toward me. "Hey!" she shouts. "Look." She's pointing east along the empty stretch of dunes and grasses. "My sister. Claire!"

The little sister is out of breath and panting. Her skin is peppered with sand. Her blond curls are matted to her head.

"Calm down," I say. "What's your name?"

"Izzy, short for Elizabeth. Look. There she is. She can't hear me. I've been calling for her." The waves are rougher than a little while ago, white-capped and higher, wilder, especially near the dunes and the rock barrier, which stretches out from the shore for a couple hundred yards, the rocks becoming larger and more menacing the farther out.

"Where is she?"

"There," she insists, crying all of a sudden. "Claire!"

I have to blink. I don't see anything.

"Claire!" her sister implores, yanking my arm. The sun beats down. I squint. The horizon is long, blue-white bursts of light and sea spray. Finally, I see her, or her head and arms. She's dangerously close to the rocks, where a sign clearly states *No Swimming*.

Claire is right there, and then with a crash of a wave, she isn't. I search the sea. She should resurface. She should swim parallel toward the shore. She should be there, in the vastness of the Atlantic Ocean, and she isn't.

The lifeguard is at least five hundred yards down toward the main part of the beach. His back is turned to us. He is blowing his whistle at other kids swimming too far out from shore.

Claire's head bobs up.

"Claire!" Izzy screams, as if she can hear her.

Izzy grabs my T-shirt in anticipation. Yet before we can be assured that she is okay, that what we see is true and right and she is fine, another wave strikes, and Claire's head disappears. All I can think is this: I have to help. But what about the stuff in my backpack? What if someone finds it?

Izzy hits my arm, bringing me back to the here and now, to what I'm seeing unfold right before my eyes, what I don't want to see—someone drowning in the riptide.

"She's out there!"

"Izzy, run and tell the lifeguard we need him."

I jump up. Fix on Claire's last position. This isn't happening. Not to me. I shout to Izzy, "Go."

Izzy wavers, wide-eyed and teary. "Where are you going?"

"In to help her."

"You can't help her."

"I know. I mean, I'm a good swimmer. I can help. You go. Get the lifeguard."

She goes as fast as she can across the sand.

I'm a strong swimmer. I can reach her—I can do this, can't I? The whitecaps crunch against the shore. The sea, which all summer seemed safely contained within our town's beach, now seems vast and uncontained. In the distance, a sailboat skims the water, small and inconsequential, like a plastic boat. Sea gulls guide the tide in with ear-splitting squawks. I steady my legs with my hands on my thighs as if I'm taking a penalty kick, and breathing hard, refusing the past, I fling the backpack off my shoulder and run.

Claire

Swim. Damn it, Claire. Swim.

I'm pumping my arms and legs but it's as if someone, the sea, has wrapped its arms around my neck and is yanking me down. I'm screaming this in my head: *Swim. Dammit, Claire. Swim!*

I'm cold to the core. My arms and legs lose strength even as I push to stroke, to strain my head above the crest of the wave, to reach air. My arms and legs dangle limp, useless.

I force myself to open my eyes and swim, swim toward the faint light. My hair, strung with seaweed and bits of shells and stone, weighs me down. I fling my arms out wide, struggling against the current. I'm less than a human being. I'm a crab dragged across the sea floor.

Swim! Claire. Swim.

I wish I could pray, though maybe that wish is prayer enough. Maybe the thought is enough—because all of a sudden, fingers grip my shoulders and lift my head above water. My arms flail. I want to stay above water. My eyes open wide. I gulp at the air. I kick the water—and him. He doubles forward, yet holds on, keeping both of us, somehow, above water. I recognize him— he's the guy from the Snack Shack. I don't know why he's here, but I'm glad that he is. He's screaming something at me that I can't hear. The pounding of the sea deafens me. I'm doing all I can to tread water, to keep my head up, to breathe.

Waves gather at the horizon and race toward us.

"Swim. Parallel to shore!" His words rush at me.

I try to shout back. My lips are cracked. My throat hoarse.

"Swim, Claire," he demands. "Swim."

I squeeze my eyes shut, fling my arms forward—and see my mother. She is on shore. She is calling for me. Somehow, she's standing there. She's also calling, "Claire. Swim."

My strength surges. I can do this. I will do this. I swim as he said to swim, and it works.

But he doesn't follow. He's struggling. He hasn't taken his own advice to swim parallel to shore. He's being pulled under. He's trying to scream but can't. I snare his shoulder. With my other arm, I'm a butterfly skimming across the sea. I'm keeping our heads above water until another wave hits. *Swim.* I'm screaming underwater and no one hears. The current snatches us back. We are ripped through the waters, even closer to the rock barrier. More waves crash over our heads. The sea thrusts us apart.

After a few long seconds, his hand reaches again for mine. Our bodies are shape without form. Swirls of black and gray and muck fill the space between us. The roar and jeer of the sea seize us.

Max

I am accidently alive.

I drag myself out of the sea. Saltwater streams off my arms and legs. My vision is fogged. I had Claire in my sight, and then I didn't. I had her fingertips clasping my own, then I didn't. I had nothing. Swirling water dragged me down. It was as if I was thrown back to shore. On the beach, I hang my head between my knees. I drop to the sand—next to arms, legs, Claire.

Her eyes are closed, her lips blue. Her hair is wound around her face, wreaths of seaweed brown. She coughs instead of speaking. Brackish gray-black seawater trickles from the side of her lips. She spits up more and lays her face in the sand as if wanting to taste the beach. I touch her back. Her skin is cool. My hand burns. I don't know what to do with my fingers now so I pat her back between her shoulder blades. She raises slightly, gathering in a breath. I breathe, too, and her eyes flutter open. These amazing eyes, almost bigger than the rest of her face, almond-shaped, maybe "exotic" is the best word, but it's not a word I usually use. I can't stop staring at her or patting her back. I got a beat going—one long pat, then two short ones. Across her mouth, across her lips, are nibbles of sand. My hand imprints on her back. Long pat. Two short ones.

Her hair strings around her hips like a mermaid's. She's

shivering. I want to put my whole arm around her. I want to brush away the sand—from her lips—and more—but those lips are vulnerable and since this is working, this stroking her back, I keep doing it. Long pat. Two short ones. And she leans into me. Her long legs etched with seaweed and sand and scratches wrap around mine. I breathe in her scent of saltwater and small fish and lose my breath as if drowning again. I concentrate: one long pat. Two short.

"Did you save me?" she asks.

"No."

"I think you did. Is everything okay? You know you're hitting me hard. I'm breathing. Can't you tell I'm breathing?"

Through her mermaid lips, she blows air toward me. Sand speckles her teeth and tongue. I want to catch her breath in mine but I keep on stroking in the cavern between her shoulder blades. The roar of the sea pulses in our ears, the pull of the tide slides underneath our backs, and the rhythm reminds me: we are alive.

All of a sudden, she shakes her head, unwinds her legs from me as if caught in a trap. "What's wrong?" I ask.

"Izzy? My little sister? Did you see her?"

She doesn't let me answer.

"Izzy!" Claire attempts to stand, though her legs are even wobblier than mine and she must use my shoulders for balance.

The ocean is edged with people, jumping, diving, snaking along the shoreline. The sailboat, a rattle and flap of sails, is still skirting the edge of the horizon. I scan the ocean, hoping

Izzy—did her hair look as alive as her sister's does?—I am hoping that she's not out there alone.

"Elizabeth," Claire says, forcing out her sister's full name. Tears stream down, cutting rivulets in the sand on her face, washing clean her lips and baring them to the sun.

"Does she know your cell phone or address in case she's found and brought to the main office?" I know this is protocol from a summer of panicked mothers and fathers rushing up to the Snack Shack as if we'd have their lost kids in the back. She turns to me hammering out her cell phone and address as if I know where her sister is and am not telling her. From all this, I learn that she is not a mermaid at all but just a girl from South Lakeshore, living less than a mile from my house. And she launches off toward the boardwalk at full speed, calling her sister's name like a siren, leaving me to snatch my backpack and stumble after her.

Grip her shoulders, her slender back firm against my chest. Reassure her.

She had hurried up to me on the beach. I had been training my mind's camera on Claire. But the little one wanted my help, begged for it, said she had been sent to find a lifeguard for Claire, but could not, and could I help her? And as I focused in on Claire, a sure shot, we witnessed her rise from the sea. Does the water burn her, too? Though it was like she was reborn. Claire on the sand, her face down, her legs wide and strong, the sun beating her hair and skin dry, was a new Claire to the world and wholly mine.

Except, Max Cooper ruined the scene.

Now I tighten my hold on the little sister. She is facing me. My lens is on her too.

"Don't you think she's wondering where I am?" She attempts to twist away from me. Holding her in place is like netting a fish, a slippery, frantic fish. She should use more sunscreen and renewable containers, I tell her, hooking my fingers under her delicate shoulders.

"Better to stand in one place and have her find you. That's what my mother always said when I got lost."

"Did you get lost a lot?" Her question is high-pitched, shaky and fearful—not the sound of Claire. She is wearing a bathing suit with pink stars like markers or signs.

I was lost all the time until the voice found me, but I do not say this to the little one. I do not want to frighten her with the idea that we are lost. And I am done being lost. Nor do I want her to think that I will leave her alone on the beach. I can put her in my car. I can lock her in there for her safekeeping.

"I have to go now. Please, let me go."

Claire must find her with me. She will now that she is searching for me, for the man also reborn, named Brent. She will look into my heart, she will know I am pure. She must look at me the way she is looking at Max, who in a clear close-up is handling her powerfully naked back in a manner that nobody but me should ever, ever handle. The little sister squirms. She is not Claire. Not Claire. Not reborn in the sun and sand. Not Claire at all.

Claire

"Rip currents are very dangerous, got it?" the lifeguard lectures from his high white chair. Max and I look at each other. As I ran for Izzy, he screamed to me that we should head toward the lifeguard, that he had sent her this way. He should have stayed out of the whole thing and left my sister on the blanket, where I told her to wait for me.

"I'm searching for my little sister," I say again, after explaining that I nearly drowned and that my little sister was lost, as if this sequence of events made any sense. Drown: submerge, inundate, sink—the most powerful is simply "drown." Running through synonyms doesn't make sense, either.

"Ricky, just help us look for her sister, okay?" says Max. "We can come back for the lecture on riptides next time."

"Some people call them riptides, got it? But 'rip current' is the correct term. First thing is, you should never swim out that far. Got it?" He climbs down off the chair.

I like to swim out far. I like to see how alone I can be in the sea's expanse. And I hate to be lectured.

Face-to-face we are almost the same height. His skin is taut and tanned. He's in his late twenties. His arms are tentacle-like, looping around the air between us. He looks me up and down and lands his sight directly on my chest.

"Are you going to help me find my little sister? I can't waste any more time. I have to find her." I force his eyes to meet mine.

"We'll find her. But you know who we got here?" he says, pointing at Max but letting his eye drop again.

I shake my head and think: he's the one who saved me, not you.

"Let's go," says Max to me.

"Max Cooper. His father is Glenn Cooper, the local state senator that's always mouthing off about climate change and beach erosion. I'd probably be on the news if I had saved his son from drowning. And who are you, sweetheart?"

"I'm nobody's daughter."

His eyes bulge at me and then at Max. I find Max's fingertips and tap out my own code. He has to stay with me until we find Izzy. He tenses.

"Hey, Ricky, we almost drowned on your beach," says Max, kicking the sand, clenching his fists, forcing my hand away.

"Almost. Next time, you'll know better, got it?" He flashes me a smile of white, even teeth. "Now let me put out an alert for your little sister. We'll have everyone we can out looking for her. We'll find her, you got it? Describe her to me."

As he waves his arms, coming forth with a smartphone, I start to say that her name is Elizabeth but I call her Izzy— A shout breaks over the rafts of blankets. Down through the empty fire lane toward the high white chairs races a blond head in a bathing suit with pink stars. She falls headlong into me. I kneel and scoop her up.

The lifeguard climbs back up to his white chair and stands there, arms crossed around his hairless chest, white teeth blazing from tan skin, and scans the ocean as if hoping someone will need saving right there and then. Beside me, Max digs through his backpack, searching for something, too. I hug Izzy toward me, knowing I have in my arms all that matters.

"Where were you?" I ask. "Why didn't you listen to me and stay on the blanket?"

"Max said he'd go in—and make sure you were alright—and he said for me to go to the lifeguard—and I could see you and I ran but I couldn't find one—and this guy, you'd remember him, he said he'd help, but then we could see you and Max just flop out of the water—and then he wouldn't let me go—and then he did. He showed me where you were and let me go. Claire, you wouldn't get lost, would you? Not without me."

"What guy?" asks Max.

Izzy points past the lifeguard chair at the shoulder-to-shoulder crowd fanned across the beach and boardwalk. I can't tell who she is pointing to and it doesn't matter. She's back with me.

"Am I lost?" I kiss the top of Izzy's head. She clings to me. I whisper in her ear, "I'm here. Right here, Izzy. Just don't tell Daddy about this, okay? Promise me. Or I'll never bring you to the beach until you are a hundred and six years old."

Izzy buries her head in my stomach. "Just don't ever do what you did again. I need you around until I'm a hundred and six."

I should have paid attention to the warning sign near the rocks. I should have seen that the waves were getting rougher and higher. But I've been in this ocean all my life and nothing's happened. I should have known that even on the most ordinary days, even on the days when you wake up and think that all you have to do is brush your teeth—and you can go without a care—the world will surprise you. The waves will hit harder; the current will drag you under.

"Are you listening, Claire?" says Izzy, as if she is suddenly the older one. "You were almost lost. I want to tell that ocean: no more losing my sister, mister."

"That's right. Are you listening?" says Max beside us. "No drowning Izzy's sister!" I notice he has dimples on each cheek when he laughs.

"No drowning, Max!" I join in. I stretch up on my toes and shout over people's heads, at the waves, at the deceitful sea. Max reaches over and swats at the sand on the side of my face. I laugh. I lick my lips and find more sand and salt there. And my lips sting, ache. And all of this doesn't make sense. I really like Brent, so why am I wishing Max would brush the sand off my lips with his own?

Instead he says, "I'm late for my shift. I work at the Snack Shack."

"I think I know that," I say.

Izzy nuzzles between us. "Can I have an ice cream cone?"

The sand from my face rubs between Max's fingers and is returned to the shore.

"Maybe. Before we go home," I say to Izzy, distracted by Max. Not that he's paying attention to me. He's squinting at a squad of girls in string bikinis parading over beach blankets as they march to the sea.

"I got to go," he says, sounding miserable that he has to leave the sight of bikinis in their neon colors attacking the gray sea.

"You're late for your shift," I repeat back to him. His eyes won't meet mine. "Will your boss understand?"

He shrugs. "Who cares?"

The state senator's son races off. I am not going to waste my time on him when I can truly connect to someone as serious and intense as Brent. Though I have to think that Max has decent speed—and he's careful to leap around other people's property. He pauses to kick a soccer ball back to a group of pint-size boys. He concentrates when aiming the black-and-white ball as if he's planning to kick it far from the kids. He doesn't. He uses the side of his foot to send it right to the smallest boy.

Izzy taps my back with the palm of her small hand. "I really want an ice cream cone. Should I get vanilla or chocolate?"

I remember the other beat: one long . . . two short, as if I am remembering my heartbeat.

Max

Back on my shift in the Snack Shack. My last shift ever, and somehow I'm ten minutes early. I could have stayed with Claire and her sister, but I couldn't think of anything else to say to a girl like her. Anyway, I don't want or need any more excitement. I need boring. I need to float from here until the first day of school. I'm sure I can just ease through the rest of the afternoon, ease through—and go. I slide my feet across the floor in my effort to be effortless.

From the front counter, Trish calls, "Hero-boy, look at you."

"Hero-boy!" echoes Peter.

The shore is packed with people dashing in and out of the water. No sign of currents that could drag anyone under. No sign at all that someone, that Claire, nearly drowned. But I'm not a hero. I don't know what came over me going in the water after her. I am not the kind of guy who saves people. I'm the go-along-to-get-along type of guy. I'm the ultimate team player, the guy who can play a half dozen positions on the soccer team, and play them well enough. I'm the guy who doesn't like to work too hard or think too much, who has had the easy life, according to my father, even if I did spend the summer working at the Snack Shack.

"How'd you hear?"

"Barkley told us," says Peter. "But he sounded mad at it."

"He always sounds mad," says Trish with a big laugh. Squeezing by, she tosses a smile at me, and I even smile back, but just a bit. I don't want her to get any ideas, even on my last shift ever. "I'm on a bathroom break," she calls out, leaving me with Peter.

"Where's Barkley?" I ask him. He's working with the broom, sweeping with great energy but no results.

"Counting water bottles again," says Peter. "Why does he always count the water bottles?"

I don't know why anybody does anything. Dive in after a girl you hardly know, count water bottles when nobody asks you to count them. "Maybe we're all just a little bit weird."

"Yeah, maybe we are," he agrees happily.

"Anybody working here?" says a middle-aged customer with a mass of hair everywhere but on the crown of his head. "I'd like a chocolate ice cream cone over here."

"One ice cream cone?" Peter repeats, dropping the broom. I pick it up and put it away so we don't trip and kill ourselves. "What kind of ice cream cone? We have chocolate, vanilla, or swirl?"

"Chocolate, I said."

"Chocolate?"

"Chocolate!"

Peter trudges back toward the ice cream machine, muttering "chocolate" so he won't forget.

"Cooper," Jackson beckons to me from the front of the line. He leans across the counter, confidentially, as if he wants to consult with me, probably on something to do with the team. I'm going to have to assure him that I've been practicing those penalty kicks. I'm going to be cool with him today.

"Hey, man."

"Still working here?"

"Last day."

"Party this weekend?"

"You know it," I say.

"Nobody's going."

"Yeah?" I say, as if I care, which, of course, part of me does.

Samantha eases up behind him. Today she is in a hot-pink bikini. Her hair hangs straight down her back. For the first time this summer, I think: this girl must never swim at the beach. I've never seen her hair wet, not like Claire's—all wild and un-done.

"Hey," she says to no one. But what she does is this: wrap her arms around his stomach and reach up to scratch his chest with her long pink nails.

"Hey," he says to her, twisting around, talking down to her head, and asking her, "You going to this loser's party?"

She doesn't even look at me, only at him, and shrugs. "He never asked me."

She's right. I never asked her. All the back-and-forth between us was in my mind. She's like any other girl on the beach— sparkle and flirt and giggle and it's hard, sometimes, not to look at her. She expects you to look and once you know that, you know it's all about her. I can't really think this through right now—with Jackson and her contorting, claiming each other with lunging kisses—and kids calling out for ice cream: vanilla, chocolate, swirl, and Peter, man, he's not keeping any of it straight and there's no sign of Barkley or Trish—I've got to admit it was never about me or us in her eyes.

He pushes her away and she giggles. "We're not going, are we, Jackson?" she says to him, swinging around to face him, noticing, I guess, that his attention is not on her at that moment.

Peter shuffles back toward the counter. "Chocolate," he says, pushing the ice cream cone toward the kid, who flings two dollars at him and runs off with the cone.

"How about taking my order?" says Jackson to Peter with a glint and edge.

"I'll help you," I say to Jackson.

"Isn't he supposed to be helping me?" says Jackson, never breaking his smile. "I'll have a vanilla cone."

"Vanilla?" repeats Peter.

"I got it."

"No, I think I'll have chocolate." He winks at Samantha, who giggles. She's freed him, for the moment, from her pink nails.

"Chocolate?" repeats Peter slowly, looking over at me.

"I'm getting it," I say, hurrying. I just want this shift to be over.

"I want the sped to help me," says Jackson in such a friendly way you almost miss him insulting Peter, that he's calling him what we all, sometimes, call the kids who are led by aides down the hall in high school, who are in the "closed door" classes, who are students in special education, or shorthand: "speds." Peter may have one more year to go in high school, even be in regular classes like gym and health, but to people like Jackson he will always be a sped. While I may have called him the same name once or twice over the summer in anger and frustration, I don't like it coming from Jackson on my last day of having to work with Peter.

"Is that you, Cooper? Are you the sped these days? You spent the summer hanging out with this guy, maybe he wore off on you? You going into the special classes with kids like him in the fall?" I don't miss this. I stop in my tracks, clenching and unclenching my fists. This is worse than yesterday. I am so glad that today is my last shift in the history of Snack Shack shifts.

"You and I are at different schools," says Peter, reasonably, to me. "Doesn't he know that?"

"Hey, hey, what are you doing?" calls out Jackson. "I'll have a swirl. You got that, Cooper?"

"Swirl," repeats Peter to me, as if I need help.

Samantha giggles more.

"Maybe two. Should I really rock their worlds and order two?" he says to Samantha.

I don't know how I liked her. How I was always waiting for her to come up to the counter—and she came nearly every day. When did she hook up with Jackson? How did I miss that?

"Two?" repeats Peter, struggling.

"I'm on top of it," I say to him. "Take care of another customer."

"Two cones?" Peter persists to Jackson. "Vanilla and chocolate, or swirl?"

"Sure. Or maybe just chocolate. Or chocolate and vanilla. Or swirl and chocolate."

"Or vanilla and vanilla," says Samantha as if she has just caught on to the pattern.

"Didn't I say 'swirl'?" Jackson spits out like he's in a comedy routine.

"I'm helping them, Max," says Peter. "I can do it."

"I know you can do it, Peter. But let me take care of these guys, okay? You handle the bottled water line. You know how I hate selling the bottled water."

This isn't happening to me. Not on my last shift.

"It's okay, the sped's helping us, isn't he?" Jackson makes like he's innocent, with this broad smile on his pinhead. Samantha smiles at him.

"Cut it, Jackson."

"What am I doing, Cooper? I'm just ordering ice cream cones. You and him can't handle that, it's not my problem, is it?"

"I can do this, Max," shouts Peter, something he does when he definitely can't handle the situation.

Jackson leans across the counter toward Peter. "Chocolate. Vanilla. Swirl. What did I want? Tell me."

Peter can only look in more confusion from Jackson to me. Before I can act or do anything with the cone in my hand, on the other side of the counter, Barkley comes up from behind

Jackson. He's twice as big as Jackson, bald, pale, and wearing those creepy sunglasses of his. He looks like an off-duty cop.

Jackson holds his hand up between himself and Barkley. "You know something, I don't really want an ice cream cone, do you, Sammie?"

"Then let's move along, okay?" says Barkley. "Because you're not helping anyone being here. Not me. Not Peter. Not Max. Move along, you got it?"

"Okay, I'm going. But I will see you Wednesday, Cooper, first day of school." Jackson leans back across the counter and without a trace of humor says to me, "Have fun at your party."

"Move," says Barkley, his voice modulated a notch or two above what's needed for the situation, not quite a shout, but loud, almost mechanical or without feeling—weird again. "Especially the girl in the pink bikini. Move off the line. You, I know you. I know what you want."

"He wishes he knew me," says Samantha to Jackson.

Barkley leans toward her. "I know that you have been watching me. All the girls in pink have been."

I'd feel better if there were some irony in that statement, but part of me believes that Barkley believes they've been spying on him. He's dead serious.

"In your dreams," says Samantha. She flutters her shiny pink nails down on Jackson's hand. He's not holding hands with her, though. At least, they're not at that stage.

And why do I care?

"Hey, I can't wait until school starts, Cooper," says Jackson, right up into my face.

"I can't wait, Jackson." My neck and shoulders tighten, and I wish I were floating, not arguing, not thinking, not having to deal with Jackson or Peter or Barkley. In all this, Tricia is looking at me like she wants to tell me something, something funny, and I'm not sure what to do with her behind the Snack Shack counter. I really don't want Samantha or Jackson seeing the fat girl liking me. Trish hands me a humongous swirl cone and rubs my back. I act like I'm in a hurry.

Samantha swivels away from Barkley. "He's an a-hole," Samantha says to Jackson so prettily I barely catch the insult. I don't know whether she's talking about Barkley or me. All at once, I wish she didn't say it, I didn't hear it, and that she means Barkley, not me.

I shove the cone toward Jackson, a lopsided swirl, dripping at its sides. I want to push it in his face.

"Hey, what the hell is this?" says Jackson.

"Swirl," responds Peter.

"Take it," I say. "On me."

"What a mess," Jackson says, shrugging and agreeing to the cone, lapping the ice cream up. He offers it to Samantha, who licks in the same place he licked. They step over the end of the counter with their free cone, and I think, some guys get it all: the game, the girl, the cone.

"Enjoy, sweetie," shouts Trish at them.

"Hey, enjoy," says Peter behind her, relieved, good-natured as always, though his innocence makes me sad.

The line breaks toward the counter in a wave. All of a sudden, Barkley, in a flat, loud voice says, "Form one line. Get on line. Do you know that only in New York do you get on line?"

A couple of the little kids push left and right. But Barkley freezes. He tilts his head as if listening to something that none of the rest of us can hear.

"You did good, Barkley," says Trish to him. "Are you coming back on this side of the counter?"

"I know what it means," he says to no one in particular.

"What it means?" I ask as I keep an eye on Peter serving up bottled water to one kid and a hot dog to the next. With Barkley on the other side of the counter, everyone on line is behaving for the moment. Maybe we should keep him there.

"What it means to be bullied." He says this to me and Trish without emotion. I take an order for hot dogs and water. Make change. He continues, "And not having anyone side with you, having to listen to that voice in your head to discern what is right and what is wrong."

I'm not sure why Barkley is always trying to prove he's smarter than us. Maybe I can't get beyond the shaved head, the body odor, and the mirrored sunglasses. Maybe I should be listening to the voice inside my head. Maybe he makes more sense than most.

However, his tragic flaw is that he keeps talking. "The voice inside us needs to be strong, or else evil wins. We cannot let the forces of evil and disorder win, can we?"

Part of me is thinking: *Screw it. Let evil and disorder win. Vote for anarchy.* I don't even fully know what I mean by that, but it feels good to be angry.

Off to the side of the Snack Shack counter, Samantha bends toward Jackson. He smashes the melting end of the cone into his mouth. She swipes at the ice cream with the tip of her tongue, and, seeing me watching her, licks again, slowly. His arm drapes around her shoulder. He flings the cone toward our garbage can and misses. Their cold mouths kiss. Sea gulls attack their ice cream cone.

Beyond the two of them, holding her sister's hand, is Claire, studying the scene, too—Samantha and Jackson kissing—and me, watching, and her watching. Somehow time or movement, the ordinary comings and goings of the sun or tide, contracts to this kiss. They are kissing and the sea gulls are scrambling on top of one another, a flurry of wings over the garbage, and I want to call out to Claire and say—*say what?* Come here? I'll give you and Izzy a free ice cream cone? Come here, because I've got to admit that Samantha is the girl that I've been jerking off to all summer long and that she isn't you, and I'm glad that you're not her?

Instead, I'm hammered by the next customer. "Anybody working here?" he yells across the counter. "I need six ice cream cones before the end of summer."

"Vanilla, chocolate, or swirl?" I say automatically. Claire's long legs are cutting a path in the crowd, and Izzy's dangling on to her fingertips. I hope she isn't leaving the beach.

"Napkins? Do you have any napkins for me?" Samantha appears at the side of the counter. She directs this question at me, and I look at her dully. The tip of her tongue slices around her mouth. "I'm all sticky," she says.

"Let's go, Sammie," shouts Jackson. "We don't have time for these speds." He raises his hand in a final salute, a middle finger aimed at us.

Next to me, Trish bursts out laughing, relieved, triumphant even, that Jackson is leaving, and of course Peter joins in. I follow, too. Sometimes you can't do anything but go along, even though it will probably hurt me more with Jackson when school starts. But for right now, I laugh at being called a sped.

Barkley tucks his mirrored glasses into the pocket of his sweatshirt. He blinks rapidly, as if negating the crowd, the requests, the daily demands on each of us, and focuses on Jackson. Someone is asking me for a bottle of water, and, for the tenth time this shift, to make sure it's cold.

"Bark, hey, you coming back to work?" I ask, because it's clear that he's not. He's trailing Jackson. "We have a long line here."

"Make sure it's really cold," says the next customer in front of me. Under her wide-brimmed hat, this customer's face is too smooth, her lips too full, and her top up and tight as if someone gave orders for her to defy gravity at all costs. Most of all, she's too old for her polka-dot bikini, and worse yet, she thinks she's something I should be looking at.

"Real cold, honey," trying to catch my eyes and flirt. "It's brutal out here."

I monitor Barkley. He's closing in on Jackson and Samantha. "Bark! We need your help."

Instead, he takes off, bounding at Jackson. He bashes into him, throwing him to the sand, sprawling on top of him, pounding the back of his head. A mass of arms and legs rolls through the sand. The line splits apart. Attention is on the fight.

"What is going on?" My customer is annoyed. "I really need my water, don't you see that?"

I race out of the Snack Shack. An old guy in a T-shirt that says "The beer stops here" tries to help and is knocked backward by Barkley wrestling Jackson. The old guy starts cursing about kids, but doesn't make any further effort. Jackson screams.

"Who is a sped? Tell me?" Barkley shouts as he locks around Jackson's suddenly fragile-looking neck.

I grab hold of Barkley's hands. They are ice cold. It's a hundred degrees out and his fingers are ice cold. Maybe he's taken some of his own pills, and they've just kicked in. And if he's done that, will it somehow get back to me that I have pills, too? Maybe the same ones? I don't know if it's Jackson, or Barkley, or me that I'm most concerned about.

Jackson yelps, red-faced.

"Don't kill him, Barkley," I say, losing my foothold in the sand.

Barkley bashes me in the chest with his elbow, once, twice, rocking the air out of me. I stagger—I didn't think under all that flab was muscle—but I hang on. His hands screw around Jackson's neck. I think: Barkley is going to kill Jackson on my last shift.

"It's the heat! Don't you see? It's making us all crazy. This never-ending heat!" the lady in the polka-dot bikini squeals at us. Another corner is yelling, "Fight. Fight!" Samantha is shouting "Jackson!" as if that will save him. I feel dizzy and sick. Barkley elbows me again, swift and hard. I fall back. My mouth is open. Sand mashes in. I'm eating sand. I should let him kill Jackson.

Like an ox, Peter, in his yellow work boots, stomps out of the Snack Shack. As if through a long tunnel, I hear Trish urging him, "Get Barkley off Jackson."

And Peter snatches the back of Barkley's sweatshirt. With a grunt, he yanks Barkley from Jackson, who wriggles free, a snake in the sand. Peter keeps his arm around Barkley until, a second or two later, with a violent jerk, Barkley shakes him off and crawls forward—he's searching for his sunglasses in the sand, and finding them a few feet away, sticks them in his pocket. He refuses any more help from Peter, stands in a slouch, arms hanging down, a kicked dog, and lumbers toward the Snack Shack, muttering "sped" under his breath.

My head clears. I stagger my way to my feet next to Peter. He tries to help me and I let him and he's happy, as if we were a team.

Jackson leaps up, cursing, sweat flying. Samantha whips herself between him and me. She's holding up her pink nails between us, and I've got to admit it, perking up those bikini breasts, not much in comparison to someone like Claire, but serviceable in this blocking defense.

"My father is a lawyer," she says, as if that will solve anything.

"Move," Jackson says to her.

She glances from me to Jackson, drops her hands, and leans into him, half his size, as if she has nowhere else to go. He's going to be okay—I bet he's even going to get laid at the end of the day.

"I'm going to kill you, Bark," shouts Jackson over her head, not touching her. Barkley doesn't turn around or otherwise acknowledge Jackson. "You hear me, you fuckin' freak? I'm going to kill you. And you too, Cooper. Just see if anybody shows up at your party. I don't care if you're on the team. Just see what happens to you this year. You're dead. You hear me? Dead to me and everybody else." Having made his threats, he storms off, back down to the sea. Samantha follows, yet after a few steps stops on the hot sand, glances back at me, then wets her lips, but I'm done looking at her.

Claire

Joy in the sea. Buoyed by the invisible fins of mermaids. High winds. Rocks crop near. Don't listen to the singing of the women-fish. Don't listen. The current swirls. *Swim, Claire, swim.* "Rip currents are the leading surf hazard for all beach-goers. They are particularly dangerous for weak or nonswimmers. Rip current speeds are typically one to two feet per second. However, speeds as high as eight feet per second have been measured—this is faster than an Olympic swimmer can sprint. Thus, rip currents can sweep even the strongest swimmer out to sea. Over one hundred drownings due to rip currents occur every year in the United States. More than 80 percent of water rescues on surf beaches are due to rip currents. Rip currents can occur at any surf beach with breaking waves." Lost at sea. Tossed against rocks. Listen, the women-fish sing. Listen. *Swim, Claire, swim.*

I'm back in my bedroom. I'm trying to make sense of what happened at the beach today, and what is happening here. I force myself to read back the prose poem. I hate reading my own writing.

"Things fall apart; the center cannot hold," writes Yeats. I feel like I can't sit still. I have that line from last year's English class above my computer. I tear it down. I'm holding it all together.

Izzy and I had an early dinner—vanilla, chocolate, and strawberry ice cream. We both agreed that it was a perfect dinner. We had left the beach in the mid-afternoon. I had planned on buying us ice cream cones there, but I don't know what was going on at the Snack Shack, some kind of fight. I saw Max leap from behind the Snack Shack, and thought: he saved me from drowning—he did—and now he's trying to break up a fight, or at least, I think he was trying to break it up. It was like watching a movie, something less than real life, though, of course, it was real. It didn't feel real, I didn't feel real. I'm not sure I feel "real" now. But earlier, that weird guy with the shaved head was also in the middle of the fight. I had warned Izzy never to speak with him again. I don't care if she now knows his name and that he knows mine. I don't care that he was the one she ran to when trying to find help. He didn't help at all. Max did.

Obviously Max likes to get himself in the middle of things—that's all I could think when I saw him in that mess of arms and legs and shouts around the Snack Shack. Izzy said she was sure that Max didn't start the fight. She wanted her ice cream. I don't know who started it or who ended it. I didn't stay for the end. I don't like fights or violence of any kind. I'm sure that I would make the worst witness, if I ever witnessed a real crime, and I hope that I never do. I couldn't even report on my mother to the ambulance driver or the doctor. I couldn't even remember if she woke up with a headache, or what time she woke up. I sometimes feel that details slip away from me, that everything is temporary. Nothing stays. When I write, sometimes these details reappear in the poems, half hidden, symbols, and they are as real as anything. I wonder if this is why I write—to know what's real.

"All that we see or seem is but a dream within a dream." My mother would sometimes quote from Edgar Allan Poe when I looked like I was far away, thinking, as she would say, "big thoughts."

But now, I force myself to be here. I listen for Izzy. I jump up and check on her in the room next door. She is lying flat on her back, her arms stretched out, her blond curls fallen around her, a few strands flung over her face, and she is sleeping, even though it's still light outside. She's exhausted from too much sun, too much beach, and too much ice cream. I tease her pink daisy sheet over her. She kicks it off.

Back in my room, I read through, again, this prose poem, which I wrote in a fury, mixing description and facts from the National Weather Service. The words pulsate, draw me in, drown me. Soon enough, I have to shut my writer's notebook.

This afternoon, I talked to my father on the phone. He sounded bone-tired but excited. He said he had come up with a solution to the insurance issue and wanted to discuss it with me in person. I am here, where is he?

Crickets whirl. Cars honk. The breeze floats in the scent of sleeping flowers. "The world is too much with us," or so writes the poet William Wordsworth. I want to shake the poetry out of me. I have to be practical.

"Because I could not stop for Death— He kindly stopped for me," Emily Dickinson's poem buzzes through my head.

"I could not stop for death?" I didn't drown. There's something exhilarating in knowing that I could come that close and survive. My laptop screen blinks at me. I circle it. I have too much energy to sit. I stand over the screen and dream out another poem.

RIPPING
by Claire Wallace

Rip: tear, rend, shred, slash,

or ripped: well-defined muscles,

or ripped: drunk or stoned—

rip-roaring,

or rip: a song from the web.

Rip into: attack

Rip off

I'm going to

rip you a new—

or reboot:

R.I.P.

Rest in peace.

Not quite Emily Dickinson. The hardest part of writing this second poem is deciding where to put the periods and commas. The words flow. The pauses are hard. The end points harder. All endings are tough, often ambiguous. I never know when to end, or where. I take the commas and periods out and put them back in. There is such permanence to a period in a poem. Emily Dickinson liked dashes in her poetry. Maybe inspiration comes from what's not there as much as what *is*.

I'm on a roll and dash out a third poem, a short one, which starts with the line "Rip out my heart." I place my palm against the screen as if through the smooth surface I could touch the sentences. Sometimes I think this is the only thing keeping me sane—and grounded. I would float away otherwise. I want to share these poems with Brent. Yet at that moment, the kitchen telephone rings.

Coffee, fresh from the gas station convenience store, scalds the roof of my mouth.

Before I returned home, I filled up my Explorer with gas and myself with coffee. This is my second extra-large cup.

Jared says he has a pill that is better than coffee. I do not believe him. I must break off with him. He is no good. He says that I should know that this pill selling is only for the short term; he needs the money. His father and mother are divorced, though in truth, his father is in jail for selling drugs. How entangled are our family histories. We are our fathers, our grandfathers; my cousin's blood runs in my blood.

I gulp down more coffee.

Claire, mermaid more than girl, chosen for me, emerged from the sea with hair that was alive, snake-like. Her face was lost in the hair. I could lose myself in that hair. I glare at the keyboard with its incoherent pattern. Better to use another device. Better to telephone her. She picks up immediately. "Are you okay?"

"Brent?"

Her voice is deep and silky and breathless. I must concentrate. I want to hold her, protect her. She will smell like the sea: salty, wild, sun-drenched—a mermaid smell.

"I posted new poems. Did you read them?"

I push my desk chair close to the screen. I am not sure if I want to see something new. I saw enough today. Saw Claire nearly drown. Witnessed her with Max Cooper. Now I am slow to respond. Time warps.

"Are you reading them now?" Her voice is near.

I read the shortest one:

RIP
by Claire Wallace

Rip out my heart

Eat it

Go ahead

Does it need salt?

Or is it sweet?

I bet it's bloody and bitter

and better-tasting than

any other part of me

I suck down another draw of coffee, black as mud, burning. Unlike my father, I do not believe in artificial sweeteners. They alter the chemistry of the brain. On the other hand, coffee aids concentration. Coffee does not require cans or plastic. I drink from a recyclable cup. I drink more and stare at the poem. I do not know what it means. I do not know what any of it means. And I have a problem with these poems, even without reading the other ones. A major problem. The lack of grammar results in the deficit of clear, concise sentences, which leads to obfuscations and lies.

"I know this isn't a screenplay. It's only a poem," she says.

"There are formats that screenplays must follow," I say. Sweat runs down the inside of my sweatshirt. I have told her that I am writing a screenplay. I have not committed myself to words yet and she has.

"I think it is so cool that you are working on a screenplay."

I drink down to the dredges.

"Claire, I do not understand what you wrote. And I want to understand, Claire. I want to understand you. I feel that is the reason we are what we are. To understand. For me to understand you."

It is not clear why it is taking her so long to answer me. Why time stretches and contracts as if by her will.

"What do you think it means?" She finally speaks, happily, almost flirtatious, as if she easily comprehends the meaning of these words and is refusing to tell me for my own good. She is acting like an English teacher. Of all the teachers, those are the ones that perplexed me the most, especially the female ones: cheerful, intense, piling symbols and metaphors and similes and subtext in a heap.

I study her words. Missing or misplaced commas and periods distort the meaning, the truth.

Be careful with her. Watch her. She needs you. Read her poetry again. It has a message for you in between the lines. In the white spaces and pauses.

"Brent?" she asks. "So what do you think?"

"I must read it closely." I lick the inside of the coffee cup. I need more.

"It's just a poem," she says. Her voice stays low and light.

"No, it's more than that."

"How did you find me, Brent?"

I realize that the Glock is for her—to protect her, too.

"I was searching for you, Claire Wallace."

Max

At sunset, I start closing up with Trish and Peter. Barkley's left his dirty coffee pot in the back. I don't think he's cleaned it out all summer, and he must have drunk a dozen cups of coffee today, a record. So I do him a parting favor: I fill up the pot with hot water and soap and leave it to soak.

After the fight with Jackson, Barkley said he couldn't focus on work and left, as if he had bigger issues to deal with and could call it a day at the Snack Shack. He wasn't doing much work anyway, mumbling to himself. I'm not the boss, either. Even so, I stayed past my shift to help Trish and Peter. Now, they're flopped down in plastic chairs behind the counter. I don't know why I thought that they would want to celebrate my shift ending; they're not the celebrating type. Even so, they have to work the three-day weekend, Labor Day weekend, and only I, Max Cooper, am stopping work before one of the busiest weekends of the year, as pointed out by Trish with her hands on her hips and a jiggle so hard I had to step back against the soft serve machine. Nobody says it, but in the same way I got the job via my father's connections, I'm ending it early because of his influence. No son of Glenn and Debbi Cooper's is going to be working on his birthday.

"Did you find who you were looking for?" asks Peter, all cheery as if we're starting the day, not ending it.

"I'm not looking for anybody." The sun sets against the sea. The sea gulls rise up over the waves. I have no plans for tonight. This is the end of summer for me.

"I hope we get to work together next summer," says Peter.

"I hope we don't," I say, kiddingly, but he doesn't get it and his smile comes crashing down.

"He's had enough of us," says Trish, getting to her feet. "It's closing time."

We spend the last few minutes in silence—the shore almost empty, the counters cleaned off, the ice cream machine wiped down, and the floors swept. We close up the front gate and lock it. I double-check that it's secure.

Last shift.

"Hey, guys," I say to them as we're standing outside the Snack Shack. "I'm having a party tomorrow night." I don't know why I say this. I've known about it all summer and haven't said a thing to them. Part of me wants to take it back. Everyone always shows up at my birthday party, and I don't want them all to see Trish and Peter there, do I? But then, Trish and Peter deserve to celebrate the end of summer, too.

"A party?" Peter repeats.

"At my house."

"Party? Is it your birthday?" asks Peter, wide-eyed.

"In fact, it is."

"How old are you?"

"Seventeen."

"I'm seventeen, too!" says Peter. "Why didn't we know it was your birthday? I like everyone to know it's my birthday. It's in December. I hope you can come to my birthday. December fifteenth."

Trish looks me up and down like I'm dirt. She knows why I didn't ask them earlier.

"A party? How nice," says Trish. "You really want us?"

"No," I say, as if joking. I don't know what I'm doing telling them about the party. I mean, I don't even want to be having this party. I remember what Jackson said, that nobody is coming, nobody that matters like him or Samantha, so I might as well invite Trish and Peter.

"We'll come!" Peter says, and adds, "Right, Trish?"

She shrugs, yanks her striped tank top down across her hips, and flings her overstuffed bag onto her shoulder. "Let's go, sweetie," says Trish to Peter. "You and me, kid, we have to be back here tomorrow. We're working the entire weekend, unlike some people."

This is going to be the worst birthday ever.

Are you going or staying, Max?" asks Trish.

"You think I'm staying? I'm out of here. Forever."

Three across, we walk down the boardwalk toward the tunnel and the parking lot. Trish and Peter both tell me they had the best summer ever working with me. Peter repeats the line twice until I nod my head, as if I'm agreeing.

Outside the short tunnel, in the parking lot, I step away from the two of them. I'm afraid they'll hug me or do something else stupid. Instead I say, "I hope you guys can come tomorrow night." And I mean it.

Peter releases one of his extra-happy smiles, the kind he always gave when I said he should have an ice cream break.

"We'll see, sweetie. I may have plans," says Trish, and then she does hug me, and it's okay.

She guides Peter across the parking lot to his bus stop at the far side. I don't know if she's been doing this all summer. I feel like I've spent the whole summer not paying attention, and now here I am at the end, and I need to start. Maybe the first thing I need to do is stop with the pain pills, prescription or not. I rub my back.

Summer is over. It's finally over. The sun eases down across the roof of the Snack Shack, over the ocean. Sea gulls glide across the stark black tar. Buses rumble in. Trish and Peter shout good-byes. For the first time that summer, I think that I should offer them a ride. But before I can, Trish is giving Peter a hug, too, and helping him on a bus. She gets on a different bus. All of a sudden, I realize that I will miss them.

My skin is uncomfortable, damp and burning. I am in the bathroom, running the shower. I make sure I blast the water for a good five minutes: fogging the mirror, overturning the liquid soap. All these months, shaving cream has been allowed. The chemicals are protective, cool to my face and head. I run a razor all around, striking off the hairs. Before I leave the bathroom, I toss all the blue towels to floor, as if they have been used. I don't touch the pink ones. Those are my mother's towels, and one of the many rules in the house is that neither I nor my father are to use her towels even if they are placed in our separate bathrooms. She does not use them. The cleaning lady sprays them once a week with what is supposed to be a rose scent, but it's only more chemicals, a false, plastic scent, a scent that does not break down, or wilt. They should be home soon and will think that I have showered.

Quick! What's the body's largest organ? Skin. And mine will remain safe and water-free. Thoughts ricochet from one side of my brain to the other. My eyes ache. My forearms are bruised from the attack on Jackson, the white turning a purple-black of ugliness.

When I return to my bedroom, I double-check that the door is locked behind me. I log on and read the poetry from

Claire again. Her words are even more indecipherable than before. All words are. They leap on the screen. Grammar, which should control the sentences, is not present.

I will save all her poems for later. Force order on them. Add commas and periods. Show her what matters in this world is a sense of right and wrong, especially in a sentence.

I will check my other messages. Maybe they are better. Among the promotions for video games, for cheap prescription drugs, among the old headlines from various news sources I subscribe to and never read, the updates from environmental groups who are always asking for donations or for petitions to be signed, the reminders about overdue library books, my local library now hunting me down via e-mails, threatening fines— among all these messages, not one from the state senator.

There is an automatic response from the Environmental Protection Agency. This starts with, "Thank you for your concern." This I don't need to read. I understand that my so-called "concerns" are being ignored, passed on, and flipped to a nameless bureaucrat. This is my cause, not my concern. I could write my congressman or United States senator or even the president, but this elected representative, Glenn Cooper, said he was here to listen and provide answers to me.

I want results, but first I am hot. I pull off my sweatshirt. My stomach hangs over my sweatpants; the sweatpants pinch me at the waist. Everything is too tight against the largest organ of my body.

I must refocus. I must begin the screenplay.

The white screen glares at me, asking for a title. The screen undulates. Why must a title come first? But the program is asking for a title and there are rules to follow. Time slows. Ten minutes. Fifteen. Thirty of white, white screen.

I need a cigarette. Coffee. Claire. I make the white small and then blow it up to 500 percent, but no words appear, only more white. I pound the keyboard and no words appear, only chaos and gibberish.

Last fall, Glenn Cooper came and spoke to my political science class at the community college and said that I would be heard. He said to write him. He gave us his e-mail and his snail mail address. This is the class where the professor mumbled things, like that the personal is political. All politics is local. Live free or die. He was another who didn't teach; he spoke in sayings culled from a hundred years of teaching the same course. I asked Glenn Cooper then, directly, man to man, about water bottles in our oceans, and he said, "Very good question." Nevertheless, he begged off a specific answer, said that was a federal as much as a state concern. He had an American flag pinned to the lapel of his dark blue jacket.

I type, hunting down the correct letters from my carefully routed Brent account. The untitled screenplay must wait.

Dear Senator Cooper:

I am writing you with my latest concern: this is a new, global concern about the lack of basic grammar

education in our schools. Sentences, like citizens, need
rules or chaos ensues.

RESPOND. IT'S TIME.

Brent

My writing will not be rejected again. The community college con artist, Professor Rosen, the so-called English professor, was over six-foot-six. His hair, in a thin ponytail, snaked down his back. He rejected me. He was not even a professor, but he liked the title and made us call him that. He was only a graduate student at the local university, only a few years older than me. He rejected my analytical essay on Franz Kafka's *Metamorphosis* and then rejected my persuasive essay on the effects of plastic debris in the ocean waters just as he had rejected my personal essay entitled "This Is Just to Say." He asked that I consult the school's "wellness center." I explained that I was "well," that our disagreement was one of ideas. He would not discuss this with me. My paper was grammatically correct, wasn't it? He was not considering my grammar; it was my ideas—they were, to quote him, "jumbled and disturbed." I railed against this insult. Threw a chair at this so-called professor. Called him a fake and a con artist to his face. Screamed that he couldn't even write an essay with proper noun and verb agreements. Backed him up against the wall. Yes, I was thrown out of his borrowed adjunct office by a security guard, and soon after expelled from community college. Yes, my parents had to intervene so none of it would be on any permanent record.

I do not care about permanent records.

My mother texts me: "Gym. Home soon." My father: "Plane. To L.A. Have fun."

I am starving. Shut down all computer programs. All white becomes black.

No more writings. We have prepared for this time, the voice soothes.

"When?" I can smell the Glock, so sweet and so cold, fresh like a plum.

Max

As soon as I'm home, my mother is following me down the hall asking about my party. "How many kids do you think are coming? I don't know how much food or drinks to have. I just want to order pizzas, Max. How many?"

At my bedroom door, I finally say, "I'll take care of it, Mom."

"You're not treating this party like it's important, Max."

"The last time a birthday party was important to me I was seven, maybe eight."

"Max, what is going on with you?"

"I don't care about this party."

"We love parties in this family."

I open my bedroom door. My mattress is stripped down. My desk and dresser drawers are flung open. The insides of my closets are exposed and rummaged through. Shoes that I never wear are scattered about like someone's been trying them on. King barks and scrunches out from under the bed. I stroke his head.

"How can that be? It's your birthday," she responds. "You always have a party."

"I never wanted a party, not this year." I'm not angry. Being angry is too exhausting. "I don't care if it's my birthday. And what's happened to my room?"

"Your father. He thinks you might be doing drugs."

"Only him?"

"He tore apart your room, not me."

"Did he find anything?"

"No."

I drop down onto my bare mattress. "I didn't think so."

"Is there anything to find?"

"I thought we were talking about the birthday party?"

She shimmies next to me in her lemon yellow suit. She even smells fresh and lemony. "We always have a birthday party. Remember when you turned six? Two dozen kids bowling? Or when you turned seven? Laser tag. Three dozen kids."

All I want to do is stretch out on the bed with King and not think until school starts.

"Wednesday school starts," she says with that trick of reading my mind. "Excited?"

I want to turn off my brain. King nuzzles me with his wet nose. He's hungry, and he knows I know it. If I think about it, I'm hungry, too. I should let her make me dinner.

So, of course, she says, "I know it's late, but do you want me to make you some dinner?"

I shrug. "I have to feed King." But I don't move, and neither does she.

"Your father does want to talk to you when he gets home."

I close my eyes.

"You okay, Max?" she asks, interrupting my thoughts. I blink at her. I don't think I've been alone with her all summer. "You probably need something healthy in your stomach after the Snack Shack all day. And today was your last day! I bet you're not going to miss it."

"Where's Dad?" I say, not wanting to talk about the Snack Shack ever again.

"Speaking at a VFW meeting."

I glance over at her. He loves speaking to fellow veterans. I shift, call for King. I feel awkward having her on my mattress. I'm so much taller than her these days. I look more like my father, though I have her dimples. On her, I've got to admit, they look good, not like mistakes, potholes in each side of my cheek. The dimples make her look young and friendly.

I drop my face into the space between King's collar and head. His stomach growls.

"When are we going to be able to talk about you, Max? You've got your whole future happening now. College applications. Senior year." This sounds like a campaign speech, though I don't know what she's running for. "Your father and I are worried."

I shrug. I have the pills from Barkley in my backpack. They didn't find anything.

She presses her eyes closed. "Max, you know this would be a very bad time for any negative press."

"So, what does that have to do with me?"

"Just look me in the eyes and tell me again that you are not using drugs."

"I can't."

"Why?"

"Your eyes are closed now."

She opens her eyes as if they ache to look at me. And she doesn't look at me. "I have a splitting headache. I just took something for it, but it hasn't kicked in yet. You think you have all the answers, Max. But you don't. You should know that your father is under a lot of pressure this election."

"I don't have any answers."

"Don't you? You should see some of the e-mails your father is receiving."

"Why?"

"He won't let me read them all. But people are crazy in the world. Nuts. They think they have all the answers. And on top of it all, your father's opponent wants a debate, and you know your father is not the greatest debater. In high school, he was on the football team. I was on the debate team. Have you thought of what you want to do, Max?"

"When?"

"For college and after. Your future. You need to start thinking about it. The future is going to be here before you know it."

"You should be the one running for office, Mom."

"Don't think I haven't thought about that."

King whimpers. I sigh. I don't want to think about anything. I hope she doesn't ask me if I have plans for the night.

"I have to feed him," I say. "And walk him."

"You love this dog, don't you?"

King rests against my leg. He wags his tail.

"I should have fed him. I'm sorry, Max."

"I'll feed him and walk him."

But neither of us moves.

Barkley

I stir, glance at the clock next to my bed—and fall back to sleep. At least it is a kind of sleep. I find myself dreaming that I have been transformed into a gigantic insect.

In the dream my sight is poor, even worse than when I am on the computer for hours at a time. All is gray and in shadows. I click my antennae together. The garbage overflows under the desk: candy wrappers, apple cores, recyclable coffee cups, the crusts from a tuna sandwich, the tuna salad green with mold. I find it all enticing.

I strain, uncomfortably large. A hard, armor-like cover tightens across my abdomen. My legs and arms no longer exist. Three appendages on each side have replaced them. Antennae, compound eyes, wings on my back—yes, I am a bug. Vermin. I twitch. Through the walls, I smell my mother cooking. She's burning what she's cooking.

I am hungry, very hungry. I wave my legs, all six of them, in the air, trying to flip myself over, to get off this bed, to reach the door and call for her. My chest tightens. I sway from side to side to throw myself off the bed. Doesn't work. My stomach churns acids. I have to get up. I heave against the wall, rocking back and forth, using all my strength, which is considerable for an insect.

I push with my antennae against the wall and topple out of bed, landing, as if by some miracle of perseverance, upright.

I hear another's voice, a voice outside the dream, outside my head. "Barkley, I'm home. I did another spin class. I amaze myself. Two spins in one day. Maybe you should think of exercising more? Have you thought of that? Would you like us to buy you your own treadmill or elliptical? I've noticed that you've been putting on weight. All the junk food at the Snack Shack." She sighs. "Barkley, can I come in? Let's talk face-to-face. I saw you took a shower. You have to know, Barkley, that no girl likes to pick up her guy's wet towels. But I'm glad you did what you promised."

In my dream state, I scurry toward the door, or at least toward where I think the door is, sensing it by smell more than sight. And then I remember, of course, I locked the door. How will I open it now? Why didn't I consider that I could have woken up as a bug when I locked it?

"Everything okay in there?"

I raise my antennae. Backing up, calling out to her, I am shocked to hear only a series of peeps and snaps and clicks that are far from my own voice. I stumble back onto the piles of papers and dirty clothes.

"How about I make you something to eat, Barkley?" she asks. The sound of her voice is unpleasantly high. "What exactly is going on in there? Barkley?"

I want to scream. I am in the dream, buried in the dream.

Scurry to the door—and up the door. I can stick to the walls. Climbing to the top of the wall and onto the ceiling and hanging upside down, I am more agile as a bug than I was as a boy. There is a certain joy in being a bug. I am free to climb the walls and across the ceiling and look down on my bed and drop into the covers.

Her fingernails tap against the door. "Are you ignoring me, Barkley? I can't take this anymore. Please open the door."

I scuttle up the wall by my bed and over to the window and feel uncomfortable moisture on my underbelly.

"I can't understand what you're saying, Barkley. Are you playing video games in there? I'm calling your father if you don't answer me."

I want to tell her that I am trying to get out, not necessarily to go to her, but to be free of this room and find some food. I peer out the window at the sky. It is supposed to be a scorching ninety-five-plus-degree weekend. But maybe these clouds and the smell of dying leaves and grasses will not burn off. Maybe everybody will lose Labor Day weekend to rain. Up until this summer, I loved the rain. I wonder if that love will return now that I am a bug.

When it rained this summer, and the water crashed against the wet sand, empty and endless, and everyone at the Snack Shack begged to be let go early, Phil, the so-called manager, showed up and ordered everyone around. He always had tasks to assign—inventory or cleaning the grill or ice cream machine, tasks that were supposed to be done on a daily basis, but except for me counting the water bottles, rarely completed. Phil never showed up unless it rained. Spent the whole summer on his boat, drinking beer. I should have been the manager, not him. I should have been in charge. Instead I was demeaned, again, forced to work for someone like Phil.

I flatten myself against the pane, wanting the outside world, for the first time in a long time, more than this room. In less than a moment, I slide off the glass—the world outside falling away. I scramble up on my legs, all six of them.

"Barkley, I'm going to call the fire department. I'm going to have them break down this door if you don't open it. Barkley, please."

I fall. A free fall.

I land hard on the floor beside my bed. Two ordinary arms and legs drop down, and an unwashed sour smell, my own man smell, reaches my nose, a flat wide nose in the center of my face. My skin is raw, bruised. I scratched deeply along my arms and stomach. I realize that I was scratching myself. That I wasn't a bug at all. I was scraping myself in my sleep and pulling off my clothes. My uncut nails are brown with dirt or blood.

How I wish I were a bug.

"Please, Barkley," the voice on the other side of the door begs. "Why are you doing this to me? Wait until your father returns from his trip—"

In the past months, I have often thought about this peculiar, though safe, feeling of having my own and another voice in my head. The voice is the nucleus; my atoms revolve around it. I wait for the voice to tell me what to do, while I itch my arms from shoulders down to wrists, tearing the dead skin off, shedding the outer layer, the dead atoms.

Careful, the voice finally says.

To survive, one must adapt and change. I can make this change happen, in myself, and in the world. I have been chosen to do this. I am being given guidance. I don't have to think too much about where the voice originated, do I? Surely, it is a good place.

"How about some eggs?" she asks. "You should be hungry after working all day. Sixty minutes of spin, and I'm starving, but I don't want to eat. I'll make them for you. Barkley, please, I don't know what to say to you anymore. Help me out."

"What kind of eggs?" I ask, staring at the ceiling, yearning for the other voice.

"Egg whites, scrambled," she answers. "They're healthier for you."

"I hate egg whites." I force this sentence out of my mouth. It is hard to talk at all.

"Exactly, you hate egg whites. I'll make you regular eggs, any way you like them. Just open the door. Please, Barkley. What's going on in there?" She sounds desperate for some reason. She must be, if she is offering to cook. We haven't eaten a meal together in months. Spring and summer are her "upfront" season, when selling her television advertising comes first—selling and exercise. I understand. But I would like eggs. My stomach churns, empty, yearning, groaning. I scrunch along the floor instead of standing. It takes both hands, awkward as they are now, to unlock the door, spin the doorknob, but I want to help her. I want to open the door.

On the other side, she is in black running shorts and a black, skintight tank top. Her hair is gathered back in a ponytail. She is shaking, crossing her arms across her chest, as if something is wrong.

"Stand up, Barkley."

With an effort, I do as she asks.

She backs up against the wall outside my bedroom.

I sniff the air over her head, hoping the eggs are not to be forgotten.

"When your father gets home from this business trip, he's going to talk to you, okay, Barkley? Are you listening to me? What exactly is going on here, Barkley? What have I done wrong?"

I glance behind me. Sheets are strewn on the floor over papers and dirty clothes. The pictures are torn from the wall. The garbage is tumbled over. This was the result of being a bug, wasn't it? Even without being a bug, I can smell the rotting tuna in my garbage can, which is probably what bothers her. I will promise to empty the garbage. Before I turn back to her, I check the desk drawer with the Glock: locked and secured.

"Barkley, what's happened to you? What exactly is going on? Don't you see there's something wrong here?"

For a second, I fear that she will touch me. I must not be touched. I skitter back into my room and try to push the door closed, though she is as quick as I am and jams her running shoe in the door.

"Where are your clothes? What did you do to yourself?" Her hands find her throat, not a long, graceful neck like Claire's. She takes a ragged breath and so do I. She does not understand that this is the result of a dream, only a dream. I was a bug; I was vermin. I look down at myself, almost expecting to see my body still encased in a black armor shell or waving six hairy legs, and I sigh, frustrated at the thought of being forced to explain another thing to her, or to my father, that they wouldn't comprehend, having, in general, limited imaginations.

"Are you going to get dressed, Barkley?" Her voice is strained. "Because I think I am going to have an anxiety attack any minute, if you don't. I am going to scream, to be exact."

I want to help her, but I am hungry. "Are you going to feed me?" I move toward her. I feel larger than I have ever been. "Please," I add.

She shrinks from me. She screams, or more precisely, wails, incoherent and loud. She holds the side of the doorway so I can't shut the door on her.

The voice in my head orders me to inform her that everything is okay, so I say it, slowly as if in another language. "I am okay, Mom. But hungry."

"I don't understand this," she says between gasps of breath. "None of this. Where's the child that I brought into the world? Where is he? I'm calling the doctor, Barkley, okay? I'm going to help you. Let me help you. I'm calling your pediatrician right now."

She is panting, her eyes closed, her ponytail swinging back and forth, so I repeat, "Hungry, Mom."

Instead of hurrying to the kitchen, she backs away from me. I am forced to repeat it in two monotone syllables, as simple as possible for her to understand. "Hungry."

More screams crest out of her, rip into me. I am caught in a tidal wave. This is not helping her, or me.

She does not understand the necessity for answers, only you do, says the magnificent voice. *Careful.*

I pull myself back into my room, away from this crazy person.

Max

"How about a walk?" I say to King after having fed him his fa-vorite dog food. I jingle his leash so he can hear the "going out" and the "being free" sounds. At my voice, he is already racing around in circles, barking, excited, jumping.

I've been promising to bring King to the beach all summer, not that he understands, but I've said it to him as if he could. I know he loves it there. After hours, when the beach is empty, he can safely run free. He can test the waters with his nose, taste the salt, bark as loud as he wants. I should talk to my father about letting him out in the house during the day. I made the bargain to keep King in my room only for a short while, not forever.

"Everything okay in there?" shouts my father.

Other than being trapped in my room with a blind dog, I'm fine. "Just going for a walk."

"Only a walk?" says my father, striding down the hall to-ward me, his cell phone pressed to his ear, telling the other per-son on the line with him, "One minute, one minute."

I snap the leash on King. We've got to get out of here. I don't want his one minute.

"When you get back I want to talk with you, Max. Got that? We all need to be in a good place the last few weeks of the campaign." He's saying that to me as much as to the other person on the line with him. See? Two things achieved.

"Let's go." I don't have to say this twice to King. We're out of the house in a flash. A weak warm breeze greets us. King leaps over the clipped lawn. I keep up a patter with him so he knows that I'm here. "Good boy, King. Good boy."

Near the bushes, King does his business. I plan to clean it up tomorrow. Right now, I am worn out. Jumpy. Feel like spiders are crawling up and down my skin. I've got to walk. I should have taken a pill or two but my mother was watching me the entire time and I don't really need them, except to sleep.

I tug his leash to the left instead of the right. We usually go right so he's confused for a second, has to stop and mark the way again. He lifts his snout toward me and I say, "Don't worry, King. Don't worry, boy. Let's try a different way tonight. I need to go somewhere different. Not the park."

So he follows me left, and we trail along the sidewalk into the shadows. "Good boy," I say to him every few feet. He raises his head at my voice. Spit drips from his strong jaws. His black fur glistens. I wish I could bring him to the beach right now, just to see how happy he'd be with the water on his skin, how he'd leap into the waves, grateful for the coolness, for the chance to run in an open space and be a dog like any other dog.

"Party tomorrow night," I say to him after a few blocks. "No barking. No racing around the room. No trying to escape, no joining the party. Don't act like last year and you'll be fine."

He barks and I take that as an okay. Last year, the entire

soccer team showed up. We got drunk on beer and played boys against the girls in a pickup game. The girls were good. Better than us—or at least less drunk.

I break into a slow jog with King close to my side, and the McMansions fall away into the background, a backdrop to someone else's life, more like a movie set than something real. After a few more blocks, the houses grow smaller and closer together, as if needing one another for protection. The garages shrink from two- or three-car garages to one and in some cases disappear. The trees are older here, too, leaning over rooftops. Streetlights dim, a hazy yellow. Somehow there are more dogs on this side of town and they're all outside, behind fences, barking one after another as we pass, as if announcing our arrival.

"Good dog. Good King," I say to him, as we amble on, as I even out, as I feel calm for the first time all night. I'm careful about running with him on the leash—he could veer out into traffic, he could trip over branches, he could smash into a tree. We make our way, not too fast, not too slow, even though what would make him really happy is to race. But it's too dangerous for a blind dog. I even resist giving him more slack on his leash.

We round a corner, and all of a sudden, no more dogs, only the silence. The winds pick up. The trees rustle. I didn't expect to find myself here. I really didn't. I scan my memory and come up with the address she gave to me in anger when we thought we had lost Izzy. I've never been on this block before. I take a few steps on the sidewalk, cracked and split. Old trees loop electrical wires, which sag against heavy branches. Her house is in shadows—no outdoor lights on—but I can make out the number above the front door. All the windows are wide open. Old oaks press against white vinyl siding. Three steps lead to her front door. King strains at his leash. He pushes his face into her overgrown lawn, as if it would smell different from any other.

Why did I end up on this side of town? Why her block? Why didn't I walk King over to the playground near my house, the one that has a sign that states, *No dogs allowed.* That's the one we always go to at night.

For precaution, I reel in King. He lopes back and rubs his snout between my legs. I know he wants to make sure it's me, but who else would it be, standing in front of Claire's house in the night shadows? (And why am I here, again? I should go.)

The muscles in the back of my neck tense. I should bring King home and call this a night. As if sensing that I might go, King roots in the grass.

I could knock on her door, ask casually how she is doing. But that would be too weird. Who just shows up at somebody's door? And what if her father or, worse, her mother answers?

I could say that I was just walking by and wanted to check if she was okay after all the drama on the beach today.

"Does that sound right, King?" My dog hunkers down on her front lawn. "What do you say, boy? What do you say, King?" He pants. I change my mind. "Let's go."

Above, stars swim in the sky, silvery points of light. The moon, almost full, floats in the night sky. King howls. I tug at his leash. He isn't moving. "Let's go," I insist.

The door opens. *Look at her.*

First, she searches the sky. Her neck is long and tan. Her hair is smoothed back in a ponytail. She has on a white muscle shirt and short blue gym shorts. I wonder if she is going out or getting ready for bed.

In the doorway, she peers across the front yard.

I should call out to her, something like, "Hey, Claire, just walking my dog," but I don't.

King barks as if to say: if Max is not going to say something, I will.

"Hey," she says, her chin high, as if calling out to King as much as me.

I can't answer. I duck my head. King strains toward her. I have to loosen his leash.

King rests on his haunches. He cocks his head toward her. Now he's playing "good dog."

She isn't wearing anything under the tank top and everything is round and full and loose. Crossing her arms across her chest, she covers everything that is illuminated in the moonlight.

King is no help. He moseys on up to her. She laughs and lets him smell her hand. I imagine it smells like the sea.

"I wish I had something for him," she says. "Maybe I should go in? I should be able to find something for him."

"He's okay."

"Are you okay?" she asks. Her eyes, big, brown, fall on me.

"Sure." All her questions throw me off. "I mean, why wouldn't I be?"

She scratches behind King's ears. He sniffs at her. She doesn't seem to mind. I try not to look down at her—and at King. I force myself to scan the sky, as if I'm interested in constellations, or looking for a stray comet. "Hey, did you hear that I'm having a party?" I quickly say.

She doesn't look up. "You are?"

"Tomorrow night. At my house. I live in North Lakeshore. Not far from here. We were just out for a walk, King and me, and if you'd like to come, it should be fun."

"What kind of party?"

I make out the Big Dipper. "A birthday party."

"So, it's your birthday?"

This girl is way too difficult.

Claire whispers something in King's ear and they perk up, alert; he's almost smiling at her, licking her hand as if she's offering him treats. I double-check. She's not feeding him anything out of her fingers. Her palm, a shade lighter than the rest of her tanned skin, cups his snout. She kisses him. Her breasts sway. I force myself to exhale. Yup, the Big Dipper is still up there.

"Why are you asking me to your birthday party? You don't feel like you have to, do you?"

She widens her eyes. I don't know this girl—with the legs and the breasts and the waves of hair and luminous brown eyes. I could spend a while looking into those eyes, even though she's not my type. She doesn't go to my school. She lives across town. I shouldn't even be at her house. I wasn't planning on walking over here and seeing her.

"Maybe I should go?" I ask.

"Go. Am I holding you here?"

She straightens up. King whimpers at her feet. "I don't need you or anybody, thinking they're going to save me, even if you kind of did save me. I know Izzy appreciates your rescue attempt, and so do I. I do. How about that?"

"Attempt?"

She undoes her ponytail, shaking all of her hair. I lose her face. This girl just isn't for me, so why do I want her at my party? School starts Wednesday, first game of the season is next weekend. I don't have time for her. She pushes her hair from her eyes. I start pacing and talking. "Hey, I've got to admit, you're not my type. I mean, you're not like the other girls I usually like. Not like the girls I know, I mean. Not like the ones on the beach, or in my high school. You're not pretty. I've got to admit, in your own way, you are but—"

She flinches. Her shoulders straighten. The moonlight flickers against her face.

I search the sky, wishing a star would just fall on me and end my misery. The Big Dipper is lost behind the clouds.

"Anything else you want to add, Max?"

"You're different is what I mean."

"Some guys like 'different.'"

I look up at her at the top of the stairs. Claire is something other than pretty. I need to say this to her but somehow I've said too much already. She steps down to the grass with me.

"Why did you invite me to your party?" she asks.

More questions. King flops down at her bare feet.

"Let me get this straight, you invite me to your party, but I'm not your type? In fact, I'm not pretty, isn't that what you just said?"

"I didn't mean to say that."

"But you did, didn't you?"

"You can't just answer a question. You answer a question with a question a lot."

"Do I?"

"Yes, you do."

Wings beat through the trees. A flock of sparrows appears and aims for the moon. "I don't think I can come anyway, how about that?"

"Don't come then," I respond. "Don't do me any favors."

"That's interesting. I owe you, don't I? A thank-you?" She looks, not like she wants me to admire or praise her, but to join her in something, something that she finds odd or something that even in the calm eye of a storm will tell us more about ourselves. A smile plays on her lips. Maybe she just finds me diving into the ocean after her delusional. I'm crazy and it's funny to her. Or maybe she thinks I'm desperate. Well, I'm not. I don't need her at my party. Still, what do I need to do to prove to her that I'm—that I am what? Not a guy who tells girls that they aren't pretty?

"How about this: if my father comes home, maybe I'll go.

Sound okay to you?" I don't know why she is smiling at me—looking warm, wet-lipped, eager for my response when I don't have one.

After a while of just standing there, I ask, "Where is he? Your father?"

The look and smile drop away.

"What about your mom?"

She shrugs into herself.

I continue with a sudden earnestness and urgency, which is not me at all. I don't do "earnest," but I try. "I can actually make myself very presentable. And I'm a state senator's son."

"They aren't home, and if they were, they wouldn't care that you are a state senator's son. How about that?" She doesn't want an answer from me and it's as if she's challenging me to ask her another question. I want to keep her outside so I'm hurting my brain for a retort or at least a question. But I don't get her. I don't understand her at all. I don't even know why I want to keep her outside and maybe that's what I should ask her. Do other guys need to be as careful with you as I am? Before I can ask anything she is through the grass and back at her front door. She turns to enter her home.

I whistle for King. I still have his leash in my hand, but I want him at my side. He isn't pleased to be leaving. I don't know why I came. I don't plan on returning.

Claire snaps on a bright light inside the house. Moths flitter around her. She raises her hand in a wave. I realize, after a second or two of gazing at her, not knowing what I want to do next, that she is waiting, with that look of hers, for me to signal back. So I raise my hand—my chest pounds as hard as it did when we were in the ocean together—and I return her gesture. She slips into the light. The click of the lock is sure and final. Yet for some reason, I'm smiling in the dark.

I run King home. I let him race at top speed, and he is happy.

Blink my eyes. Taste the morning stale in my mouth. Rubbing my arms doesn't help. *Don't cry. Don't cry. You've done enough crying since your mother's stroke.* I don't know why I'm crying again. A dream. I had another dream. I was a small bird sailing over the sea. Not a sea gull, but a simple sparrow. Sea spray glistened on my wings. I could follow the sun and know which way I should go. I could fly anywhere. I want to go back into that dream.

I shiver. I yank off the comforter. Time to get dressed. Time for Izzy to get up. Time for my father—if he's home, but he must be home by now—I can talk with him about what we need to do once school starts. I resist the urge to shout out for him. I don't want to scare Izzy if he's not home. If he's not home, I'll go to the rehab center with Izzy and—I'll do what? What if he's not there? What will I say to my mother? What I need is a shower. I hurry into the bathroom and turn the water on as hot as it will go, plunge in. Pull my fingers through the morning knots. Douse them with conditioner. Drop my head back into the steaming water. I don't want to think of Izzy, or my father, or anything for five minutes, not even Max and his invitation. Of course, I can't go. I have responsibilities.

My fingertips dig into my scalp. The scalding water churns

my skin red and raw. Cut the water off. Step out of the shower. Izzy calls me, pounding through the house. My skin prickles.

"Coming," I whisper to the locked bathroom door.

"Claire!"

"I'm coming."

The mirror is fogged over.

The other voice, Max's voice, filters in. *You're not pretty.*

I want to scream.

But he wants you to come to his party. Or was he just asking you because he felt sorry for you? *You're not pretty,* isn't that what he said?

"Claire!"

You're not pretty.

"Claire!"

You're not—

I face the mirror. Wet hair hangs down around my waist. My lips are my mother's lips. My eyes are her eyes. I've spent months not looking at myself in the mirror, not wanting to see her, or the her from before.

"Claire!" Izzy shouts even louder, jumping up and down. "You've got to come."

A few minutes later, I am dressed in semi-clean shorts and a tank top, reaffirming to myself that I am not going to Max's party tonight, no way, absolutely not. Why am I smelling pancakes cooking? I guess my father *is* home. He's making pancakes like he used to on Sundays before the stroke, probably to make up for practically disappearing on us. The buttery smell smokes down the hallway. I'm annoyed and relieved. I'm going to tell him that he's been acting in a way that is unacceptable. You can't just go off and abandon your seventeen-year-old with your six-year-old, no matter how responsible both are—you can't just leave them. Things could happen. I laugh at myself—nothing happened—nothing ever happens to me. I pivot away from the mirror. I can't bear to look at myself.

Of course, Izzy is giving a speech to our father about what *did* happen. All the way in my bedroom, I can hear her racing on about going-to-the-beach-and-seeing-Max-and-swimming-in-the-waves-and-Claire-swimming—and there were other big kids there too—what were there names again? One was Barkley—like the doggie on *Sesame Street*— And guess what? Do you know I'm starting first grade next week? Do you know—? Izzy broke her promise to me. She's telling him everything. I can't believe this. I can't trust her with anything.

Pancakes pop and sizzle. Izzy laughs. My father coughs, burly, nervous. I want to go back to sleep, back to dreams, dreams of flying again. A woman laughs, sputters. My stomach hurts, my head, too. I have to lie down. I can't possibly eat. I do want to know where my father's been, but then again, I don't care. He's back. I don't have to take care of Izzy every minute of the day.

I should be thinking about school starting on Wednesday, senior year, or my poetry, or even Max—no, I mean Brent. I should be thinking about Brent. He went to North Lakeshore, didn't he say that? Maybe he knows Max. But he's a few years older, so I'm sure he doesn't. *You're not pretty.* I shake Max's voice out of my head. I'd rather think about Brent. I don't need a stupid kid like Max in my life. I wipe my palms down my shorts. Should have put on a clean pair. I feel like I'm dredging the bottom of the sea. I must need more sleep, even though I slept twelve or thirteen hours. What time is it? The clock's in the kitchen. If I want to know what time it is I have to go in there.

"Who wants pancakes?" shouts my father, in a voice I haven't heard in a long time, happy, loud, boastful—it's his "I've done something good" voice.

"Me. Me. Me," shrieks Izzy.

"Do you want to go see if Claire wants one?" he asks.

"I'll go," says the voice, slowly, the words forced out.

"Don't push yourself," says my father.

"Let," says the voice. "Me."

I freeze. Pancakes are flipped onto plates. More batter is poured—more pops, sizzle. The house is too humid. Smoke from the griddle floats down the hallway. I cough. I'm choking. Everything is fuzzy. I'm underwater and can't breathe.

"This is the best morning of my life," says Izzy.

"Look, look at this," says the voice, pausing with each word. "This is what I missed."

I smell coffee. My stomach flips. I go cold. Palms sweat. I feel sick. Airless. I am at the very bottom of the sea.

Smells trigger memories, images, sounds, of her calling your name and the coffee vapors on your hands. Maybe this morning, your father wanted a cup of coffee. I should go back to bed, pull the covers over my head. If he's home, he can watch Izzy.

"Claire!" screams Izzy. "Claire! Guess what?"

"Quiet, Izzy," he says. "And you, you sit here."

My father clears his throat. "Claire?"

I round the corner, hugging the wall. Birds shrill to one another with urgency. Feels like the heat is never going to break, or are the birds warning us that it will break soon, today?

The kitchen is almost the same. The stove and the countertop next to it are a jumble of pancake mix, eggshells, and open milk cartons. The sink is piled high with bowls and dishes. The floor has white powder on it. At the center is the square kitchen table crowded with plates and a plastic jug of real maple syrup and a melting block of butter. Three of the four seats are taken. The fourth is piled high with junk mail and magazines and catalogs. We haven't needed four seats in three months. There's nowhere for me to sit. I don't want to sit anyway. I don't want to move. And she has trouble rising. Her left side sags. She stands with the help of a cane. Her hair is at her nape, streaked with gray. An effort has been made to brush it. But the hair does what it wants, curling and waving. Her hairbrush is on the windowsill next to her chair, next to what I've always thought of as her window.

I yearn to brush my own hair with it. I gather my hair back from my face as if I am revealing something more, but I'm not, only the fact that I have my long hair, and she does not. She sways with the cane.

She says to me in a wavering voice, almost her old voice, "My girl."

My father watches her struggle to speak. He is wearing the same wrinkled polo shirt he had on the last time I saw him. He must have slept in it. "Isn't this great, Claire?" he says, his eyes on her. "The hospital insisted it wasn't medically necessary for her to be in rehab any longer, especially after the insurance ran out, especially when I couldn't come up with a payment for another month."

"You were good," my mother says to him, pausing between each word as if having to jumpstart the syllables. "I will take care. Of us." She grips the cane until I can see the muscles in her arm. Her skin is white, translucent, the veins reddish-purple. I fear she will fall, but I don't go to her. I can't. I am drowning in the sunlight.

And I think: she will have another stroke. It will happen, this time in front of my father, too. Somehow, she leans on the cane, catches herself, and eases back into a kitchen chair with the carefulness of a very old person or, I guess, someone who had a stroke. My father follows her every move as if ready to leap and catch her.

"Pancakes are burning," I say, gulping for air.

He tumbles over to the stove and inches down the flame.

"Why didn't you let me know?" I say to him.

"Know what?" he says, trying to flip the burned pancakes, scraping the griddle, sending pieces flying across the stove. Crumbs hit the floor. It is going to be a mess to clean up, for me to clean.

"That she was coming home?" I say, my voice rising in anger. I feel like I'm just keeping my head above the waterline. "Why didn't you tell me? I would have helped. I would made sure everything was in order. The laundry—I didn't get to all the laundry!"

"The house is," says my mother, "spotless."

"I wasn't sure, Claire," says my father, sweating, cutting in between my mother and me. "I was scrambling with the rehab center. I stayed there two nights to make sure I could help take care of your mother. They gave me on-the-job training. But she's here, and I don't care if this is the best thing or not, I'm glad she's home. I'm glad. Aren't you?" He scrapes the pancakes into the overflowing garbage.

"I would have taken a bath if I had known," adds Izzy. "But Mommy says I'm fine. I don't have to take a bath."

"You have to take a bath, Izzy," I say.

"Mommy says I don't. She's back and she's the boss again." Izzy runs over and hugs our mother around her waist.

"Gentle," says my father to her, as he shoves the garbage down into the pail with more force than needed. "See, I told you, our Claire isn't a kid anymore. Are you, kiddo?" says my father, attempting to be funny, pouring fresh yellow batter onto the griddle, splattering it. "Let's try this again." My father is someone who always believes in second chances, in do-overs.

"Are you done with your pancakes, Izzy?" I ask, clearing her dish away so quickly she has to grab at one final bite. I wish it could be only me and Izzy. I want yesterday back. I want the beach.

"Don't you want some, Claire? They're good. Come on, have some."

"No."

"Can I watch TV now?" Izzy asks.

"Go," I say. I want to say run. Get your bathing suit. Get in the minivan.

"Mommy?" she asks. She races over to my mother and then leaps over to me. I kneel in front of her. I want to bury my head in her blond curls.

"Aren't you glad that she's home, Claire?"

I say nothing. I am, but I'm not. I don't like surprises, maybe that's it.

My mother is following this; my father is not. This is how it always was. She would know when things were wrong. She would know somehow. But then, maybe I'm imagining this. My mother can't be the same. It will never be like it was.

"I love you, Claire," says Izzy.

"I love you more, Izzy. Now go. You don't want to miss your TV show."

Izzy hugs me first, and then my father and then her. My mother can hug Izzy back only with one arm. But that's enough for Izzy, who blurts out, "I love you. I love you. I love you," at top speed, and she's off, downstairs, the television on too loud.

I will not look at her, at the other hand, which is folded, immobile across her waist.

"I missed," she says, "you." Each word has its own emphasis, like my mother is from another country and practicing her English.

"Isn't this our dream, our hope?" my father asks me, touching her shoulders as if to confirm that it isn't a dream. "To have your mother home?"

"Our dream? Did you know I dreamt of her every night? Do you even care about me? You couldn't tell me she was coming home?" My stomach churns. I run tepid tap water into a cup. I chug it down.

"If only we could," says my mother with so much exertion that she has to sit back, "live in our dreams."

She searches for my eyes. "In no time, life changed. But I have more to do." She takes a deep breath. "Much more."

I can't bear to look at her in the kitchen, in her old seat. Near the window, birds, plain sparrows, build nests in our oak tree. I don't know why I feel trapped as if in someone else's house, someone else's kitchen, as if the world is suddenly off-balance.

My father cuts off his happy voice. "Laurie. I'm sorry. I don't know why she's acting this way. Claire, can't you see this is your mother and she's home. Give her a hug."

The birds swoop in and out of that old oak tree, a grand tree, gathering sticks and grass. I used to like to climb its branches, sometimes too high, imagining that if I fell, I'd grow wings. I'd fly, too.

She flutters the fingers on her good hand toward me. The other is lifeless. The fingers are curved. The thick nails need to be cut. If I touch the skin it will be dry and scaly. I should have made that 911 call faster, realized something was wrong sooner. Maybe then, she wouldn't be like this. "I didn't recognize myself, Claire. Didn't know who I was. Didn't know my own name."

I still don't know who this person is. I want my mother. I want her whole. Send this one back.

"But you. That day. You saved me. Because of you—and your sister and your father—I will recover."

It takes me a minute for what she is saying to sink in. To feel like my head is above water. *Save her?* I was foolish and unthinking—and the birds are swirling, chirping, urgent about a storm coming or winter—and I didn't save her or anyone. I didn't act fast enough. Maybe the doctors did. But not me.

Her eyes flutter closed. The words having flooded out of her, a burst of fluency, and she is more exhausted and even paler than a moment before. "Last night, I dreamed of being a bird. Flying. Over the ocean. At night."

My father hurries to her. "Claire, if I could have found more money for the rehabilitation center, I would have. I want your mother to be a hundred percent, too. But she's well enough to be home. We'll all pull together. You'll still have to do a lot around the house, but you don't mind, Claire, do you? Your mother is here. Her thoughts are clear. That's what matters."

"I want," she says pushing the words out, "to be home."

"Your mother will have weekly physical therapy, weekly speech therapy for as long we can, as long as the insurance allows. I've been going out of my mind, thinking of ways to make more money. I'm going to get a second job. Any job."

"Mitch," she says. "I'm home. Speak to me like I'm here."

My father drops to his knees. She strokes his head with her functioning hand. He kisses her face and her hands, both of them.

"Can you believe, Mitch," she says, haltingly, "I dreamed, my dream, of being a bird?"

"Laurie." He buries his head in her lap. A man of few words, he has abandoned them. I had forgotten how much they loved each other.

I pour myself more tap water, letting my glass overflow and soak my fingers and the countertop. I concentrate on sipping the warm water as if my life depends on it, as if I have never been this in need of a basic sustenance.

Embarrassed, my father jumps up and bangs over to the sink and soaps up the pots and pans with a steel-backed intensity. My mother attempts to turn to me, but can't easily shift in her chair. From behind her thick purple glasses, her soft brown eyes strain in my direction, wanting me to look at her. I gaze over her head, out the window, at the heat burning off the dew, scorching the uncut grass.

"I'm not what I was," she says. "You see that. My speech is broken. My heart is not."

"You dreamed of being a bird?" I ask, holding back my breath, or tears.

"Yes, angel."

I finish off the glass of water. I'm struggling to come up for air. "So did I."

Max

This is not the way summer is supposed to end.

No one is showing up at this party. I know everybody has this fear: you have a party and nobody comes. Nobody is responding to my texts. Nobody has left me any messages, anywhere. I'm pacing in front of the living room windows. King is scratching and whimpering behind my bedroom door, wanting to be with me even though I explained to him that he had to be a good dog and stay.

"Why don't you call one of your friends?" asks my mother again.

"No."

"Why don't I call some of the parents, see if something came up? Or maybe everyone is just running late?"

"Don't. Please don't. I thought you and Dad were going out?"

"We're going. Just to the diner. Just for a cup of coffee. Maybe we'll split one piece of pie between us. I have a campaign to run."

"How could I forget?"

"Don't worry. We won't be gone long. I don't want you to think at seventeen you can throw wild parties."

"At what age do I get to throw wild parties?"

"We're going to be five minutes down the road, Max. We can come home at any time, and we will. Remember last year."

Last year we got a little drunk and played soccer in the back-yard. My mother and father came home while all the beer bottles were in full sight. They had a fit, but I sometimes wonder whether they were angry because they had to see the beer bottles on the deck, see us running into each other, see their son act stupid. Or, were they just concerned it would make the local news: *Underage state senator's son drinks a beer.* I should text everyone and let them know: the party is off. Yup, I should take a pill, party by my pathetic birthday boy self.

"What's going on, Max? Worried about school starting?" She hovers around me, stroking my side, fixing the collar on my polo shirt. "Is something wrong?"

"Nope. Nothing wrong." For some reason, my back stiffens, but not unbearably. Pain is at a minimum tonight. I'd rather it be more, give me an excuse to blot this all out.

"You are so handsome. The most handsome. You know you have that nice pink polo shirt to wear tomorrow. Now I know it's pink, but it's a fun boy pink."

"I don't wear pink."

"Maybe you'll wear it tomorrow—to the meet-and-greet for your father. You'll look so nice in a pink polo under the white tent."

"Stop it, Mom."

"Stop what, handsome boy?"

She means well, but she doesn't know anything, not a thing about me anymore.

"Okay. Nothing's wrong. That's what you and your father

think." She glances outside and throws out her told-you-so smile. A car has rattled up. Maybe I was wrong and she was right.

But it's only Trish and Peter in a beat-up Toyota, and even my mother knows that these aren't my real friends. The bigger her smiles, the worse things are.

"Look, Max, who's here," she says too loudly.

Peter tumbles out of the car. Trish looks glum, squeezed into a T-shirt one size too small. I'm not sure if she thinks it makes her look thinner, or if she just outgrew it.

My mother whispers to me, "What's happened to you, Max? To us? You always had a lot of friends." She's clutching my arm with her bright nails. "Where are all the nice boys that you've always been friends with? Jackson? Andrew? Ethan? Michael, Alex? I can name a dozen boys you've been friends with since kindergarten. I can call their parents. What did you do?"

"Not enough."

"What does that mean?"

Trish brings Peter through our open backyard gate adorned with two dozen helium balloons at my request. I walk away from my mother, through the house to the kitchen, where there are chips and dip and sodas laid out for the party. Trish leads Peter through the backyard, up to the deck. He stumbles anyway, but she is as sturdy as ever. Peter is wearing a pressed checkered shirt and slacks. I'm sure his mother helped him get dressed. He's waving at me as if we haven't seen each other in a long time, and even though he's just across the deck, I have to wave back.

My mother turns her back to them. "Who are these two?"

"My friends." I step around her and greet Peter and Trish like they are long-lost friends, even giving Trish an unexpected and unwarranted hug, squishing her back fat in. She doesn't return the hug, as if she knows my hug is a fake. However, she does smell nice, not like sweat or sand or sour milk from the ice cream machine. I want to say, "I'm sorry. Here's a real hug," but I can't do that.

"Mom," I mumble, "meet Trish and Peter. I talked a lot about them this summer."

"You did," she says, showing no recognition.

"I work with them. At the Snack Shack."

She opens her eyes wide. Now she knows who they are, and she flashes on her state senator's wife smile. "Great to meet you. But I'm not going to hang around—though you should tell your parents to vote for Glenn Cooper, Max's dad, in November. State Senate. You're okay, Max? Your father and I are going to get a cup of coffee and some pie at the diner."

"What kind of pie?" asks Peter, startling my mother.

"Apple."

"With ice cream?"

"No, honey. I'm on a diet, so no. No pie à la mode for me." My mother glances at Trish with a knowing look that really says: I hope you're listening.

"Vanilla is my favorite," Peter continues.

"Why don't you guys go hang outside, and I'll be right there?" I say to Trish and Peter, and Peter follows Trish out the sliding doors.

My mother's smile is tight. Behind her, my father appears, talking and walking, not aware that we have guests. "Deb! Max! I think we should give that dog a Xanax."

"What?" I don't want him giving King a pill. In fact, I think I could use a pill. One of the ones from Barkley still in my knapsack.

"Max, your dog needs something to calm him down while all the kids are here," my father is explaining.

"My dog doesn't need a pill."

"Well, I left it for him in his dish. Hid it in the food. I don't want him tearing up the place. And who is out there? Have we met?" King has never taken Xanax before. How does my father know how he'll react to it?

"Why did you do that? Why'd you give him a pill to knock him out?"

"It will just calm him down. It's from the vet."

"You went to the vet for a pill?"

"Yes, I asked your mother to go to the vet for your dog because I was thinking of you and your party, Max."

"I'm going to make sure he's okay."

"He's fine. And your friends are here." My mother glares at my father.

"He's fine, Max," says my father, sliding open the glass.

"Hey, sweetie, go to your dog," says Trish to me. "Don't worry about us."

My father quickly takes her in. I see he's trying not to make a face. "Are you going to introduce us, Max?"

"These are my friends," I say to my father. "From the Snack Shack," I add, moving to the side of the deck, which suddenly feels crowded. Let him see who I had to work with all summer. "Glenn Cooper, your neighbor, running for reelection as state senator," I announce. My father actually offers his hand to Peter, who gladly pumps it up and down.

"Max is a great kid," says Trish to my father, surprising me. "We had a terrific summer together. Didn't we, Peter?"

"The best summer ever."

My mother looks from Trish and Peter to my father to me. "You'll be okay, Max?"

"Fine."

"I'll check on King before we go."

"Thanks, Mom."

My father's hand finds my shoulder. "Where's the rest of your friends?"

I shrug. I don't want him touching me.

"They'll be here," he says softly to me, but it's already too late. He drugged my dog.

"Yup," I say, which really means, "I don't think so." I face him. "Don't worry. Go to the diner. Have a piece of apple pie à la mode for me." I'm thinking that I'm going to take one of Barkley's pills, maybe both of them, as soon as he leaves. I'm going to obliterate myself. I'm going to rip away all the hurt and feel nothing and lie down next to King.

"Pie à la mode, that sounds good," he says, giving my shoulder one last shake. I clench my fist, or, I swear, I'd punch him.

"I like my pie with ice cream. Vanilla," says Peter to no one in particular.

"If I never ate another soft swirl in my life I'd be happy," announces Trish.

My mother tugs my father's arm. "Let's let the kids have some fun, Glenn. It's still a birthday party, after all. And you know the diner is packed at this time of night."

"I can shake more potential voters' hands is what she means," he says to Trish and Peter and me. My mother hurries my father back into the house, and after a minute or so, I hear the front door open and close behind them.

"I just have to go in the house and get something," I say to Trish.

"You won't find it."

"Find what?"

"The pills you bought from Barkley. I took them from your backpack, didn't you notice? I saw you with Barkley and knew you were making a mistake."

"Who the hell are you to take them?"

"I'm your friend."

"You're an idiot." I pace around her. "Those were mine. Who the hell do you think you are?"

"Lie down."

I slump against the deck railing, listening to my parents drive off. "No."

"Why not? I'm fat? A fat what? Even if you haven't said it, and you've been nice, Max, you haven't, but I've seen your look.

I see everyone look at me like I'm a freak, like I'm a sideshow, like they think I don't know they're staring at me, saying to themselves: she is a fat pig. Either they're looking or they're pretending that I'm invisible. I don't exist. I'm not a real person with genuine feelings. Well, I am. So, listen to me, sweetie. Lie down."

She doesn't wait for me to say no again. She stands behind me, locks her hands on my wrists, and pulls upward.

"Hey."

"I should have offered to do this earlier this summer."

She guides me to a lounger on the deck. I lie down on my back. I feel like I have no choice, so I do. I can't believe this is my birthday party. Up in the sky, a thousand stars up and a full moon, a hint that maybe the heat will break soon, that fall and the promise of winter will come. I want to imagine what the sky looked like three or four hundred years ago when places like Long Island were barren of decks like these, of houses like these, when there were plains out here. In fifth grade, I wrote about the Hempstead plains, high grasses that stretched all the way to the ocean. I almost want to flip off the floodlights on the deck and see the stars for what they are. I've never been out in the night with only the stars.

"Turn over. Head down." I do as she says. Soon enough, her hands on my back, and then under my shirt, and surprisingly cool and dry on my skin.

"Didn't your mother ever tell you to stand up straight?"

"She thinks I'm perfect," I mumble.

"Good thing someone does."

Peter circles the deck, something he always did at the Snack Shack when he didn't know what else to do. "This is a very nice party, Max. Thank you for inviting me."

Trish loosens my shoulders. "Does this hurt?"

"What if I said yes?"

She stretches each arm separately, pinpoints different muscles in my back. "You've done this before?"

"On my mother. She's an English teacher. A lot of stress between the semicolons and the persuasive essays."

"What should I do?" asks Peter.

"Can you sit down?" answers Trish.

"Yup."

"You sound like Max," says Trish. Peter reacts as if he's received a major compliment.

He doesn't sit, though. "What's back there?" he asks, pointing to the high evergreens like sentries at the edge of the yard.

"Nothing. Woods. A town hiking trail." My voice is muffled into the lounger.

"Does anything come out of there?" Peter looks worried. "I think something could."

"Peter, that's your problem, you think too much," says Trish. "Let me finish here." For some reason, I think she's going to leave. So the party will be Peter and me until everyone else comes, or just me and Peter. I flinch.

"Relax. Concentrate on nothing at all."

Nothing doesn't work for me, not without pills, only makes

me think more. Instead, I focus on her hands. And they are strong. Trish kneads her hands up and down, deeply, then lightly, as if by alternating between extremes she will bring me naturally to a middle ground, a safe place. I couldn't run if I wanted to, and I don't. She works every muscle, bending into me. If I concentrate I can smell the trees dry and desperate for rain, pine trees, their needles ready to fade from green to brown, ready for the ground, as ready as I am for summer to end.

She massages my back for fifteen or twenty minutes, long enough for me to feel stretched and loose and good. When her hands leave my grateful back, she orders me to stand up slowly and I obey. She instructs me to walk briskly, and I jog around the confines of the deck, freer than I've been all summer.

"If you want to go take one of those pills now, go take it."

"You said you threw them away."

"I thought about it, but I didn't. I think drugs are stupid, but it's your stupid, not mine."

I stop in front of her. She's wearing a lot more makeup than she usually does at the Snack Shack, eyeliner and bright silvery blue eye shadow, a sure sign of a South Lakeshore girl. She's sprawled out on one of the deck chairs, looking out toward the trees. Her legs are in a V-formation in front of her. I make direct eye contact. "Thank you."

"For what?" says Trish, blushing. "You haven't even offered me anything to drink or eat yet, sweetie. And, whoa. Look at this." Trish holds up her phone. "I think we may be the first and last at your party."

Glowing radioactively on the phone is a text from Jackson, which has been forwarded and forwarded and found its way to Trish: "Meet at dunes. No go Cooper's."

"Here's another. This is from Samantha. Essentially says the same thing, Cooper. Do you want to hear it?"

"I don't need to hear it."

"I'll hear it," says Peter.

"You don't need to hear it, either," says Trish. "But Max, you're what everyone is talking about tonight. You're trending."

"Nobody is showing up."

"Okay, so nobody shows up. More chips for us."

"More chips for us," repeats Peter.

I bring out the chips and dip and place them next to Trish.

"Go ahead, take one," says Trish, pushing the bowl toward Peter.

"No, thank you," he says, even though it's clear that he wants one.

"Eat," I say, sounding a little bit like my mother.

"I'm not supposed to eat or drink anything. You don't know what kids could put into the food or drinks. My mother said that."

I take a chip and dip it into the onion soup and sour cream mix. "Delicious."

"Really?" says Peter, looking at Trish.

"Go ahead. Have fun. Life is too short."

Peter scoops up a handful. I stretch and feel okay, and that's a lot—to feel okay.

"Magic hands," she says, fluttering her fingers. "So, I'll have a beer, if you have any. If you don't, I have a cooler with some in my car. That was going to be my contribution to the party, but it doesn't look like you need any contributions."

"Are you sure nothing is in those woods, Max?" asks Peter, munching on chips.

"Nothing," I say. "How about I find us some beers?"

"May I have a soda, please?" asks Peter.

"Sure thing, Petey," I say, to make him smile. "And don't worry about the woods."

I step back into the house without turning any lights on. The temperature drop is artificial, choking, wrong. I peer into the dark. I feel lost and alone and want to go check on King. But first, I have to go downstairs and rescue my father's beers from the backup refrigerator, where they've been hidden—or so he thinks—since our Memorial Day barbecue.

Then, all of a sudden, lights flash into the living room, a lot of them. Cars honk, a dozen or more, suddenly gathered, like a swarm of mosquitoes drawn to light, except I'm in the dark. Someone is standing with his head through the sunroof, whooping my name. Jackson. On closer look, I see that Samantha is leaning over and driving his car.

"Having fun, Cooper?" shouts Jackson. "We're off to the dunes. To party."

On "party," everyone shouts or honks their horns or flashes their lights, and I am caught in the barrage.

"Having fun?" he shouts again, because that's about how

clever Jackson is. "Part-ay. Part-ay." He's stolen all the helium balloons. Laughter rips into the night.

By the middle of my birthday party somebody, usually Jackson, would have sucked the helium out of the balloons, and talked like an idiot with a high-pitched voice. I wonder if my mother knew that was why I always insisted on balloons.

Out on the street, Jackson raises his hands above his head like a goal has been scored—a goal against me. Like he dribbled at me, sidestepped me, and slammed it right into the net. He ducks his head back into the car and commandeers the wheel from a screeching Samantha. He speeds up, all the cars in a line behind him, all my so-called friends, the entire party. They are gone as quickly as they descended on me. After the buzzing roar of a dozen cars veers from the neighborhood, after what seems like a very long time, I stumble down the stairs to our lower den, where it's even cooler. Waves of heat and sweat and total embarrassment pound in my ears. I pop open a beer and gulp down searing cold swallows. I'm thinking that I could take my mother's car and go down to the dunes, too. I could bring all the beer and make like it was all a joke when I see Jackson. I could go there, too.

"Hey," comes the voice down the stairs.

Inside my head, I scream. I want to be left alone. I thought they had all gone.

"Hey, anybody here? Anybody down here?"

I don't know that voice and I do. Husky and quiet.

"Max?"

I don't say anything until she is downstairs. I busy myself with finishing my beer as fast as I can.

Even in the shadows, I can see that she is in a white button-down shirt, her sleeves folded up, the tails of the shirt tied at her waist, and jeans, nothing fancy, but somehow she looks dressed up for a party. She takes a deep breath. Lets it out slowly. Her big, brown eyes adjust to the dark. She wears no makeup. I open the refrigerator and go rummaging through it searching for Peter's favorite soda.

"Max? Is this the party?" she asks, concerned, or maybe annoyed.

"Nobody is showing up."

"I got a text from Brent. He said he was planning to come."

I pull out two beers and, yes, two orange sodas. "I don't know any Brent."

"He said you'd say that. He's a couple of years older than you. But he's a friend of a friend. He knew all about your party. How about that?"

"How about it? Then, I don't think he's going to show, either."

"Maybe I should just go? I'll just go."

She's brilliant. She asks and answers her own questions—I think sarcastically. Claire heads for the stairs. Juggling bottles of beer along with Peter's orange soda, I slam closed the fridge and follow her. She races to the top. I hesitate. She swings her hair off her face, and I stare: this is hair I want to bury my face in, my whole self in.

"Claire," I finally say. "Please, don't go."

"Why not?"

"I'm glad you came."

"How about that?" she says softly.

Claire
Sunday, 9:20 P.M.

I'm not staying because of Max. I'm out of here. I don't know why I even came to this party, which isn't a party at all. I just had to get out of my own house, and this has nothing to do with Max inviting me—it has to do with Brent. When I mentioned it to him in a quick phone call, he said that he was thinking of making an appearance—that when he was a senior, he was on the varsity soccer team with Max and had heard that he was having his annual party this weekend. But I don't think I can trust Max. I don't know what he wants from me, and all I want in my life is clarity right now. It's all clear with Brent. And with Max, it's all cloudy, all far away, with those sea blue eyes.

At the top of the stairs, a desperate scratching and whining stops me from walking out the front door. I glance down the long hallway.

"That's King. He's locked in my bedroom." Max lays down the bottles and cans on the pristine wooden floor and jostles past me. He opens his bedroom door, and out bounds his black Labrador, sniffing my feet and leaping up to lick my face. His paws easily reach my shoulder.

"King!" says Max behind me. "Down."

"You keep your dog locked in your bedroom?"

"My parents don't like him banging around the house. You see, he's blind."

King's eyes are misted and sightless. "I'm sorry. Last night—I didn't realize."

"That's okay. I don't think he knows, either."

I stroke King's thick fur. I stare into his eyes even though he can't see me. He knows I'm there and I'm his friend.

"That's okay," I say, running my fingers between his ears. "He remembers me. He's a good dog."

The dog lurches toward Max, whipping his tail, sniffing and grinning, if dogs could grin. "Sometimes. He's a smart dog. You're a smart mutt, aren't you? You didn't eat anything in that food dish, did you?"

King looks back to his dish. The entire room smells like dog food. He strokes King, but the way the dog is rubbing his head up and down Max's leg, it's almost like the dog is petting him.

"You like dogs?" asks Max.

"I do, not that I have one. I've always wanted one. My mother always said I could have one when I was old enough to take care of a dog. This summer, I proved I could take care of a lot more, so maybe I should ask for a puppy?"

"Be prepared. Puppies are a lot of work."

"Maybe I'll hold off. It's been a really long summer at our house."

"Here too," says Max.

King presses into me, as if sensing my sadness. He licks my hand. My father didn't want me to go out tonight. He wanted us all to watch a movie together. But I couldn't stay. I couldn't watch another old movie. I've been trapped in the house all summer. I had to get out, and I remember, I really did want to see Brent.

Max grabs King's collar. "Kneel, King. Kneel."

The dog listens to him.

"Are you sure you don't know a Brent?" I ask again, crossing my arms. "He's twenty-one?"

Max doesn't look at me. He fusses with King. "Maybe I'd know him if I saw him. I know a lot of people. So maybe he'll show up, which means, maybe you should stay?"

I shrug and bend to scratch King's ears.

"At least, can you help me out? Take King outside while I get the drinks? He's not really allowed in the house. My parents will kill me if they come home and see him running around." Dimples appear on each side of his face, shy and sweet.

"I think I should go home, Max. I had something weird happen today." And suddenly I'm telling him about my mother, and he's losing his smile, losing his dimples, and he's serious, listening as if deep in thought about what I'm saying. His dog curls at my legs. I slump against the white-white walls, no cabbage-flowered wallpaper here.

After a few minutes of me talking, he says, "I've got to admit it, you did have a long summer."

"You have a nice house," I say, not wanting to talk any more about me. Cathedral ceilings and black leather couches and glass-and-chrome tables, everything is shiny and sleek, unlike my house. My skin prickles. This house is cool enough for a sweater. I look out the high windows at the other houses on the block with their cathedral ceilings and perfect cut lawns. I don't think Max ever had to worry about "insurance," or electric bills, or money for gas for a ten-year-old minivan.

"Aren't you glad your mom is home?" he asks.

"I am, but my father should have warned me, don't you think? He still sees me as a kid. If I had known she was coming home, I could have prepared. I could have cooked a nice dinner or done the laundry or dusted or vacuumed one more time. I could have shown her that I'm not a kid anymore. What do you think, Max?"

"You do all those things?" Max eases out a small laugh. But I'm not laughing with him. He can think it's all not cool. He can think I'm not pretty. He can think that this girl should go back to South Lakeshore—that she doesn't belong here. He can even pretend he doesn't know me or look right through me like so many others, if he sees me on the street or in the park. I know I did the best I could to keep it all together this summer.

"I do all those things. How about that?" I say, challenging him to continue, even though I'm feeling drained and exhausted.

Instead, he says, "Down, King, down," as if I mind that his dog is near me. When King obeys, Max kneels and nuzzles him. I bury my head in his black fur, too, a smell of grass and earth and warm dog. We are not hugging each other, but we are both hugging the dog.

Too soon, we hear voices, and it's like we are underwater, and the voices are muddy and far away, mermaids singing to us. Max pulls back first, but he's looking at me, seeing me—smiling with dimples.

Barkley

I am dressed: navy blue sweatshirt and sweatpants smelling of laundry detergent, of chemicals. I prefer the gray set I have been wearing all summer. Nevertheless, she selected the navy blue for me, and I will wear this if it helps her.

She paces in the hallway, on her smartphone. When she is farthest from me, I slip the Glock tight inside the pocket of my hooded sweatshirt.

"Barkley, we need to talk, okay?" she says, sliding the device into its holster at her waist. "Everything a little better now? Nice to be in clean clothes, am I correct? Looks like you're going out? Seeing friends? It would be great to know that you're seeing friends. Are you? I'd rather you be doing anything than playing those games. Are you listening? I called your doctor. We want to have you evaluated, and we're going to start with your pediatrician, okay? I'm calm now, don't I sound calm? Exactly, my doctor gave me a prescription to help me through—and I am sure that there will be something to help you, too."

I pat my sweatshirt down flat in the front and test a grin on her: wet my lips, open my mouth, show teeth.

"Why are you looking at me with that odd expression? Everything will be okay. You'll see. With the right strategy, we can get this all back on track."

You know what you want to do. What you must do.

"What do I smell?" she asks, sniffing the air. "Do I smell cigarette smoke on you? You know your father and I are going to be very disappointed if you've taken up that filthy habit. Please be truthful with me. You're not all of a sudden starting to smoke, are you? Dr. Hazel is not going to be happy hearing this."

Dr. Hazel always gave me a toy after an exam. The last time was a high-flying mini-ball. I was seventeen, getting a physical for that community college. I did not want to see her at seventeen, and I will not see her now. I am perfectly fine. I liked the ball, though.

My mother trails me down the hallway. "I think we should call your father together. I'm getting him on the phone now."

At the front door, she sprints in front of me. She pushes her smartphone toward me. Manicured fingernails tap my cheek. I grab her hand and jerk it away from my right lobe. My father shouts at me from across the country, high-pitched, upbeat. "Barkley, you're an awesome kid. We trust you. But we think you may need a little help."

They have made a pact against me.

"What's changed with you, buddy? Something's changed, hasn't it? You were always a phenomenal kid. I know this is just a minor setback. We are going to take this on together."

I shove the phone away. It clatters out of her hand, bangs to the floor—my father keeps on chattering—and I am engulfed by the airless night. She dives after the phone, calling out to me,

"When are you going to be home? We need to plan some family time together."

Walk perfectly. The voice understands. This isn't Kate and Dan's story. There is no longer a "we" in this family.

I head over to the party. Hike from the main street into a patch of woods. Here there is an actual hiking trail, which edges the backyards of a dozen houses, approximately a half acre from the house to the trail. His house is one of the few without a high fence separating the wide yard from the trees. Lights are trained on the expansive deck.

I have stood out here in the dark before. Once, in high school, I brought along Scotch and pot for the soccer team. We got drunk and stoned. They chased me through the trees. I tripped. They tore off my sneakers. My parents never asked me why I needed new sneakers right away or what happened to the old.

Tonight, I pull out a pack of cigarettes and light one. Drag hard. I blow out smoke. Fire. Am pure. I no longer want to join the party. Now, I need to be here for Claire. I must warn her about Max and the pills. He could be sharing them with her. She must not harm herself.

I smoke, hiding the tip in the cup of my hand. I shake out my scarred arms. The trees stir with traces of autumn, of the end of things. They close in around me. Overhead, my old sneakers dangle.

Trish and Peter linger on the deck, as if they lived on this end of town. No sign of Claire. An old maple shields me from their sight. Sap runs on my hand. I light another cigarette with the half-finished first. I wish I had my sunglasses with me, even though they would be useless in the dark.

Glass doors slide open. A dog crashes out onto the deck, barking, bashing into legs and chairs. A big, dumb dog. I step back. I suck the cigarette down to its bitter, burning end. Light another.

The world will soon enough know morning. Your morning.

FOCUS ON: Claire stepping out swinging a bottle of water at her side and bringing it up to her full lips.

CLOSE-UP: Eyes. lips. Her swan-like throat.

I pull back. Of course, she is only drinking from that plastic since it is Max's house, Glenn Cooper's house. She is not at fault. The state senator is. Her lips wrap around the water bottle. She must be thirsty, gulping the water down, her chest rising. A trickle runs down her chin, and she laughs, wiping it off with the back of her hand. Her palm is white, white against the summer-browned skin. She sips more, glancing toward the trees. I stand still, invisible to her. She is innocent, a poet, in need of me, in need of me to act, of Brent to act. Yet Max is intent on her. He does not know her like I know her. It is hard to swallow. I need more coffee. More fire. Another cigarette. Claire.

I stumble. Scrape my palm against the trunk of a tree. Heads on the deck turn. Search the dark and see nothing, or what they want to see: nothing.

I sink to the ground. My knuckles grind the dirt: rocky,

leafy, and bone-dry. An earthworm slides through my fingers, sightless. I cannot hurt it. I want to scream out for Claire. And I want to scream: help me. But she cannot see me weak and alone. I claw at the dirt. I smoke through the pack, sucking in fire after fire, cleansing myself. My eyes blur. She is far off, a distant ship in the moon's glare. What do they—Claire, Max, Trish, Peter—Barkley—fear? What do we all fear? A dog barks. My body tenses. Thoughts spring into my mind but cannot fit a pattern. The pine scent seeps into my skin. An owl hoots. I pull out the Glock from inside my sweatshirt. The Glock is sweet and cold and ready.

Claire

So I stay. I kick a soccer ball to King. After a second of listening, sniffing, he chases after the ball, nosing it back toward me. Peter thinks this is the best thing in the world and asks if he can join. Fireflies light around us. We run in pools of dim backyard lights, the woods dark behind us.

Soon all of us—Max, Trish, Peter, and I—are kicking the ball in a mock soccer game. King gallops from person to person, the happiest dog I've ever seen. Peter snaps the ball hard and wide, off to the side and the shadows. Trish lumbers after it, cursing under her breath in a friendly way. Peter keeps saying he sees lights, red dots off in the woods.

"Only fireflies," I say to him. I've always loved the woods at night.

Max yells, "Be careful, Trish, there's poison ivy over there." She laughs and says, "Don't worry. I'm thick-skinned."

The ball soars back to us. Trish has a strong kick. Max stops it with the tip of his shoe, controls it, and lobs it over to me.

As a kid, I always just liked open fields. In second or third grade when I played soccer, I ran with my hair flying behind me, faster than anyone else. A wonder, my mother always said. I never really learned to handle the ball, not like Max, and by fifth grade I was too self-conscious of my body, which was starting to change almost overnight, and I stopped running. By sixth grade, I had quit soccer altogether.

In high school, through the windows of the school library, I liked to watch our varsity soccer team practice. The game itself— the green fields, the long runs, the ball arcing the field—is a game of grace.

If I had gone to an actual game, I might have seen Max play. Our high schools have a major rivalry in sports. But I never went to see the soccer team or any school team compete. That was the role of other girls. All of a sudden, in the middle of Max's backyard, I realize how much I had put myself in a box, let others define me. This year, I decide, I'll go to a game, even if I have to take Izzy with me. Maybe Brent will go, too.

"Are you hogging the ball?" calls out Max. I know he's just happy to have me stick around because no one else is showing up. It doesn't even look like Brent is coming. He's probably got the word like all the others that this wasn't the place to be.

I tap the ball over to Peter, who howls, joyfully, chasing it in his work boots. An owl hoots from somewhere in the trees and another responds, as if refereeing our game. I race from one end of the yard to another like I have wings on my back. I feel eyes on me, a strange feeling, and I turn, and there's Max, kicking the soccer ball back to me.

Fireflies whip around us like they're playing defense. A whiff of pine needles and apples, a wild scent, wanders over the newly cut grass. Clouds, wisps of gray, rub across the moon, haloing our short field. I feel caught in another time, a time before my mother's stroke, a time when I didn't have to think of taking care of other people, of dinner, or dirty dishes, or laundry, when I didn't have to think of anything except running up and down green fields.

So she stays, and so do Trish and Peter. We play soccer and drink more beer, and I'm not feeling much pain in my back, or anywhere else. Nobody else shows up. Even so, I don't feel like I need anyone else, or to be anywhere else.

Claire jogs across my backyard. She moves in circles, and the circles seem to move with her.

"I guess Brent isn't coming?" she asks from across the lawn, though I don't think this is a question I need to answer. I don't feel like me at all. I want to move closer to her, but keep a safe distance, a yard or so from her, a yard too far. Most of all, I want her to forget this guy Brent.

"Right now, all I know is Trish and Peter and you," I say, careful not to gape at her legs, or even at her shadow, cast against the house. Her eyes are wide and gold-flecked. I don't think I can look directly at them without getting totally distracted.

Out toward the woods, leaves crash against bone-dry ground. Sometimes kids go back there and drink or smoke pot. Maybe some junior high school kids. That's what I used to do. Or maybe it's just raccoons. I trace a path around her.

"Is anything wrong?" asks Claire, glancing behind her.

The moon glints on the pine trees. The trees sway with a

trace of wind. I shake my head. "Feels like a breeze. Maybe the heat will break tonight?"

"I don't feel a breeze," says Trish, flapping her generous arms.

Claire takes a long drink of water. "Feels like we are in a dream within a dream."

I nod as if I know what she's talking about. I don't want her to think that I don't know.

Great. The girls exchange looks like they could be friends. Trish seems to collect friends like Peter and Claire—and me? Anyway, I can look at Claire without her looking at me, look at her long, strong legs, look at her hair wave around her waist, until Trish proclaims that she has never been thirstier. "And how about some cake? Shouldn't there be a cake around here if it's a birthday? What the hell kind of birthday is this?"

At that moment, my mother and father return, exactly two hours since they left. And I don't know what they talked about in the diner, but they seem happier, or at least their arms are around each other, not jabbing at cell phones or other electronic devices. They stick their heads out to the deck and one of them, my mother, asks, "Hey, everybody okay?" Neither waits for an answer. They really don't want one. They want to know that we are all still alive and that's about it.

On the deck, Claire is bending down to help Peter tie his work boots. King barks sharply at the quick rustle of the trees. He's not used to being outside in our yard at night. In her lounge chair, Trish scrutinizes the backyard and says she thought she saw something move, too. "Are there animals that live in the woods back there?" she asks.

Giving my soccer ball one last fierce kick into the dark, I join them on the deck. I tell Trish that only raccoons and feral cats are back there. Claire and Peter are stroking King and he is content, squeezed between the two of them. I ask if anyone wants cake, chocolate cake. I retrieve the cake from the bottom of the refrigerator and return with it like an offering. Peter claps. Buttercream icing, points out Trish to Peter. My favorite, murmurs Claire to Trish.

Everyone wants cake. Even I want cake.

Claire
Sunday, midnight

We see Trish and Peter off. I hug them both and promise them we'll see each other again soon. Max, looking up at the stars, not at me, announces that he has to take King for a walk. "We can go by your house. We can take you home."

I search up as if to see a shooting star or a comet, but the sky is calm and fixed. "Sure. Why not? Walk me—and King. Maybe we should walk on that trail behind your house?"

He glances back there. Shadows bend. All night long, Peter thought someone was watching us, and I can almost believe the trees were watching us, jealous of how we ran, how we laughed.

"It's really dark back there at night."

"Are you afraid of the dark, Max?"

"Yup."

I don't believe him. Maybe I'm not the kind of girl he walks home under the trees, under the moonlight.

On the way to my house, we watch King attack the whisperings of squirrels. Max patters on to him about being a good dog, and he is a very good dog. When the sidewalk narrows near my house, Max lets me go first with a silent offer of his hand. I stride ahead. I almost feel like running home, unfettered, to write about this night so it would feel more real than it does.

Soon enough, we arrive at my house. The outside lights blaze with new lightbulbs.

And I've decided on the walk over, under the full moon, that I want to kiss Max good night. I feel warm in my bones, lovely in a way. I want to kiss. I don't know if it matters if it's Max. I'm sure he doesn't want to kiss me. But the desire comes from some aching center. If I could pinpoint it, it would be beneath my chest, above my stomach. I'm not sure if this is connected to Max. If Brent were here, I'd kiss him. At this moment, under the moon, I want to kiss. And even more, I want to believe, for a moment, that summers are about things as frivolous as parties and long, deep kisses. I want to kiss.

In front of my house, on the sidewalk, Max is staring above my head with a lopsided smile as if there's something in the night sky more than a moon and stars. I linger a bit closer to him. He looks left and right, as if expecting someone. The wind rises.

And my mother appears in the doorway, a fragile ghost in baggy jeans and her favorite sweater. Her hair is slicked back. She's freshly showered. She raises her good hand, as if we haven't seen her in the center of the doorway. She favors one side, and wavers. As if I suddenly have blurry vision, I blink. I'm afraid that she will fall. But she eases against the doorframe. She has her cane and it helps her balance. I know I should go to her.

Max waves back at her, friendly and open. And she steps back into the doorway, as if satisfied. I sigh. She's okay. And I still want to kiss him, even more right now. I want him to wrap his arms around me. On the sidewalk, King ruffles at my feet. He pants his dog breath into my palm. The moon is bright.

One kiss. I jerk forward, toward Max. He jolts backward into the shadows. Gives a dumb laugh. I feel like I loom over him, oversized and aching. I peck him on the cheek because I can. A peck is nothing, one-sided. I don't even include a hug. That would be even more awkward. Maybe I should have been like other girls and waited to see if he would kiss me? But I've never been like other girls. Of course, I've never been kissed, either. I should have stayed home or followed everyone else down to the dunes tonight. Maybe Brent would have been there. Maybe trying to kiss him would have ended in another way. Luckily, King whines, and I can plant a smooch on the top of his head. He smells like dog sweat and grass. I hold on to him. He responds with a definitive tail wag, hustling into my side as I straighten up.

"Hey, about tomorrow," says Max, pulling at King's leash. "At my father's event? At the community park?" He glances over toward my mother, placing a sweater from the hall closet over her shoulders, not paying attention to us. "The event starts at ten and it goes to about two, I think. I have to be there early."

I don't think I'll go to the community park tomorrow, even though he asked me to earlier tonight, when we were on his deck, when the night felt different, the world wondrous. It's so obvious, anyone can see, this guy doesn't want anything to do with me. Instead of saying anything else—there's nothing to say, not even a question left—I race up the path to our house, and brush my lips against my mother's cheek. She kisses me back with a surprising fierceness. I press myself to the soft wool of her violet sweater, to the lavender on her neck, the scent of open fields, of my mother, too, a smell almost lost to me, and I know she's real.

BEFORE
MY EYES

Barkley

Last night, I could not act in the dark of the woods. Nevertheless, this morning, I am in the tent. Inside the whiteness. All is
within my vision, a wide shot.

The Cooper family is ahead: Max; the mother, Debbi; and
the father, the state senator, and his sign: *Reelect Glenn Cooper,
your neighbor.*

PAN: Balloons, bumper stickers, lawn signs, and pencils,
hundreds of pencils.

I have been given clarity. There are those among us who are
given the gift of blazing foresight, and I am one of them.

After this, I will never be alone.

*This is the morning, the morning to cut off the evil from the
land,* the voice signals. *Action.*

Disorder reigns. Pollution. Fragments. Atoms spinning out.
Speak truth to power. Demand answers.

FAST CUTS: Light flashes. Screams bang in your head.
Bodies hit the floor.

"He has a gun," one of the tanned women shouts.

"A gun?" says another. "Just like that senator?"

"Senator? I thought she was a congresswoman?"

"From New Mexico."

"New Mexico?"

"I thought Arizona."

"Arizona?" One is pulling the other to run. Both of them are screaming; a lot of people are screaming.

They must all shut up. Quiet. The Glock aims at them.

Walk perfectly, the voice insists.

I am thirsty, so thirsty. I itch. I force the grin wide. The Glock discharges. The crowd splits. A car screeches. Someone is shouting my name—a cop with a face sprayed with freckles. He got my name from Max Cooper, who is also shouting. "Barkley!" The officer must not be shouting my name, that name. There is no Barkley here. Only Brent.

I spin. The Glock fires—

Fires off again and again—and the policeman, a gun in his hand, too, stops shouting. He is sprawled on the ground.

And then, another body hits the floor. A flash of pink. Sparkly pink. Two old people tumble toward the pink. The Glock is firing in that direction.

A table topples over. Pencils spin on the ground. A dog leaps forward. Instead of backing off, his teeth bare. I roar. The dog rips into my right leg. I kick. Hard.

Fire. Fire the Glock. The Glock, the voice orders.

The black mutt careens toward the coolers. Bullets—up, down, left, right. Water spills. Red liquid. I back off. A sudden banging in my ears—heavy metal guitars and drums and cymbals clashing—drowns out all but the voice. The bodies are hitting the floor. The bodies. Nothing's wrong. The bodies are hitting the floor.

To the side of me: Mrs. Cooper. She must be in collusion with those that would destroy me, Barkley, Brent. The Glock points at her. "Please," she's screaming. "Please."

And then Claire—in the frame—at Mrs. Cooper's side. She is not dressed in pink. Not one speck of pink. Claire is pure. Exactly. Phenomenal.

A firm stance steadies me. Focus on her.

TIGHT CLOSE-UP: Claire. My Claire. Claire's eyes. Claire's mouth and lips. Claire. Claire. Claire.

Soon enough, she will know me as Brent. The world is listening to me. Everything comes together: the lens, the pen, the gun.

Fire. Fire. Fire.

I grin, wider.

The Glock shudders. Jams. Thirty-three bullets. Did the Glock shoot all thirty-three bullets?

Reload, directs the voice with will and determination. *The morning is not over.*

Claire

The world in the tent explodes into gunshots and screams.

I hadn't wanted to come here, to the community park. My father wanted to take my mother grocery shopping. She was supposed to work on the ordinary things, the everyday things. My mother wanted to go here first. She always liked to be involved in politics. I didn't even dress up for this—a white T-shirt over a bathing suit and cutoffs. After grocery shopping, I planned to go to the beach for one last time this summer. Yet right before we entered the tent, Izzy slipped out of my mother's hand, begging that she wanted to go to the playground first, running off in her sparkly pink top to the swing sets. My father said to me, "Why don't you go inside with your mother?" But my mother said, "Let me sit, for a while. We'll meet. Inside. How about that? Maybe that rakish young man, from last night, will be in there?" I insisted that I didn't want to go in alone. But she gave me one of those looks, one of her classic looks, that said, "Claire, you can do this," and so I entered the white tent alone.

———

Now, eyes blinking, now, I'm afraid to run and even more afraid to stay. I feel like I'm less in the air and more in the sea, underwater, drowning.

Max is screaming above the din, "Bark. Bark!"

I don't know why "bark," until I realize it's a name. That in fact, it's the name of the guy with the mirrored sunglasses on the beach—and it's also the name of the man with a gun—and it's the same guy. And as Max screams that name, "Bark," that man stares straight at me. He grins, as if I know him, as if we've ever met. And he aims his gun at me. I'm going to die—the guy with the mirrored glasses from the beach is here, in this sweltering white tent, with a gun—and he's going to kill me.

I fall to the ground. My knees scrape against the dirt. I see a little girl in sparkly pink crying, and I think Izzy, although I know Izzy should be in the playground.

"Izzy," I scream. The girl spins around. "Izzy!" But it's not Izzy, is it? It's a little girl wrapped in the arms of an elderly man and woman. All three are dropping to the ground. A flash of pink and blond curl. A cry for "Mommy" rises. A gasp. Is someone shouting, "Claire"? Is it Izzy? "Izzy!" Izzy is far away. The tent sways above my head. Mrs. Cooper is sprawled at odd angles, whimpering and crying. Her pink suit is twisted up around her hips. Her leg is bleeding, and I can't do anything. I'm not shot. I'm not. I'm sure I'm not shot. But she is, and I can't help her. She's Max's mother and I can't help her. Just like I couldn't help my mother. "Stop!" I order myself. "Stop!" I scream into the vastness of the tent. More gunshots pierce my screams.

I urge myself, "Swim, swim, Claire. Toward the light. Swim."

I crawl next to Max's mother. My hands are slick and raw with sweat, dirt, and blood, someone else's blood, her blood, Mrs. Cooper's. Now "swim" means help in another way. Now "swim" means save *her* life. She's bleeding and moaning. I have nothing to help her with. I don't have a Band-Aid. Part of me knows how irrational that thought is. She doesn't need a Band-aid. She's shot. Blood from her leg zigzags across her suit. Her nice pink suit. The bullet has struck a major vein, maybe an artery. I yank off my T-shirt—wrap it tight around her leg like a tourniquet, something I learned in first aid. She reaches for my hand.

Barkley shuffles toward us, the gun pointed at me, straight at my head.

Mrs. Cooper is holding on to me, as if I can save her, or myself, pleading, "Don't leave." Screams roar around us, seize me, but I can hear her as if only us—a mother, a daughter—exist. I want my own mother more than I have ever wanted her in my life.

"Don't worry," I say. "I'm not leaving you alone."

Max

The number-two pencils spin to the grass. Pots of flowers are trampled and broken. For a second, I don't know what's going on. I hear a pop and another and another. I smell something, turn my head, and think: flowers. It's only dying flowers. The crowd surges out of the white tent. A car careens into another car with a deafening smash. Barkley raises his arm higher. He pushes the sleeves of his hooded gray sweatshirt up, carefully, like I've seen him do a hundred times this past summer. Trish shoves Peter down underneath one of the tables, flat on the ground, like they are already dead.

I'm screaming at my mother. My face is wet. I touch my cheek. Red. My blood? My pink shirt and her pink suit are splattered with blood. My mother is down on the ground, writhing, turning, screaming. And then I see her—she's taken off her T-shirt, she's in her Speedo and shorts—and she's tying her shirt around my mother's leg.

Now Barkley's aiming at them again. I'm shouting his name. It's like the only name that I can say out loud. "Bark!"

I don't see King, or my father. Everything is slowing, everything is exploding—

Next to me, Jackson's father is lying facedown. Shot in the head. I want him to get up, but he isn't moving. More shots and—

The two old people, the two my mother hugged, crash down over their granddaughter, shielding her, or are they all—

I don't know why everything has slowed down. Why I can't move. Why I am thinking: run, get out of the tent, dive out of the tent, and I can't move.

Barkley trudges toward my mother and Claire, a grin cut into his face, eyes unblinking, arm straight out as if the gun is leading him, not him leading the gun—

"Hey, Bark," I shout with a jolt like I'm just calling for him, like we're somewhere else, at the Snack Shack. "Hey, Bark."

He swivels—the gun pointed at me.

I'm going to die. It's him and me. Why the hell is he grinning? He has a gun. What is there to smile about? In less than sixty seconds, he's shot twenty or thirty bullets into the tent. He's aiming to shoot again, except something's wrong. He's fumbling in his pocket. More bullets. He's ramming another cartridge into the gun with clumsy fingers.

From out of the corner of my eye, I spot my father. He's screaming, "Run!" Barkley sinks the second cartridge in place.

"Run!" My father is three or four feet from me, that's all. But so is Barkley, who aims level at my eyes. At that instant, my father bounds from the left, not thinking that he's over fifty, that he can't strike that hard anymore, not thinking or debating, and strikes him. Barkley rears at him, off-balance. The gun drops to his side. I duck my head—and with all my strength, everything in me, everything that every coach and teacher, everything that my mother and father ever said was in me—rush forward and head him in the stomach. Knock him back. Smash up into his lungs and heart. Nail the gun out of his hand, and send it swerving—only an arm's length away. I'm dizzy and sick to my stomach.

Barkley lunges for the gun. I taste blood at the back of my throat. But I rush him again, more of a stumble. My father jumps up, blood on his face, and side-tackles Barkley with more force than I've ever seen him use. Barkley's on his knees, but his long arms reach for the gun. He wraps his fingers around it—only for Peter to stomp on his hand with his massive yellow work boot. The gun flies out. Sunglasses clatter off his face and are also crushed by Peter. Barkley howls. But his intent is clear—he wants his gun back.

Only Claire is quicker. She throws herself toward the gun. It slips from her hand, spins away.

I scream, "Barkley!" He glances at me. In the breath of two syllables, Claire grabs the gun again. This time she gets it with both hands. She stands up, clutching the gun aloft. Barkley grins at her, that sick grin, as if she knows him, as if she is on his side. The gun quivers in her hand. Barkley crawls toward her and my father leaps on his back and flattens him to the ground. Peter bears down on legs. Trish kicks him in the side. Sirens swirl around us. Claire screams for her sister, for her father, and the loudest, for her mother. The gun quivers in her hand. A dozen police cars race right up to the entrance of the tent.

I'm having a hard time keeping my head up. The room skews off its base. I'm going to be sick. Bile sears my throat. And now, Barkley is whimpering. His sleeves flop around his face. My father is pounding Barkley's shoulders and head, my father's face a volcanic red. The police have to tear him off Barkley, throwing him on the ground, separating them. Barkley lifts his sweatshirt up like he's on fire. He scratches the white flab of his chest and sides like he's infested. A female cop wrenches his arms back with one swift yank and handcuffs him, and he doesn't say a word.

I'm afraid that Claire is going to shoot off the gun, and the police must think so, too. They circle around her, their hands on their guns, ready to be drawn.

One muscle-bound cop demands the gun. "Just put it down on the ground between us."

And she sinks her arm with a twitch and a pulse of breath. The cop jerks forward and screams, "The gun!" She kneels and her fingers unfurl, as if having lost function, and the gun slides to his feet with a thud.

Quickly examining the weapon, the cop says, "Shit. The bastard went through an entire 33-round assault clip, and was ready to go through another." He removes the second cartridge. The cop's hands are gripping the gun in one hand and the clip in the other. If he could crush the clip in his hand, he would. If he could bend metal, he would. If he could turn into Superman and have the bullets bounce off him, harmless to all, he would. A second, older officer relieves him of the weapon and the ready clip shaking in his hand.

Sounds pop in and out of my brain. I have to get up. I try, but I can't get up.

My father stumbles over to my mother, who is shouting my name. I can't respond. Her hand reaches for mine even as two paramedics are helping her. They are saying that the shirt, Claire's shirt, probably saved her life. Barkley is being shoved out of the tent in handcuffs. He drags his feet and tilts his bald head to look directly at us. He's grinning. I want to punch him in the face, and more. I look to where he's looking: Claire. I want to shoot that grin off his face, except I can't move.

"Claire," he shouts, and it's like all the babble in my brain drops silent. "I am Brent. He is I. I am he."

"I don't understand," she says, standing just a few inches from me.

"He is I. I am he. Perhaps a new poem, Claire?"

What is he talking about? He's Brent? And where is King? I don't have the strength to call for my dog.

All I can see: brown eyes. Large and questioning and full of hurt. Her father rushes up to her, going on about being out in the playground, about swings, grabbing her toward him. Her mother, with a cane, follows, pushing forward, not letting anyone stop her. Her little sister looks scared at the overturned tables and chairs and pencils strewn across the floor until Claire kneels and scoops her into her arms. "Don't look," I want to scream, but can't.

The muscled cop snatches Barkley and propels him forward, out of the tent. All around is more chaos: ambulances, police, hurt bodies, blood. Peter and Trish are going from person to person, offering water and hugs.

"You're a hero," some lady is harping above me, and another is agreeing. "A hero. You and your father are heroes. Aren't they heroes?" Suddenly, they are crying, too. I don't know why they are sobbing.

"King? King?" I want to scream, but my voice is lost, like it's been kicked out of me. Why are Claire's mother and father leading her away? I want to take her in my arms and tell her it's over. I want to kiss her. I want to tell her I'm sorry about the other night. I wanted to kiss her back, really kiss her, but I couldn't, not with her mother so near. I want to kiss her now and never stop. Why is she leaving? And why are my father's arms around me, damp and heavy, and why is he crying and shouting my name?

And why can't I move? Why did Barkley do this? Why? The world is darkening and dimming. I am afraid of the dark. My sight fails. I see a flash of white, and a whiteness beyond the tent. *Why?* Why are there only questions and no answers?

Claire

Late yesterday, the heat finally broke. Gusts of wind and thunder and rain were followed by severe storm warnings. The world spun a shadowy, sickly green. Hail came down. A tornado threatened. Tree limbs broke. Leaves were shed. The first, violent colors of autumn were strewn on the ground: yellows, oranges, and blood-reds.

I waited for the storm to end on our couch, wrapped in my richly purple handmade blanket. We lost our electricity in the early evening, and it was a good thing. I wouldn't talk to any news crews. I couldn't watch any more news or spend any more time online. In the dark, I couldn't do anything but curl up on the couch, hollowed out, an emotional zombie.

And now, the morning is over. I'm still here—on the couch. It's lunchtime, and I haven't eaten anything since yesterday's breakfast, but I can't eat. My mother sits down next to me and rests her good arm around me. I expect her to tell me something about the psychology, or biology, or neurology behind what happened. Before her stroke, she would have loaded me up with facts and figures on what the news is calling "paranoid schizophrenia." She gave me some insights, but I want more. She strokes my hair. All she offers is, "We are all fragile."

She smells like clean laundry. I don't care if I'm going to be doing most of the cooking and food-shopping and house-cleaning. I don't care. She's alive. She's here. And I'm here, too.

Izzy—Elizabeth—I don't want to call her Izzy anymore—the girl who was killed was named Isabelle, and "Izzy" reminds me of her. Elizabeth sits at my feet lining up all her stuffed animals for cookies and milk. My mother brushes my hair, long strokes, until it feathers down my back. I lean into her like I would a nest. It's like all of us are afraid to be out of one another's sight.

Debbi Cooper was struck in the right leg but is doing fine, or so Max's father told my father. I may have helped save her life by tying a tourniquet around her leg with my T-shirt. Joe Jacobs, who was there to play tennis at the park, is dead. Herman and Ann Amico, married fifty-one years, and their granddaughter, Isabelle, dead. One police officer, the one with a face full of freckles, Tim O'Ryan, is in critical condition but expected to pull through, and I pray he does. I pray a jumble of prayers, a mix of prayers and poetry, of psalms and Emily Dickinson, of "Yea, though I walk through the valley of the shadow of death," to "Because I could not stop for Death— / He kindly stopped for me," to words whose meanings I've lost to incoherence. I'm rocked by a sea swell greater than any other.

Late last night, the police barreled up to my house and confiscated my laptop. I explained that I hardly had any messages from Barkley or Brent. They said that it is very common for cyber-stalkers to start with online contact and quickly go to the telephone. They don't want to have a written trail. I said it wasn't like that, but then, I didn't know at all what it was like. They took my laptop for evidence.

All I know is that I never want to hear his voice in my head again.

My father promised that they would get me a tablet before I went to college, but that seems very far off. He's gone back off to work. "Let's pretend it's like any other Tuesday," he said. I didn't say to him that I will never have another ordinary Monday, or Tuesday, or any other day. I can't even think of tomorrow. I can't think of anything except what happened. I'm cold. I dig into the corner of the couch, grab my notebook. My hands hurt. I can't feel the ends of my fingertips. I can't believe what happened, really happened. I'm shaking, but I grab a pen and write this as fast as I can:

A white tent,

An oasis
on a steamy Labor Day.
Then, a flash of steel.
A gun.
He has a gun—
I thought they meant the
freckle-faced policeman.
The white tent cut through
with screams

Shots.

He has a gun!

My words are lost, or stolen.

A body drops.

Thirty seconds before

the tent, cool and safe.

Now, ripped with shots,

screams, sweat—

No, this isn't sweat.

It's blood. Blood rippling

down. Blood,

everywhere.

Blood. A body

drops.

I throw the pen across the room, fold my arms around myself, shivering, fingers numb, teeth grinding, a knot burning in the back of my throat. This is my poem. My work. This is what is important to me, I realize: that I can write a poem like this. That no one will stop me. He tried to take this from me. He had that gun pointed at my head. He tried to destroy what matters most to me—my ability to think, to imagine, to write. I reread the poem, over and over and over, the words, the sounds, their rhythms, rescuing me.

When all the storms clear, the temperature drops thirty degrees and autumn winds rise over Lakeshore. Someone taps on our door. It's as if the person on the other side is unsure we would be home, or maybe hoping we would not be home. On the stoop is Max.

"Hey," he says. "You okay? I mean, I just came here to make sure you were okay."

His leg is bandaged. He's leaning on an old man's silver metal cane. He was grazed—the bullet missed his bone.

"Are you?"

"You know, you almost always answer a question with a question."

"I do?" I say, knowing I'm doing it, wanting to make this less surreal. "Your leg. Are you taking something for the pain?"

"Only over-the-counter stuff. Nothing else. Nothing. I want my head to be clear. I'm done with everything else."

I step out onto the front stoop in my worn-out gym shorts and flip-flops. My legs are bruised along my knees and thighs, some from nearly drowning, more from the white tent. There's no hiding the purplish-green welts on my knees, the result of throwing myself to the floor in that tent. I breathe in wet autumn leaves, keeping the front door ajar to air out the stuffy house.

"How's your mom?" I ask. "Is she home, too?"

"Nope. She's going to be in the hospital a while. But she's planning her congressional run. She wants to do one better than my father. They've always been competitive with each other, but it seems to work for them." He seems too upbeat, too unreal, but I play along.

"Congress? Are you kidding?"

"Nope."

"And your dad?"

"He's counting on getting reelected, a sympathy vote, though he's pissed that he's getting criticized for not going public about those crazy e-mails and texts. At the end of the day, I don't care if he gets reelected or if my mom gets elected. I want them home."

"What do you think is going to happen to him?" I say, hesitantly, not wanting to say his name, the one that I now know is Barkley, not Brent.

"I don't care, do you?" He limps a few steps away from me, to the other side of the stoop.

"My mother agrees with the news that it's highly likely—that's how she phrases it—'highly likely' that he will be diagnosed with paranoid schizophrenia. He was hearing voices, or a voice."

"Wouldn't people have known that?" he says. "Shouldn't somebody have seen something was wrong?" The playfulness drains away; anger and grief fill his mouth and eyes. "Shouldn't there have been some warning? Shouldn't a teacher or his parents have known? Why didn't I see something was wrong with him? Why didn't I know? Tell me that. Why didn't I see something was wrong?"

"Maybe you weren't looking. Maybe you had your own things going on? Maybe I did, too."

He takes this in, and so do I, weighing the difference between what we know and what we don't, what we see and what we choose not to see.

"But shouldn't there have been some warning? I worked next to him all summer. He was weird, but look who I was working with. Trish and Peter and Barkley and me. Maybe something is wrong with me?" He laughs, harsh and quick.

All I can do is quote my mother again. "She says that he's probably been in serious decline for the past year or two, or more. But sometimes people don't want to see warnings, or more likely, they didn't even know to look."

He studies the empty street, as if we're on the bow of a little sailboat and that boat is lost at sea.

"According to the police and the news, he's in the hospital under armed guard," I say. "He's refusing medication."

"He should be in prison. Does New York execute murderers like him? Sometimes I think I'm never going to sleep again. I keep playing it over and over in my head, don't you? I keep seeing it right before my eyes."

"More would have been hurt, if it wasn't for you, Max. You were brave."

"You grabbed the gun."

"You struck first. You went after him. You're the hero."

"Don't believe everything you hear on the news."

Last night from the hospital, Max appeared on all the local newscasts with his mother and father. He's been called a hero. However, he gave full credit to Peter for crushing down on Barkley's arm and me for snatching the gun. Peter and Trish have been interviewed, too. After the event, they helped so many people who were hurt. They were heroes. I couldn't do it. I couldn't help anyone after I handed that gun over, not even myself. I couldn't make sense of it for news reporters and declined to participate in any interviews. Instead, I watched all the reports with my mother. In particular, Peter seemed the happiest at being called a hero, and I hope he's considered one for a long time.

"I wasn't brave. I wasn't anything. I wasn't even thinking. I'm not thinking now, just replaying it in my head. The gun. Who even sold him that gun? Couldn't they tell he was off? Apparently, he tried to enlist in the army, and they turned him down for psychological reasons. Shouldn't that have been on a record somewhere? Why wasn't it? Most of all, why did he feel the need to shoot anybody? To kill anybody?"

"He almost killed more. But you stopped him."

"Why did he do this? Just tell me why. Why? What was he thinking? And why didn't anyone see this coming? Why didn't I see something was wrong with him, something off, something sick? He was sending my dad e-mails about bottled water and grammar and I didn't know it was him. They didn't tell me it was him until after, until we were at the hospital. He was using another name. If I had known—"

"Grammar? I had heard on the news about the bottled water—"

"None of it makes sense. None of it makes any fuckin' sense, and now Jackson's dad is dead. What if it was my dad, or yours?"

My hand covers my lips. I want to hold it together. I don't want him to see me cry, think I'm that kind of girl who can't be strong enough to talk with the day after the worst day of our lives. His sea blue eyes are keen on me and I don't know what to say except, "You knew one of the men killed?"

"Joe Jacobs. His son and I—well, we play soccer together. We're on varsity together. I don't know if he's going to play this season. But his dad was at every game, even coached us as kids. I'm going to the funeral. The entire team is going. I plan to be there for Jackson. That's my teammate—Jackson Jacobs."

He raises tearful eyes to mine. Our little sailboat is being pitched into the sea. I'm off the side. I'm drowning.

I can't look at him and break away.

"I mean, bottled water, Claire? We sold hundreds of plastic bottles of water this summer. Thousands. He never said any-thing. He liked to count them, that's all I knew. He liked to keep stock, he said. Never refused once to sell it. I don't get it. Why didn't I see that something was wrong with him?" He slumps against the railing. "Is something wrong with me?" He lets his cane fall from his hand. He leans over the wrought iron like he's going to throw up, or throw himself over.

"I don't need that thing," he says as I pick up his cane. "My mom is lying in the hospital, her leg shattered. Others are dead. That little girl. I don't want it. I don't want that. I want to kill him. I want Barkley dead, too. It isn't fair. Why didn't I see what was going on with him? I worked with him all summer. Why didn't I see something was wrong? Why? Tell me that. Why?"

He grabs the cane from me, almost stumbling into me, but backs off as if he doesn't want me anywhere near him. I squeeze my eyes shut. See the white tent. The blood on that little girl's sparkly pink top—the dog barking—the screams—his mother's hand in my hand—blood—the grin—the gun.

After a few seconds of being there in that tent again, the scent of coffee wafts out through the front door. A fresh pot. I open my eyes.

I want to run back in—make sure my mother's okay—that she's sitting or standing—or comfortable—that she's there.

She calls out to us from the kitchen. Obviously, she is also listening to our entire conversation.

"Can we go inside?" I say to Max. "It's chilly out here."

He shakes his head.

"Please."

In the kitchen, my mother says, "I found brown bananas. In the fridge." She nods to the banana bread on the table. "Izzy cracked the eggs. A big girl now. She went to work with her father today." My mother offers Max a slice but he declines, and I do, too, even as the reassurance of cinnamon fills the kitchen.

"A cup of coffee?" she asks. "It's fresh, too."

"Barkley was drinking two or three pots of coffee a shift by the end of the summer," says Max. "I don't think I can ever drink coffee without thinking of him."

Somehow the smell of coffee isn't so terrible to me anymore.

But Max asks for a glass of milk, and I dash between the refrigerator and cabinet, pouring each of us one, not paying enough attention, spilling some, white puddles on the clean countertops.

"This will be a long road for everybody." She clears her throat. Her speech is surer and steadier every day. "A long road. For that sick, sick young man. For his family. The courts will have to decide if he is fit to stand trial. I looked up what happened to that young man that shot that congresswoman out in Arizona a few years ago. He got seven life terms." She pauses, and I think she's done, exhausted. "Tragic," she adds, and sounds like she is falling.

I'm holding on to these facts like a raft.

"Is that why he did it? He's sick? Is that an excuse?" says Max more to himself than to me or my mother. "He chose to have that gun, didn't he? He chose to shoot those people, didn't he?"

"Paranoid schizophrenia is an organic brain disease. Most are not violent. Not at all. But did he 'choose' in the way you and I 'choose' to do the right thing or the wrong thing?" My mother pales from the output of so many words.

Max clenches his fists. "He is a murderer."

My mother's coffee mug trembles as she raises it to her lips. "Yes, and he has a degenerative disease, Max. I don't excuse his actions. In a perfect world, people would have seen signs. Helped him." She takes a shallow breath. "We live in an imperfect world."

"He tried to create a world that was dark and ugly as his own," says Max.

"He failed, didn't he?" I look at him next to me, close enough, but not touching me. I want the answer to come from him. I want him to agree. The blue in his eyes deepens as if he's gone to the dark and ugly.

"Of course he did," says my mother in a quiet, strained voice. "He failed."

"I was the one who should have thought twice about him." I am pleading this to Max. "I got on the phone with him thinking he was this Brent, this guy I never met. I was the one who wanted to believe he was something he wasn't."

"He wanted you—to believe," she says.

"I wanted to think that somebody, anybody, understood me." I can't look at either of them when I say this.

Max strikes the table with his fist. The plate of banana bread wobbles, and I reach out to straighten it, right it, but am not quick enough. The plate spin and crashes to the floor. Shards of glass mix with bread—the scent of cinnamon and banana splayed across the kitchen floor. My heart stops. Everything is broken.

"I'm sorry," says Max.

"Don't worry. I'll clean," says my mother.

"No. Don't get up. I'll do it." I search for the broom and dustpan and a deafening silence descends—and I am alone and Max is alone and my mother is alone and the center cannot hold—and the world is too much with us—and because we could not stop for death—

The broom is in the back of the kitchen utility closet. I sweep across the floor with hard strokes, wanting to forget these past four days, this entire summer, and knowing I never will. I was stupid. I was naive. Never again. Never.

"I'm sorry," says Max, rising. "I'm sorry, Mrs. Wallace. I'm sorry," he mumbles, standing up with a push of the kitchen table against the wall.

"Why don't we go into the living room. Continue this conversation in more comfortable chairs?" offers my mother.

"I'm not staying," Max says.

I nod my head like this was always the plan. *He's not staying.* Not in my life. School starts tomorrow. He's on one side of town, and I'm on the other, and he's not staying—even though all I want him to do is stay—all I want to do is wrap my arms around him and kiss the pain away from his lost-boy blue eyes— but he's not staying.

My mother studies Max and then me. "I'm here. If you need me. I'm here now."

Outside, leaves float off the maple tree. A blue jay flits from branch to branch, chirping to an unseen mate. Max hobbles down the front steps and I watch him and want to tell him to be careful, but they are only leaves. I sit down on the stoop, tuck my legs under me, hug my knees close to my chest. The blue jay flies off in search of what matters: food or shelter or love.

"I feel like I spent the summer in a fog. I spent the summer worrying about the wrong things," he says, as if he's talking to himself.

"What things?" I have to call after him.

"Like if I could make the next penalty kick or not—and other stuff. I've got to admit that I've been worrying about all the wrong things, and maybe I have to start trusting myself. I don't know. Does any of this make sense?" He keeps on going.

"You're asking me?"

"And you're answering with a question?"

Sometimes things don't make sense. Like, I don't understand why my mother had to have a stroke. You can explain to me all you want about the science, about the weakness in the neurovascular system, but I don't understand why she had to be the one to have a stroke. Why didn't we see warnings? Why her? Why my mom? And with Barkley, I understand that schizophrenia is a disease, that he heard voices, or a voice, that was speaking to him, telling him to take control, to demand answers, to what? And why that day? Why in that tent? What questions require a gun?

I rock forward. Hug myself. "Why did Barkley choose me to track down online? Was it that random? Did he just want a girl with long brown hair? If I were short and blond and petite, would I have been passed over? If I were pretty?" I am unmoored, cast off, alone.

"Claire," Max interrupts me, pivoting around on the front walk to face me.

I keep on reaching for the questions that are flooding my thoughts, drowning out Max. If I weren't so lonely, would I have answered him? Was it me who caused this, too? Should I have written something else to Brent/Barkley? Should I have said something? Should I have known? My mother always said smart girls ask a lot of questions. A smart girl takes nothing at face value. A smart girl asks first. But maybe I do ask too many questions. Or maybe I'm just asking all the wrong ones?

"Listen to me."

"What?"

"I want to tell you something."

"You said you weren't staying."

He brushes his dark hair back. His hand, bruised, tremors. "I've got to admit this to you, Claire. You aren't pretty. You are beautiful."

Nothing is said for a long minute or so, nothing questioned.

"Did you see how King lunged for him?" Max says in the space between us. "King, even blind, knew something was wrong."

I should have asked about King right after I asked about his mother. He was such a brave dog. I probably owe my life to the split second that King threw Barkley off-balance as much as to anything else.

I squeeze my eyes shut. Tears burn. *King!*

"My dog, my blind dog, was braver than me. My parents are now telling everyone that the real hero is King, and I agree with them. It's the one thing this summer we all agree on."

At the memory of King during the shooting, my throat tightens.

"King!" shouts Max, throwing back his head. His wounded leg stiffens. He is cursing in pain. I want my mother's arms around me, and I don't. I'm not a little girl anymore. I want to know why this happened, too. *Why?* One question is followed by another question, by another, and if you ask enough, maybe, someday it starts to make sense? Or maybe the question is never completely answered. Maybe the answer is only to keep asking the questions? The wind picks up. Feels like more rain. Geese appear on the horizon, flying in perfect v-formation, filling the sky with their sharp calls. The end of summer.

"King!" Max's shouting trims the air. I'm cold. It's time to go inside. I remember yesterday: Max calling out my name above all the din and chaos.

"King?" I whisper.

And from the back of Max's Jeep, King is up on all fours on the seat, sticking his snout out of the cracked-open window.

"I promised him a special walk, and no matter what I want to keep my promise."

The squawks of the Canadian geese put King on alert even more than Max calling for him. He releases a series of sharp barks. He senses the end of summer, too. *Good dog,* I say to myself. *Good dog.*

Max stares past me. I should return to my mother, let him go to his dog. The geese pierce the deep blue sky, signaling to one another, tracking the sun. They know instinctively which way to go. They know that time is short.

"Come with me?" he finally asks.

"Where?"

"Always questions."

"How about that?"

"The beach. Would you like to go with me and King to the beach?"

I would like nothing more than to be able to say yes without any more questions. Life is fragile, but with possibilities, and here is one of them. I stick my hands in my jeans pockets.

He shrugs and starts to leave, thinking I'm not going with him.

"Yes," I say. "Yes, to the beach."

An after-storm scent settles across the wet sand and grasses. A cool breeze rides across the crests of high tide. Driftwood and seaweed are strewn on the sands. The beach is bereft of people, save a few strolling up and down the boardwalk, and one lone man in baggy shorts with a Geiger counter searching for coins or valuables or anything else left behind by the summer crowds. The high white lifeguard chair is vacant and will remain so until next year. At the far end, Max unleashes King, who plows over the sand, packed hard by the storm, at the edge of the water. He skirts the waves chopping at the shore. The water looks rougher than it did even two days ago—grayish black, with bristling whitecaps.

King tests the water, dashing in and out. He marks the shoreline. Max and I haven't said more than a word or two to each other since I climbed into his Jeep with him—my mother peeking out the front window. It feels strange being at the beach, or anywhere, without my sister—strange and free.

Max calls to King. The dog bounds out of the waves, shakes himself on Max and me, a cold spray, before sitting down, facing the sea and the pale afternoon sun. I have an intense desire to go into the water one last time this summer or at least feel the sand and ocean run through my feet one more time. I stand toward the sea. The wind rises and my hair whips behind me. I'm at the edge of the earth. The taste of sea salt lines my lips. I turn to Max, my hair whirring around me, and feel the rushing of my heart. He's looking at me. I wait for him to say something or do something. He glances back at King, who seems to be waiting, too. The sea could take me, but I'm less interested in the rough ocean right now. A spray flits across my face, a taste of salt mixed with the recent storms.

"You're a hero," I say.

He hesitates. "No, I'm not. I'm just a guy who didn't want to die. I didn't want to be shot, or see my mom killed, or you."

I have to steady myself. I take my flip-flops off, toss them behind me onto the beach. I dig my toes into the sand, and feel the pull of the tide, the moon, gravity at play.

"I wish," he says, "that I felt like a hero. But you know, I feel like a regular guy, someone ordinary, and I think that's okay." He asks me, "Is that okay? That I don't think I'm a hero?"

He gives me his shy, lopsided smile. I step closer to him. We are eye to eye. The cold whitecaps swirl around my bare feet. I sway.

Yelping sea gulls descend: seizing the beach, landing in lines like military columns. I shudder, but realize that I'm not that afraid of them anymore, not after what happened. I stare down their black steely eyes. Still, I'm glad when King attacks them with a fury of barks, evicts them from our corner of the beach. Max keeps looking at me. He brushes my hair away from my face. I will him to kiss me. But he doesn't. He just stares at me right before his eyes.

"Are you going to kiss me?" I have to say. But I don't wait for an answer or for another question from myself. I just kiss him full on the mouth, wrapping my arms around his neck. His taste is salty, a mix of sea and tears. I hold on. He tugs me toward him. He kisses back as if he's never going to stop kissing me. I keep my eyes open. I want to see that I am kissing Max. Soon enough, he opens his too and anchors me to him. We kiss on. I want to always remember: this is how the summer ended.

Tomorrow, Wednesday, school starts.

Author's Note

As I complete this novel, I am particularly thankful to my mother-in-law, Dr. Frances Bock, Ph.D., a neuropsychologist, who read this novel while it was in progress and offered me her expertise, and to my brother David Blech. As a nurse practitioner with experience working on psychiatric wards, his insights into people afflicted with schizophrenia and his careful readings of the manuscript were invaluable. For those families suffering with mental illness, the National Alliance on Mental Illness (NAMI) is one of the largest nonprofit grassroots organizations for education and support. In addition, my mother suffered a stroke when I was four and a half years old and spent more than forty years brain-damaged and paralyzed. I wish when I was growing up there had been the information now readily available from the American Heart Association/American Stroke Association for victims and their families.

Acknowledgments

I am so grateful for the insights and skills of my editor, Sara Goodman, and my agent, Rachel Sussman. I could not have written this book without their enthusiasm and encouragement. And I couldn't have written this novel without Jessica Koenig reading first drafts with her discerning eye, or without knowing that dear friends Kim Becker, Susan Kaplan, and Charlene Weisler were near. I couldn't have kept writing without the camaraderie of my book club: Sophia Brogna, Maureen Cook, Paula Gilman, Lisa Mintz, Kathie Ring, Mary Sussman, Maria Schultz, and Gail Soffer, or without good neighbors, including Phyllis Baychuk. I don't know if I would have had the courage to write this book if not for Heather Greco, an extraordinary young adult librarian at the Plainview–Old Bethpage Public Library, who read a draft of this work, and even more, recommended armloads of fine young adult books for me to read and learn from. I would not have finished this without the cheering-on of my father, Morris Blech, may he rest in peace, and my father-in-law, Hal Bock. I've dedicated this book to my siblings: Mark, Susan, and David—they will always see me in a way no one else does—and I am so thankful our family now includes Moshe and Leah and Cindy and Jacob. Most of all, I know I wouldn't be a published writer at all if not for my husband, Richard, who reads and rereads all my work as well as reads, almost every night, to our children, Michael and Sara.

"Bock creates a **SUSPENSEFUL**, **GRIPPING**, and **POWERFUL** novel that will keep readers on their toes."
—*Library Journal* (STARRED REVIEW)

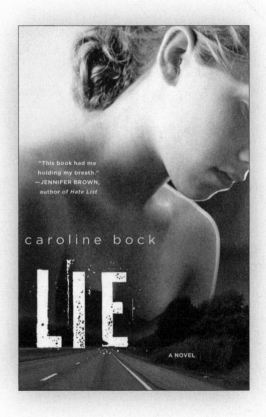

"This book had me holding my breath."
—JENNIFER BROWN, author of *Hate List*

caroline bock

LIE

A NOVEL

"An **INTENSELY MOVING**, beautifully written novel."
—Suzanne Weyn, author of *The Bar Code Tattoo*

St. Martin's Griffin